SPORES OF DOOM

SPORES OF DOOM

Dank Tales of the Fungal Weird

Edited by
AARON WORTH

This edition first published in 2025 by
The British Library
96 Euston Road
London NW1 2DB
bl.uk

Selection, introduction and notes © 2025 Aaron Worth
Volume copyright © 2025 The British Library Board

"Mushrooms" from THE COLOSSUS by Sylvia Plath, copyright © 1957, 1958, 1959, 1960, 1961, 1962. Reprinted in the USA by permission of Alfred A. Knopf, an imprint of the Knopf Doubleday Publishing Group, a division of Penguin Random House LLC. Reprinted in the rest of the world with permission of Faber and Faber Ltd.

"The Vaults of Yoh-Vombis" © 1932 The Estate of Clark Ashton Smith.

"The Great Fog" © 1943 by H. F. Heard. Used by permission of
Harold Ober Associates Inc. and The Barrie Family Trust.

"The Stains" © 1980 The Estate of Robert Aickman.

"Cesare Thodol: Some Lines Written on a Wall" © 2005 The Estate of Mark Samuels.

"The Mykophagoi" © 2025 Aaron Worth.

Every effort has been made to trace copyright holders and to obtain their permission for the use of copyright material. The publisher apologises for any errors or omissions and would be pleased to be notified of any corrections to be incorporated in reprints or future editions.

For product safety information, please visit
shop.bl.uk/pages/british-library-publishing, or the Publishing pages on bl.uk.

Cataloguing in Publication Data
A catalogue record for this publication is available from the British Library

ISBN 978 0 7123 5562 9
e-ISBN 978 0 7123 6883 4

Cover design by Mauricio Villamayor with illustration by Sandra Gómez.
Frontispiece illustration by Sandra Gómez. Images on pages 6 and 320: details from
C. Krause's chromolithographs of illustrations by Fritz Leuba in *Les Champignons Comestibles et les Espèces Vénéneuses* (Edible and Poisonous Mushrooms) (Neuchatel, Switzerland, 1890).

Text design and typesetting by Tetragon, London
Printed in Scotland by Bell & Bain Ltd

CONTENTS

ACKNOWLEDGEMENTS	6
INTRODUCTION	7
A NOTE FROM THE PUBLISHER	15
Mushrooms SYLVIA PLATH	17
The Voice in the Night WILLIAM HOPE HODGSON	21
The Fall of the House of Usher EDGAR ALLAN POE	39
The Yellow Wall-Paper CHARLOTTE PERKINS GILMAN	65
The Shunned House H. P. LOVECRAFT	89
The Purple Pileus H. G. WELLS	125
The Fiddler in the Fairy Ring JULIA HORATIA EWING	141
How Fear Departed from the Long Gallery E. F. BENSON	149
The Vaults of Yoh-Vombis CLARK ASHTON SMITH	169
The Great Fog H. F. HEARD	191
The Stains ROBERT AICKMAN	211
Cesare Thodol: Some Lines Written on a Wall MARK SAMUELS	283
The Mykophagoi AARON WORTH	301

ACKNOWLEDGEMENTS

My sincere thanks to Jonny Davidson for his enthusiastic support, and to Cerys Savinkina and everyone else at the British Library (though I may not know their names) for their work on the project. The book is dedicated to Michelle, *il miglior micofilo*.

INTRODUCTION

"Mushrooms", tweeted Jeff VanderMeer in 2023, "seem to be having a moment." It's hard to disagree. And it's not just mushrooms: fungi of all sorts have never been so conspicuous a feature of the cultural landscape as in the twenty-first century. The past decade or so has witnessed a particularly acute acceleration (alarming or exhilarating, according to your view) of this growth pattern, whether we are talking about art installations and museum exhibitions, bestselling nonfiction books, or such manifestations of popular culture as films, television series, and video games. Particularly prominent within the last category are Gothic, horror (or "sporror"), and otherwise weird stories. This is perhaps unsurprising, given the abiding weirdness of fungi themselves, at least from our perspective—the slightly unsettling conceptual niche they have long occupied in the human imagination, across the centuries and around the world.

I cannot resist a brief parenthesis here. Rather hilariously, the Victorian mycological writer William Delisle Hay upbraided his fellow Britons for their fear and loathing of fungi, which he regarded as a purely insular prejudice: "This popular sentiment, which we may coin the word 'Fungophobia' to express, is very curious. If it were human—that is, universal—one would be inclined to set it down as instinct… But it is not human—it is merely British… a national superstition. Fungophobia is merely a form of ignorance, of course; but its power over the British mind is… immense." To paraphrase Poe, however (and with all due respect to Mr. Hay), I maintain that fungophobia is not of Britain, but of the soul. ("Mycophobia" is more etymologically sound, but maybe the linguistically hybrid "fungophobia" is, perversely, more appropriate after all.) Perhaps not all cultures *fear* fungi, but the members of this particular kingdom have too many trans-cultural associations with the supernatural (the miraculous, the sacred, and the magical, including connections in myth and folklore with fairies and other beings), as well as death and decay (unsurprising, this, given their feeding habits) to be waved away as symptoms of a merely British neurosis. This is not to say, of course, that the particular anxieties fungi arouse, or can be used to arouse, cannot also be culturally and historically specific. That is always the case with the ingredients of horror. Take the vampire. There may well be something universal about this figure—vampires of different kinds can be found around the world—but if it is an archetype, it is one that can be employed to stoke fears of (say) racial otherness in one cultural context, and to play upon fears of HIV/AIDS or other infectious diseases in another.

But we were talking about fungi. What's so weird about them, anyway?

Well, how much time have we got? Their sex (and not-sex, which they also have, or don't-have, depending on species and situation) is weird. We don't need to go into that here. Some of them glow. Some can zombify other species. There's one in Oregon that may be older than Nineveh and Tyre, and it's still going strong. (Eat spore, Dracula!) Paradoxically, the more we learn about them (and there's so very much we don't know, beginning with an estimated two million unknown species), the stranger they seem to get. There's the way they have of resisting our systems of classification. We have to keep changing our taxonomies. Slime moulds aren't fungi any more (I think I thought they were). Lichens are fungi, but also plants. And of course, fungi themselves *used* to be plants, until quite recently. To be more accurate, in evolutionary history fungi diverged from plants over a billion years ago (yes, it's more complicated than that, as we'll see in a bit), but it wasn't until 1969 that the binary Linnaean scheme (in which you're either Animal or Vegetable, with nothing in between) was overthrown, granting them their own sovereign kingdom. (Revolution was in the air: it was the year of Woodstock and the Stonewall uprising.) But even before that taxonomic upheaval, fungi were always looked upon as... different. There was even something monstrous about them, the way they straddled and conflated ostensibly distinct categories. Indeed, monstrosity itself, according to one influential conception, inheres precisely in such transgressions. The monster, as Noël Carroll tells us, is not only "physically threatening"; it is also (and this is worse) "cognitively threatening." The monstrous figure blends, blurs, or eradicates comforting binaries: between living and dead, organic and inorganic, human and animal (or vegetable, or mineral), male and female. (Pop quiz: Which of these oppositions do fungi deconstruct? Hint: all of them.) Disconcertingly, too (as Lewis Carroll knew), fungi are magical agents of transformation, both of body and mind. Much as they aid in the transubstantiation of ordinary matter into such divine gifts as wine, beer, bread, and Stilton cheese, they can change us, too, through illness or intoxication. They can feed us, poison us, cure us. They can literally change our minds, loosen our very grip on reality.

Perhaps, by way of sketching out some contours of a typology of fungal anxieties, we might begin with some contemporary exemplars of what might be called the mycological weird, and then work backwards (or dig downwards) from there. There is nothing like enough room here to do more than point to a few texts belonging to this emergent canon. (Would that we could, like mycelia, cause our sentences to redouble and fold in upon themselves like hyphal threads, packing miles of meaning into a limited space.) I say "texts" not to sound academically hifalutin, but because any such list needs to include, at the very least, short stories and novels, films and TV shows, mangas and graphic novels, and video and tabletop games. More, these stories not only originate in a variety of media but frequently cross the boundaries between and among different media: take the hugely successful post-apocalyptic HBO series *The Last of Us* (2023) (which, given the timing, is likely to have prompted the tweet quoted earlier): it was adapted from a 2013 video game, which also spawned a comic book, a role-playing game, and live readings and musical performances, as well as its own game sequels. Fungal creatures, bioweapons, infections, and other hazards menace the players of other popular video games (*Darkest Dungeon*, *Resident Evil*, *Silent Hill*, *Control*). A short list of prominent novels of the fungal weird might include VanderMeer's own Ambergris trilogy (2002–2009) and *Annihilation* (2014), M. R. Carey's *The Girl with All the Gifts* (2014), Silvia Moreno-Garcia's *Mexican Gothic* (2020), and T. Kingfisher's *What Moves the Dead* (2022); myco-horror movies, meanwhile, are sprouting up so fast that it's all but impossible to keep count—in addition to film adaptations of *Annihilation* and *The Girl with All the Gifts*, one might mention *Shrooms* (2007), *Splinter* (2008), *The Hallow* (2015), *Tin Can* (2020), *In the Earth* (2021), and *Gaia* (2021). And many, many more.

Of course, sprouting up, in alarming profusion and with uncanny suddenness, is what mushrooms, at least, are known for ("Mushroom, verb, intransitive: to spring up suddenly or multiply rapidly"), and both for this, and for their equally abrupt dissolution, have they long been viewed with suspicion: R. T. and F. W. Rolfe, in their *Romance of the Fungus World* (1925), noted that "these queer fellows spring up in such profusion as to force themselves as upon the attention of even the least observant... all appearing and often disappearing in such uncanny fashion, these pariahs of the plant world have been for ages at once a source of wonder and of loathing to the uninitiated", while

Miles Joseph Berkeley, the founder of British mycology, pointed to the instinctual disgust triggered by both "the evanescent nature" of fungi "and the loathsome mass of putrescence"—had he been reading Poe's tale of M. Valdemar?—that is "presented in decay by many species." But can we historicize this sudden flush of fungal tales in our own time? Well, it's surely suggestive that particularly prominent within contemporary works of fungal fiction and film are seemingly endless permutations of body horror, eco-horror, and eco-body-horror (where is Polonius when we need him?), liberally sprinkled with apocalyptic scenarios and/or tropes of infection and invasion. All of which makes sense, given our multifarious fears (and fantasies) of the posthuman and transhuman, the spectre of environmental catastrophe, and our recent experience (and the still-present threat) of global pandemics. Fungi model, too, modes of relation (both among themselves and with other species, paratactic and hypotactic, parasitic and symbiotic) which are strange to us yet, at times, strangely familiar: it can hardly be an accident, for example, that the growing cultural obsession with both fungal and hybrid fungal-plant networks coincides with our becoming ourselves a globally networked species. Depictions of fungal life have increasingly been used as a way to explore various forms of hybridity and fluidity—of, for instance, sexuality, race, and gender. It is surely significant that women authors, who wrote far fewer fungal tales, comparatively, during the period of the "classic" weird (despite being extremely well represented as writers of plant horror more generally), have emerged as leading voices of the subgenre today. (Apparently the authorship of fiction featuring malignant vines, roots, flowers, and trees was less rigidly coded with respect to gender; the situation was doubtless not helped by the male domination of early twentieth-century science fiction, particularly in the pulp magazines where tales of extraterrestrial spores, moulds, mildews, rusts, blights, sentient mushrooms, and other fungal entities were pumped out by the score.) In short, these features of the genre would all seem to track nicely with other aspects of the early twenty-first century zeitgeist.

And yet. It is striking how many of these same themes and anxieties can be found in earlier tales of the fungal weird as well. Consider the fear of "becoming-fungus": as Anthony Camara has discussed, this is a trope that can be seen in Arthur Machen's novel *The Hill of Dreams*, which appeared in 1907 (the same year as William Hope Hodgson's "The Voice in the Night", included here). And in fact many of today's stock fungal tropes can be found in one creditable candidate for the true ur-tale of the genre, "The Story of Konnor Old House", one of the Flaxman Low occult detective stories written in the 1890s by (perhaps appropriately) the symbiotic mother-son team of Kate and Hesketh Prichard, aka "E. and H. Heron". It is a profoundly racist story, and not particularly effective (though the reader, if curious, can easily enough find it online), but interesting in summary for the overdetermined, if rather confused, nature of its mycological horrors. In the story, an African manservant is brought to Scotland, covets and frightens his master's daughter, whom he kills using his knowledge and manipulation of multiple fungal strains (an early instance of the "fungal technology" trope, central to VanderMeer's Ambergris books); the father dies soon after. The servant is subsequently overgrown with fungus himself (fungal body horror; we discover a motionless standing figure, encased in fungus, "shrouded from head to foot in faintly luminous white mould"), and from time to time appears as a mindless "shining man" haunting the house ("fungal zombie" trope); there are dangerous spores, luminous phosphorescence, "black patches" appearing on victims' faces, a melty, dripping face appearing in a patch on the ceiling—it's a virtual smorgasbord of genre tropes. True, it is not difficult to see the particular fin-de-siècle anxieties and ideologies being exploited here; exactly contemporaneous with such classics of "reverse imperialism" as H. G. Wells's *The War of the Worlds*, Richard Marsh's *The Beetle*, and Bram Stoker's *Dracula*, "Konnor Old House" racializes fungal invasion—it is pointedly "African" in its source, and reminds the detective of similar "Indian" cases. (Side note: there is an interesting essay to be written about the significance of post-colonial Britain as an element of Robert Aickman's tale of fungi, moulds, mosses, lichens—and even Marmite, that yeast-derived favourite!— included here.) But it is striking, nonetheless, how many of the same figures tend to recur over time.

And so, however apparently abrupt, however tied to our own historical moment, the above-described invasion of literary and popular culture by fungal entities may seem to be, it might better be understood as the coordinated fruiting of many bodies (to use a mycological metaphor that, I fear, has already become somewhat shopworn) out of a literary mycelium (the tangled network of filaments of a fungal colony) which has been stealthily growing below the surface, as it were, for decades. The present collection, comprised (with a pair of late exceptions) of nineteenth- and twentieth-century weird stories, is offered as a kind of guided tour of that subterranean colony. It includes early classics of the genre, as well as tales both classic and obscure (in some cases, forgotten altogether) that only emerge in retrospect as pioneering strands in that hidden conceptual webwork.

The category of the "Unheimlich" (which translates, unsatisfactorily, to "uncanny" in English) has been asked to do quite a lot of heavy lifting in literary and film studies in the century since Freud wrote his celebrated essay on the subject. Most often it appears in connection with dolls, doppelgängers, and kindred topics. But if we return to the roots of the word (it's difficult, isn't it, to think outside of roots, of rootedness?), and to Freud's understanding of its repressed duality, it would be hard to find a class of entities more *Unheimlich* in their relation to us than the members of the fungus kingdom. *Unhomelike*: deeply strange, unsettlingly alien, disconcertingly other. Yet simultaneously *homelike*: we were *once the same*, in a sense are *still* the same—part of the same clade, the supergroup of eukaryotes called the opisthokonts, containing the animal and fungus kingdoms but not the plants, from which (from whom?) we parted ways earlier, *together*. Becoming-fungus, whether we encounter it in the horror-worlds of Machen, Hodgson, or VanderMeer, is, then, really a kind of homecoming. A source of unspeakable existential horror, or a consummation devoutly to be wished. Depending on your perspective. Moreover, since our respective furcations from fungi in the primeval past, both plants and animals have *returned* to them, forging intimate and ineluctable relationships of countless different kinds—as co-travellers, symbiotes, parasites, infections, and much more. For plants they serve as a communications network, part of the "Wood Wide Web", and are vital providers of nutrients and water. And, of course, they are crucial to the processes of decay which none of us, animal or vegetable, can hope to escape. From birth to death (indeed before birth; fungal DNA is believed to be delivered to us in the womb via the placenta), then, fungi are not only among us; they are within us, all around us, and in the spaces between us. They are, one might say, waiting for us all.

So why delay the inevitable? Gathered together in these pages are some of the strangest fungal varieties to be found anywhere on, or off, the earth. And they are very, *very* eager to make your acquaintance.

A NOTE FROM THE PUBLISHER

The original short stories reprinted in the British Library Tales of the Weird series were written and published in a period ranging across the nineteenth and twentieth centuries. There are many elements of these stories which continue to entertain modern readers; however, in some cases there are also uses of language, instances of stereotyping and some attitudes expressed by narrators or characters which may not be endorsed by the publishing standards of today. We acknowledge therefore that some elements in the stories selected for reprinting may continue to make uncomfortable reading for some of our audience. With this series British Library Publishing aims to offer a new readership a chance to read some of the rare material of the British Library's collections in an affordable paperback format, to enjoy their merits and to look back into the worlds of the past two centuries as portrayed by their writers. It is not possible to separate these stories from the history of their writing and therefore the following stories are presented as they were originally published with minor edits only, made for consistency of style and sense. We welcome feedback from our readers, which can be sent to the following address:

>British Library Publishing
>The British Library
>96 Euston Road
>London, NW1 2DB

1960

MUSHROOMS

Sylvia Plath

First, a little something by way of an amuse-bouche (that's the title, by the way, of an extremely... disturbing episode of the TV series *Hannibal*, one with a strong element of myco-horror). Born in Boston, Massachusetts in 1932, Sylvia Plath died by suicide in London in 1963, at the age of thirty. Awarded a posthumous Pulitzer Prize in Poetry in 1982, she is regarded today as one of the finest American poets of the twentieth century. She wrote this unsettling little poem in November (a fine month for fungi), 1957 at the Yaddo artist colony in Saratoga Springs, New York, where she was staying with her husband, the poet Ted Hughes. In her journal she noted: "Wrote an exercise on Mushrooms yesterday which Ted likes. And I do too. My absolute lack of judgment when I've written something: whether it's trash or genius." "Mushrooms" was published in 1960 in both *Harper's Magazine* and her collection *The Colossus and Other Poems*. Plath might well have been surprised to see it included, some years later, alongside the work of such masters of speculative fiction as Isaac Asimov, Ray Bradbury, and Robert A. Heinlein in the anthology *Science Fiction*, edited by Sylvia Z. Brodkin and Elizabeth J. Pearson.

Overnight, very
Whitely, discreetly,
Very quietly

Our toes, our noses
Take hold on the loam,
Acquire the air.

Nobody sees us,
Stops us, betrays us;
The small grains make room.

Soft fists insist on
Heaving the needles,
The leafy bedding,

Even the paving.
Our hammers, our rams,
Earless and eyeless,

Perfectly voiceless,
Widen the crannies,
Shoulder through holes. We

MUSHROOMS

Diet on water,
On crumbs of shadow,
Bland-mannered, asking

Little or nothing.
So many of us!
So many of us!

We are shelves, we are
Tables, we are meek,
We are edible,

Nudgers and shovers
In spite of ourselves.
Our kind multiplies:

We shall by morning
Inherit the earth.
Our foot's in the door.

1907

THE VOICE IN THE NIGHT

William Hope Hodgson

If there is a great-grandaddy (grand-mycelium?) of the "sporror" genre, it is this. Well-known among readers of classic speculative fiction for his nonpareil tales of the nautical weird, his proto-cosmic-horror novels *The House by the Borderland* and *The Night Land* (both republished as part of the British Library Tales of the Weird series), and his stories featuring the occult detective Carnacki of 427, Cheyne Walk, William Hope Hodgson was born in Essex in 1877, ran away to sea as a young boy (caught and returned home, he finally managed to join the Merchant Marines at the age of 14), wrote both nonfiction and fiction in a variety of genres, and was killed in Ypres in 1918. In 1907, Hodgson published his first novel, *The Boats of the "Glen Carrig"*, as well as "The Voice in the Night" (in *The Blue Book Magazine*). He seems to have had fungus on the brain that year: *"Glen Carrig"*, an eighteenth-century pastiche in which the survivors of a shipwreck encounter manifold marine horrors, features ambiguous hybrid beings—apparently part fungus and part tree, with human faces—as well as a great valley of monstrous fungi whose destruction by fire Hodgson imagines in an unforgettable tableau replete with Old Testament cadences: "And during all that night no man of us slept, and the burning of the fungi sent up a mighty pillar of flame out of the valley, as out of the mouth of a monstrous pit and when the morning came it still burned." His 1912 tale "The Derelict" (included in the British Library's *The Weird*

Tales of William Hope Hodgson) features a monstrous, "mould-covered" ship. "The Voice in the Night" spawned a number of fungal-island tales (Philip Fisher's "Fungus Isle" being one successful, albeit not, perhaps, very memorably titled, example); it has also been adapted in various media, notably in the Japanese film *Matango* (1963).

It was a dark, starless night. We were becalmed in the Northern Pacific. Our exact position I do not know; for the sun had been hidden during the course of a weary, breathless week, by a thin haze which had seemed to float above us, about the height of our mastheads, at whiles descending and shrouding the surrounding sea.

With there being no wind, we had steadied the tiller, and I was the only man on deck. The crew, consisting of two men and a boy, were sleeping forrard in their den; while Will—my friend, and the master of our little craft—was aft in his bunk on the port side of the little cabin.

Suddenly, from out of the surrounding darkness, there came a hail:

"Schooner, ahoy!"

The cry was so unexpected that I gave no immediate answer, because of my surprise.

It came again—a voice curiously throaty and inhuman, calling from somewhere upon the dark sea away on our port broadside:

"Schooner, ahoy!"

"Hullo!" I sung out, having gathered my wits somewhat. "What are you? What do you want?"

"You need not be afraid," answered the queer voice, having probably noticed some trace of confusion in my tone. "I am only an old—man."

The pause sounded oddly; but it was only afterwards that it came back to me with any significance.

"Why don't you come alongside, then?" I queried somewhat snappishly; for I liked not his hinting at my having been a trifle shaken.

"I—I—can't. It wouldn't be safe. I—" The voice broke off, and there was silence.

"What do you mean?" I asked, growing more and more astonished. "Why not safe? Where are you?"

I listened for a moment; but there came no answer. And then, a sudden indefinite suspicion, of I knew not what, coming to me, I stepped swiftly to the binnacle, and took out the lighted lamp. At the same time, I knocked on the deck with my heel to waken Will. Then I was back at the side, throwing the yellow funnel of light out into the silent immensity beyond our rail. As I did so, I heard a slight, muffled cry, and then the sound of a splash, as though someone had dipped oars abruptly. Yet I cannot say that I saw anything with certainty; save, it seemed to me, that with the first flash of the light, there had been something upon the waters, where now there was nothing.

"Hullo, there!" I called. "What foolery is this!"

But there came only the indistinct sounds of a boat being pulled away into the night.

Then I heard Will's voice, from the direction of the after scuttle:

"What's up, George?"

"Come here, Will!" I said.

"What is it?" he asked, coming across the deck.

I told him the queer thing which had happened. He put several questions; then, after a moment's silence, he raised his hands to his lips, and hailed:

"Boat, ahoy!"

From a long distance away, there came back to us a faint reply, and my companion repeated his call. Presently, after a short period of silence, there grew on our hearing the muffled sound of oars; at which Will hailed again.

This time there was a reply:

"Put away the light."

"I'm damned if I will," I muttered; but Will told me to do as the voice bade, and I shoved it down under the bulwarks.

"Come nearer," he said, and the oar-strokes continued. Then, when apparently some half-dozen fathoms distant, they again ceased.

"Come alongside," exclaimed Will. "There's nothing to be frightened of aboard here!"

"Promise that you will not show the light?"

"What's to do with you," I burst out, "that you're so infernally afraid of the light?"

"Because—" began the voice, and stopped short.

"Because what?" I asked, quickly.

Will put his hand on my shoulder.

"Shut up a minute, old man," he said, in a low voice. "Let me tackle him."

He leant more over the rail.

"See here, Mister," he said, "this is a pretty queer business, you coming upon us like this, right out in the middle of the blessed Pacific. How are we to know what sort of a hanky-panky trick you're up to? You say there's only one of you. How are we to know, unless we get a squint at you—eh? What's your objection to the light, anyway?"

As he finished, I heard the noise of the oars again, and then the voice came; but now from a greater distance, and sounding extremely hopeless and pathetic.

"I am sorry—sorry! I would not have troubled you, only I am hungry, and—so is she."

THE VOICE IN THE NIGHT

The voice died away, and the sound of the oars, dipping irregularly, was borne to us.

"Stop!" sung out Will. "I don't want to drive you away. Come back! We'll keep the light hidden, if you don't like it."

He turned to me:

"It's a damned queer rig, this; but I think there's nothing to be afraid of?"

There was a question in his tone, and I replied.

"No, I think the poor devil's been wrecked around here, and gone crazy."

The sound of the oars drew nearer.

"Shove that lamp back in the binnacle," said Will; then he leaned over the rail, and listened. I replaced the lamp, and came back to his side. The dipping of the oars ceased some dozen yards distant.

"Won't you come alongside now?" asked Will in an even voice. "I have had the lamp put back in the binnacle."

"I—I cannot," replied the voice. "I dare not come nearer. I dare not even pay you for the—the provisions."

"That's all right," said Will, and hesitated. "You're welcome to as much grub as you can take—" Again he hesitated.

"You are very good," exclaimed the voice. "May God, who understands everything, reward you—" It broke off huskily.

"The—the lady?" said Will, abruptly. "Is she—"

"I have left her behind upon the island," came the voice.

"What island?" I cut in.

"I know not its name," returned the voice. "I would to God—!" it began, and checked itself as suddenly.

"Could we not send a boat for her?" asked Will at this point.

"No!" said the voice, with extraordinary emphasis. "My God! No!"

There was a moment's pause; then it added, in a tone which seemed a merited reproach:

"It was because of our want I ventured—Because her agony tortured me."

"I am a forgetful brute," exclaimed Will. "Just wait a minute, whoever you are, and I will bring you up something at once."

In a couple of minutes he was back again, and his arms were full of various edibles. He paused at the rail.

"Can't you come alongside for them?" he asked.

"No—I *dare not*," replied the voice, and it seemed to me that in its tones I detected a note of stifled craving—as though the owner hushed a mortal desire. It came to me then in a flash, that the poor old creature out there in the darkness, was *suffering* for actual need of that which Will held in his arms; and yet, because of some unintelligible dread, refraining from dashing to the side of our little schooner, and receiving it. And with the lightning-like conviction, there came the knowledge that the Invisible was not mad; but sanely facing some intolerable horror.

"Damn it, Will!" I said, full of many feelings, over which predominated a vast sympathy. "Get a box. We must float off the stuff to him in it."

This we did—propelling it away from the vessel, out into the darkness, by means of a boathook. In a minute, a slight cry from the Invisible came to us, and we knew that he had secured the box.

A little later, he called out a farewell to us, and so heartful a blessing, that I am sure we were the better for it. Then, without more ado, we heard the ply of oars across the darkness.

"Pretty soon off," remarked Will, with perhaps just a little sense of injury.

THE VOICE IN THE NIGHT

"Wait," I replied. "I think somehow he'll come back. He must have been badly needing that food."

"And the lady," said Will. For a moment he was silent; then he continued:

"It's the queerest thing ever I've tumbled across, since I've been fishing."

"Yes," I said, and fell to pondering.

And so the time slipped away—an hour, another, and still Will stayed with me; for the queer adventure had knocked all desire for sleep out of him.

The third hour was three parts through, when we heard again the sound of oars across the silent ocean.

"Listen!" said Will, a low note of excitement in his voice.

"He's coming, just as I thought," I muttered.

The dipping of the oars grew nearer, and I noted that the strokes were firmer and longer. The food had been needed.

They came to a stop a little distance off the broadside, and the queer voice came again to us through the darkness:

"Schooner, ahoy!"

"That you?" asked Will.

"Yes," replied the voice. "I left you suddenly; but—but there was great need."

"The lady?" questioned Will.

"The—lady is grateful now on earth. She will be more grateful soon in—in heaven."

Will began to make some reply, in a puzzled voice; but became confused, and broke off short. I said nothing. I was wondering at the curious pauses, and, apart from my wonder, I was full of a great sympathy.

The voice continued:

"We—she and I, have talked, as we shared the result of God's tenderness and yours—"

Will interposed; but without coherence.

"I beg of you not to—to belittle your deed of Christian charity this night," said the voice. "Be sure that it has not escaped His notice."

It stopped, and there was a full minute's silence. Then it came again:

"We have spoken together upon that which—which has befallen us. We had thought to go out, without telling any, of the terror which has come into our—lives. She is with me in believing that tonight's happenings are under a special ruling, and that it is God's wish that we should tell to you all that we have suffered since—since—"

"Yes?" said Will, softly.

"Since the sinking of the *Albatross*."

"Ah!" I exclaimed, involuntarily. "She left Newcastle for 'Frisco some six months ago, and hasn't been heard of since."

"Yes," answered the voice. "But some few degrees to the North of the line she was caught in a terrible storm, and dismasted. When the day came, it was found that she was leaking badly, and, presently, it falling to a calm, the sailors took to the boats, leaving—leaving a young lady—my fiancée—and myself upon the wreck.

"We were below, gathering together a few of our belongings, when they left. They were entirely callous, through fear, and when we came up upon the decks, we saw them only as small shapes afar off upon the horizon. Yet we did not despair, but set to work and constructed a small raft. Upon this we put such few matters as it would hold, including a quantity of water and some ship's biscuit. Then, the vessel being very deep in the water, we got ourselves onto the raft, and pushed off.

"It was later, when I observed that we seemed to be in the way of some tide or current, which bore us from the ship at an angle; so

THE VOICE IN THE NIGHT

that in the course of three hours, by my watch, her hull became invisible to our sight, her broken masts remaining in view for a somewhat longer period. Then, towards evening, it grew misty, and so through the night. The next day we were still encompassed by the mist, the weather remaining quiet.

"For four days, we drifted through this strange haze, until, on the evening of the fourth day, there grew upon our ears the murmur of breakers at a distance. Gradually it became plainer, and, somewhat after midnight, it appeared to sound upon either hand at no very great space. The raft was raised upon a swell several times, and then we were in smooth water, and the noise of the breakers was behind.

"When the morning came, we found that we were in a sort of great lagoon; but of this we noticed little at the time; for close before us, through the enshrouding mist, loomed the hull of a large sailing-vessel. With one accord, we fell upon our knees and thanked God; for we thought that here was an end to our perils. We had much to learn.

"The raft drew near to the ship, and we shouted on them, to take us aboard; but none answered. Presently, the raft touched against the side of the vessel, and, seeing a rope hanging downwards, I seized it and began to climb. Yet I had much ado to make my way up, because of a kind of grey, lichenous fungus, which had seized upon the rope, and which blotched the side of the ship, lividly.

"I reached the rail, and clambered over it, on to the deck. Here, I saw that the decks were covered, in great patches, with the grey masses, some of them rising into nodules several feet in height; but at the time, I thought less of this matter than of the possibility of there being people aboard the ship. I shouted; but none answered. Then I went to the door below the poop-deck. I opened it, and peered in. There was a great smell of staleness, so that I knew in a moment that nothing living was within, and with the knowledge, I shut the door quickly; for I felt suddenly lonely.

"I went back to the side, where I had scrambled up. My—my sweetheart was still sitting quietly upon the raft. Seeing me look down, she called up to know whether there were any aboard of the ship. I replied that the vessel had the appearance of having been long deserted; but that if she would wait a little, I would see whether there was anything in the shape of a ladder, by which she could ascend to the deck. Then we would make a search through the vessel together. A little later, on the opposite side of the decks, I found a rope side-ladder. This I carried across, and a minute afterwards, she was beside me.

"Together, we explored the cabins and apartments in the after-part of the ship; but nowhere was there any sign of life. Here and there, within the cabins themselves, we came across odd patches of that queer fungus; but this, as my sweetheart said, could be cleansed away.

"In the end, having assured ourselves that the after-portion of the vessel was empty, we picked our ways to the bows, between the ugly grey nodules of that strange growth; and here we made a further search, which told us that there was indeed none aboard but ourselves.

"This being now beyond any doubt, we returned to the stern of the ship, and proceeded to make ourselves as comfortable as possible. Together, we cleared out and cleaned two of the cabins; and, after that, I made examination whether there was anything eatable in the ship. This I soon found was so, and thanked God in my heart for His goodness. In addition to this, I discovered the whereabouts of the freshwater pump, and having fixed it, I found the water drinkable, though somewhat unpleasant to the taste.

"For several days, we stayed aboard the ship, without attempting to get to the shore. We were busily engaged in making the place habitable. Yet even thus early, we became aware that our lot was even less to be desired than might have been imagined; for though, as a first step, we scraped away the odd patches of growth that studded the floors and walls of the cabins and saloon, yet they returned almost to their original size within the space of twenty-four hours, which not only discouraged us, but gave us a feeling of vague unease.

"Still, we would not admit ourselves beaten, so set to work afresh, and not only scraped away the fungus, but soaked the places where it had been, with carbolic, a can-full of which I had found in the pantry. Yet, by the end of the week, the growth had returned in full strength, and, in addition, it had spread to other places, as though our touching it had allowed germs from it to travel elsewhere.

"On the seventh morning, my sweetheart woke to find a small patch of it growing on her pillow, close to her face. At that, she came to me, so soon as she could get her garments upon her. I was in the galley at the time, lighting the fire for breakfast.

"'Come here, John,' she said, and led me aft. When I saw the thing upon her pillow, I shuddered, and then and there we agreed to go right out of the ship, and see whether we could not fare to make ourselves more comfortable ashore.

"Hurriedly, we gathered together our few belongings, and even among these, I found that the fungus had been at work; for one of her shawls had a little lump of it growing near one edge. I threw the whole thing over the side, without saying anything to her.

"The raft was still alongside; but it was too clumsy to guide, and I lowered down a small boat that hung across the stern, and in this we made our way to the shore. Yet, as we drew near to it, I became gradually aware that here the vile fungus, which had driven us from the ship, was growing riot. In places it rose into horrible, fantastic mounds, which seemed almost to quiver, as with a quiet life, when the wind blew across them. Here and there, it took on the forms of vast fingers, and in others it just spread out flat and smooth and treacherous. Odd places, it appeared as grotesque stunted trees, seeming extraordinarily kinked and gnarled—the whole quaking vilely at times.

"At first, it seemed to us that there was no single portion of the surrounding shore which was not hidden beneath the masses of the hideous lichen; yet, in this, I found we were mistaken; for somewhat later, coasting along the shore at a little distance, we descried a smooth white patch of what appeared to be fine sand, and there we landed. It was not sand. What it was, I do not know. All that I have observed, is that upon it, the fungus will not grow; while everywhere else, save where the sand-like earth wanders oddly, path-wise, amid the grey desolation of the lichen, there is nothing but that loathsome greyness.

"It is difficult to make you understand how cheered we were to find one place that was absolutely free from the growth, and here we deposited our belongings. Then we went back to the ship for such things as it seemed to us we should need. Among other matters, I managed to bring ashore with me one of the ship's sails, with which I constructed two small tents, which, though exceedingly rough-shaped, served the purposes for which they were intended. In these, we lived and stored our various necessities, and thus for a matter of some four weeks, all went smoothly and without particular unhappiness. Indeed, I may say with much of happiness—for—for we were together.

"It was on the thumb of her right hand, that the growth first showed. It was only a small circular spot, much like a little grey mole. My God! how the fear leapt to my heart when she showed me the place. We cleansed it, between us, washing it with carbolic and water. In the morning of the following day, she showed her hand to me again. The grey warty thing had returned. For a little while, we looked at one another in silence. Then, still wordless, we started again to remove it. In the midst of the operation, she spoke suddenly.

"'What's that on the side of your face, dear!' Her voice was sharp with anxiety. I put my hand up to feel.

"'There! Under the hair by your ear.—A little to the front a bit.' My finger rested upon the place, and then I knew.

"'Let us get your thumb done first,' I said. And she submitted, only because she was afraid to touch me until it was cleansed. I finished washing and disinfecting her thumb, and then she turned to my face. After it was finished, we sat together and talked awhile of many things; for there had come into our lives sudden, very terrible thoughts. We were, all at once, afraid of something worse than death. We spoke of loading the boat with provisions and water, and making our way out on to the sea; yet we were helpless, for many causes, and—and the growth had attacked us already. We decided to stay. God would do with us what was His will. We would wait.

"A month, two months, three months passed, and the places grew somewhat, and there had come others. Yet we fought so strenuously with the fear, that its headway was but slow, comparatively speaking.

"Occasionally, we ventured off to the ship for such stores as we needed. There, we found that the fungus grew persistently. One of the nodules on the main deck became soon as high as my head.

"We had now given up all thought or hope of leaving the island. We had realized that it would be unallowable to go among healthy humans, with the thing from which we were suffering.

"With this determination and knowledge in our minds, we knew that we should have to husband our food and water; for we did not know, at that time, but that we should possibly live for many years.

"This reminds me that I have told you that I am an old man. Judged by years this is not so. But—but—"

He broke off; then continued somewhat abruptly:

"As I was saying, we knew that we should have to use care in the matter of food. But we had no idea then how little food there was left, of which to take care. It was a week later, that I made the discovery that all the other bread tanks—which I had supposed full—were empty, and that (beyond odd tins of vegetables and meat, and some other matters) we had nothing on which to depend, but the bread in the tank which I had already opened.

"After learning this, I bestirred myself to do what I could, and set to work at fishing in the lagoon; but with no success. At this, I was somewhat inclined to feel desperate, until the thought came to me to try outside the lagoon, in the open sea.

"Here, at times, I caught odd fish; but so infrequently that they proved of but little help in keeping us from the hunger which threatened. It seemed to me that our deaths were likely to come by hunger, and not by the growth of the thing which had seized upon our bodies.

"We were in this state of mind when the fourth month wore out. Then I made a very horrible discovery. One morning, a little before midday, I came off from the ship, with a portion of the biscuits which were left. In the mouth of her tent, I saw my sweetheart sitting, eating something.

"'What is it, my dear?' I called out as I leapt ashore. Yet, on hearing my voice, she seemed confused, and, turning, slyly threw something towards the edge of the little clearing. It fell short, and, a vague suspicion having arisen within me, I walked across and picked it up. It was a piece of the grey fungus.

"As I went to her, with it in my hand, she turned deadly pale; then a rose red.

"I felt strangely dazed and frightened.

"'My dear! My dear!' I said, and could say no more. Yet, at my words, she broke down and cried bitterly. Gradually, as she calmed, I got from her the news that she had tried it the preceding day, and— and liked it. I got her to promise on her knees not to touch it again, however great our hunger. After she had promised, she told me that the desire for it had come suddenly, and that, until the moment of desire, she had experienced nothing towards it but the most extreme repulsion.

"Later in the day, feeling strangely restless, and much shaken with the thing which I had discovered, I made my way along one of the twisted paths—formed by the white, sand-like substance—which led among the fungoid growth. I had, once before, ventured along there; but not to any great distance. This time, being involved in perplexing thought, I went much further than hitherto.

"Suddenly, I was called to myself by a queer hoarse sound on my left. Turning quickly, I saw that there was movement among an extraordinarily shaped mass of fungus, close to my elbow. It was swaying uneasily, as though it possessed life of its own. Abruptly, as I stared, the thought came to me that the thing had a grotesque resemblance to the figure of a distorted human creature. Even as the fancy flashed into my brain, there was a slight, sickening noise of tearing, and I saw that one of the branch-like arms was detaching itself from the surrounding grey masses, and coming towards me. The head of the thing—a shapeless grey ball, inclined in my direction. I stood stupidly, and the vile arm brushed across my face. I gave out a frightened cry, and ran back a few paces. There was a sweetish taste upon my lips, where the thing had touched me. I licked them, and was immediately filled with an inhuman desire. I turned and seized a mass of the fungus. Then more, and—more. I was insatiable. In the midst of devouring, the remembrance of the morning's discovery swept into my mazed brain. It was sent by God. I dashed the fragment I held, to the ground. Then, utterly wretched and feeling a dreadful guiltiness, I made my way back to the little encampment.

"I think she knew, by some marvellous intuition which love must have given, so soon as she set eyes on me. Her quiet sympathy made it easier for me, and I told her of my sudden weakness; yet omitted to mention the extraordinary thing which had gone before. I desired to spare her all unnecessary terror.

"But, for myself, I had added an intolerable knowledge, to breed an incessant terror in my brain; for I doubted not but that I had seen the end of one of those men who had come to the island in the ship in the lagoon; and in that monstrous ending, I had seen our own.

"Thereafter, we kept from the abominable food, though the desire for it had entered into our blood. Yet, our drear punishment was upon us; for, day by day, with monstrous rapidity, the fungoid growth took hold of our poor bodies. Nothing we could do would check it materially, and so—and so—we who had been human, became—Well, it matters less each day. Only—only we had been man and maid!

"And day by day, the fight is more dreadful, to withstand the hunger-lust for the terrible lichen.

"A week ago we ate the last of the biscuit, and since that time I have caught three fish. I was out here fishing tonight, when your schooner drifted upon me out of the mist. I hailed you. You know the rest, and may God, out of His great heart, bless you for your goodness to a—a couple of poor outcast souls."

There was the dip of an oar—another. Then the voice came again, and for the last time, sounding through the slight surrounding mist, ghostly and mournful.

"God bless you! Goodbye!"

"Goodbye," we shouted together, hoarsely, our hearts full of many emotions.

I glanced about me. I became aware that the dawn was upon us.

The sun flung a stray beam across the hidden sea; pierced the mist dully, and lit up the receding boat with a gloomy fire. Indistinctly, I saw something nodding between the oars. I thought of a sponge—a great, grey nodding sponge—The oars continued to ply. They were grey—as was the boat—and my eyes searched a moment vainly for the conjunction of hand and oar. My gaze flashed back to the—head. It nodded forward as the oars went backward for the stroke. Then the oars were dipped, the boat shot out of the patch of light, and the—the thing went nodding into the mist.

1839

THE FALL OF THE HOUSE OF USHER

Edgar Allan Poe

A Gothic classic that has been obsessively scrutinized, interpreted and reinterpreted, from every conceivable critical viewpoint (and which repays every rereading with fresh shudders), Edgar Allan Poe's immortal tale of isolation, contagious madness, and premature burial should be viewed in retrospect as an important precursor or ancestor of the mycological weird. Two successful horror novels of the past half-decade, Silvia Moreno-Garcia's *Mexican Gothic* and T. Kingfisher's *What Moves the Dead*, are both homages (in the latter case a retelling) of Poe's tale (it also forms the basis of a recent Netflix series of the same name). "The Fall of the House of Usher" was first published in *Burton's Gentleman's Magazine* (1839), then included in Poe's *Tales of the Grotesque and Arabesque* (1840).

Sitôt qu'on le touche il résonne.
—DE BÉRANGER

During the whole of a dull, dark, and soundless day in the autumn of the year, when the clouds hung oppressively low in the heavens, I had been passing alone, on horseback, through a singularly dreary tract of country; and at length found myself, as the shades of the evening drew on, within view of the melancholy House of Usher. I know not how it was—but, with the first glimpse of the building, a sense of insufferable gloom pervaded my spirit. I say insufferable; for the feeling was unrelieved by any of that half-pleasurable, because poetic, sentiment, with which the mind usually receives even the sternest natural images of the desolate or terrible. I looked upon the scene before me—upon the mere house, and the simple landscape features of the domain—upon the bleak walls—upon the vacant eye-like windows—upon a few rank sedges—and upon a few white trunks of decayed trees—with an utter depression of soul which I can compare to no earthly sensation more properly than to the after-dream of the reveller upon opium—the bitter lapse into every-day life—the hideous dropping off of the veil. There was an iciness, a sinking, a sickening of the heart—an unredeemed dreariness of thought which no goading of the imagination could torture into aught of the sublime. What was it—I paused to think—what was it that so unnerved me in the contemplation of the House of Usher? It was a mystery all insoluble; nor could I grapple with the shadowy fancies that crowded upon me as I pondered. I was forced to fall back upon the unsatisfactory conclusion, that while, beyond doubt, there *are* combinations of very simple natural objects which have the power of thus affecting us, still the analysis of this power lies among considerations beyond our depth. It was possible, I reflected, that a mere different arrangement of the particulars of the scene, of the details of the picture, would be sufficient to modify, or perhaps to annihilate its capacity for sorrowful impression; and, acting upon this idea, I reined my horse to the precipitous brink of a black and lurid tarn that lay in unruffled lustre by the dwelling, and gazed down—but with a shudder even more thrilling than before—upon the re-modelled and inverted images of the grey sedge, and the ghastly tree-stems, and the vacant and eye-like windows.

Nevertheless, in this mansion of gloom I now proposed to myself a sojourn of some weeks. Its proprietor, Roderick Usher, had been one of my boon companions in boyhood; but many years had elapsed since our last meeting. A letter, however, had lately reached me in a distant part of the country—a letter from him—which, in its wildly importunate nature, had admitted of no other than a personal reply. The MS. gave evidence of nervous agitation. The writer spoke of acute bodily illness—of a mental disorder which oppressed him—and of an earnest desire to see me, as his best, and indeed his only personal friend, with a view of attempting, by the cheerfulness of my society, some alleviation of his malady. It was the manner in which all this, and much more, was said—it was the apparent *heart* that went with his request—which allowed me no room for hesitation; and I accordingly obeyed forthwith what I still considered a very singular summons.

Although, as boys, we had been even intimate associates, yet I really knew little of my friend. His reserve had been always excessive and habitual. I was aware, however, that his very ancient family had been noted, time out of mind, for a peculiar sensibility of temperament, displaying itself, through long ages, in many works of exalted art, and manifested, of late, in repeated deeds of munificent yet unobtrusive charity, as well as in a passionate devotion to the intricacies, perhaps even more than to the orthodox and easily recognizable beauties, of musical science. I had learned, too, the very remarkable fact, that the stem of the Usher race, all time-honoured as it was, had put forth, at no period, any enduring branch; in other words, that the entire family lay in the direct line of descent, and had always, with very trifling and very temporary variation, so lain. It was this deficiency, I considered, while running over in thought the perfect keeping of the character of the premises with the accredited character of the people, and while speculating upon the possible influence which the one, in the long lapse of centuries, might have exercised upon the other—it was this deficiency, perhaps, of collateral issue, and the consequent undeviating transmission, from sire to son, of the patrimony with the name, which had, at length, so identified the two as to merge the original title of the estate in the quaint and equivocal appellation of the "House of Usher"—an appellation which seemed to include, in the minds of the peasantry who used it, both the family and the family mansion.

I have said that the sole effect of my somewhat childish experiment—that of looking down within the tarn—had been to deepen the first singular impression. There can be no doubt that the consciousness of the rapid increase of my superstition—for why should I not so term it?—served mainly to accelerate the increase itself. Such, I have long known, is the paradoxical law of all sentiments having terror as a basis. And it might have been for this reason only, that, when I again uplifted my eyes to the house itself, from its image in the pool, there grew in my mind a strange fancy—a fancy so ridiculous, indeed, that I but mention it to show the vivid force of the sensations which oppressed me. I had so worked upon my imagination as really to believe that about the whole mansion and domain there hung an atmosphere peculiar to themselves and their immediate vicinity—an atmosphere which had no affinity with the air of heaven, but which had reeked up from the decayed trees, and the grey wall, and the silent tarn—a pestilent and mystic vapour, dull, sluggish, faintly discernible, and leaden-hued.

Shaking off from my spirit what *must* have been a dream, I scanned more narrowly the real aspect of the building. Its principal feature seemed to be that of an excessive antiquity. The discoloration of ages had been great. Minute fungi overspread the whole exterior, hanging in a fine tangled webwork from the eaves. Yet all this was apart from any extraordinary dilapidation. No portion of the masonry had fallen; and there appeared to be a wild inconsistency between its still perfect adaptation of parts, and the crumbling condition of the individual stones. In this there was much that reminded me of the specious totality of old wood-work which has rotted for long years in some neglected vault, with no disturbance from the breath of the external air. Beyond this indication of extensive decay, however, the fabric gave little token of instability. Perhaps the eye of a scrutinizing observer might have discovered a barely perceptible fissure, which, extending from the roof of the building in front, made its way down the wall in a zigzag direction, until it became lost in the sullen waters of the tarn.

Noticing these things, I rode over a short causeway to the house. A servant in waiting took my horse, and I entered the Gothic archway of the hall. A valet, of stealthy step, thence conducted me, in silence, through many dark and intricate passages in my progress to the *studio* of his master. Much that I encountered on the way contributed, I know not how, to heighten the vague sentiments of which I have already spoken. While the objects around me—while the carvings of the ceilings, the sombre tapestries of the walls, the ebon blackness of the floors, and the phantasmagoric armorial trophies which rattled as I strode, were but matters to which, or to such as which, I had been accustomed from my infancy—while I hesitated not to acknowledge how familiar was all this—I still wondered to find how unfamiliar were the fancies which ordinary images were stirring up. On one of the staircases, I met the physician of the family. His countenance, I thought, wore a mingled expression of low cunning and perplexity. He accosted me with trepidation and passed on. The valet now threw open a door and ushered me into the presence of his master.

The room in which I found myself was very large and lofty. The windows were long, narrow, and pointed, and at so vast a distance from the black oaken floor as to be altogether inaccessible from within. Feeble gleams of encrimsoned light made their way through the trellissed panes, and served to render sufficiently distinct the more prominent objects around; the eye, however, struggled in vain to reach the remoter angles of the chamber, or the recesses of the vaulted and fretted ceiling. Dark draperies hung upon the walls. The general furniture was profuse, comfortless, antique, and tattered. Many books and musical instruments lay scattered about, but failed to give any vitality to the scene. I felt that I breathed an atmosphere of sorrow. An air of stern, deep, and irredeemable gloom hung over and pervaded all.

Upon my entrance, Usher arose from a sofa on which he had been lying at full length, and greeted me with a vivacious warmth which had much in it, I at first thought, of an overdone cordiality—of the constrained effort of the *ennuyé* man of the world. A glance, however, at his countenance, convinced me of his perfect sincerity. We sat down; and for some moments, while he spoke not, I gazed upon him with a feeling half of pity, half of awe. Surely, man had never before so terribly altered, in so brief a period, as had Roderick Usher! It was with difficulty that I could bring myself to admit the identity of the wan being before me with the companion of my early boyhood. Yet the character of his face had been at all times remarkable. A cadaverousness of complexion; an eye large, liquid, and luminous beyond comparison; lips somewhat thin and very pallid, but of a surpassingly beautiful curve; a nose of a delicate Hebrew model, but with a breadth of nostril unusual in similar formations; a finely moulded chin, speaking, in its want of prominence, of a want of moral energy; hair of a more than web-like softness and tenuity; these features, with an inordinate expansion above the regions of the temple, made up altogether a countenance not easily to be forgotten. And now in the mere exaggeration of the prevailing character of these features, and of the expression they were wont to convey, lay so much of change that I doubted to whom I spoke. The now ghastly pallor of the skin, and the now miraculous lustre of the eye, above all things startled and even awed me. The silken hair, too, had been suffered to grow all unheeded, and as, in its wild gossamer texture, it floated rather than fell about the face, I could not, even with effort, connect its Arabesque expression with any idea of simple humanity.

In the manner of my friend I was at once struck with an incoherence—an inconsistency; and I soon found this to arise from a series of feeble and futile struggles to overcome an habitual trepidancy—an excessive nervous agitation. For something of this nature I had indeed been prepared, no less by his letter, than by reminiscences of certain boyish traits, and by conclusions deduced from his peculiar physical conformation and temperament. His action was alternately vivacious and sullen. His voice varied rapidly from a tremulous indecision (when the animal spirits seemed utterly in abeyance) to that species of energetic concision—that abrupt, weighty, unhurried, and hollow-sounding enunciation—that leaden, self-balanced and perfectly modulated guttural utterance, which may be observed in the lost drunkard, or the irreclaimable eater of opium, during the periods of his most intense excitement.

It was thus that he spoke of the object of my visit, of his earnest desire to see me, and of the solace he expected me to afford him. He entered, at some length, into what he conceived to be the nature of his malady. It was, he said, a constitutional and a family evil, and one for which he despaired to find a remedy—a mere nervous affection, he immediately added, which would undoubtedly soon pass off. It displayed itself in a host of unnatural sensations. Some of these, as he detailed them, interested and bewildered me; although, perhaps, the terms, and the general manner of the narration had their weight. He suffered much from a morbid acuteness of the senses; the most insipid food was alone endurable; he could wear only garments of certain texture; the odours of all flowers were oppressive; his eyes were tortured by even a faint light; and there were but peculiar sounds, and these from stringed instruments, which did not inspire him with horror.

To an anomalous species of terror I found him a bounden slave. "I shall perish," said he, "I *must* perish in this deplorable folly. Thus, thus, and not otherwise, shall I be lost. I dread the events of the future, not in themselves, but in their results. I shudder at the thought of any, even the most trivial, incident, which may operate upon this intolerable agitation of soul. I have, indeed, no abhorrence of danger, except in its absolute effect—in terror. In this unnerved—in this pitiable condition—I feel that the period will sooner or later arrive when I must abandon life and reason together, in some struggle with the grim phantasm, FEAR."

I learned, moreover, at intervals, and through broken and equivocal hints, another singular feature of his mental condition. He was enchained by certain superstitious impressions in regard to the dwelling which he tenanted, and whence, for many years, he had never ventured forth—in regard to an influence whose supposititious force was conveyed in terms too shadowy here to be re-stated—an influence which some peculiarities in the mere form and substance of his family mansion, had, by dint of long sufferance, he said, obtained over his spirit—an effect which the *physique* of the grey walls and turrets, and of the dim tarn into which they all looked down, had, at length, brought about upon the *morale* of his existence.

He admitted, however, although with hesitation, that much of the peculiar gloom which thus afflicted him could be traced to a more natural and far more palpable origin—to the severe and long-continued illness—indeed to the evidently approaching dissolution—of a tenderly beloved sister—his sole companion for long years—his last and only relative on earth. "Her decease," he said, with a bitterness which I can never forget, "would leave him (him the hopeless and the frail) the last of the ancient race of the Ushers." While he spoke, the lady Madeline (for so was she called) passed slowly through a remote portion of the apartment, and, without having noticed my presence, disappeared. I regarded her with an utter astonishment not unmingled with dread—and yet I found it impossible to account for such feelings. A sensation of stupor oppressed me, as my eyes followed her retreating steps. When a door, at length, closed upon her, my glance sought instinctively and eagerly the countenance of the brother—but he had buried his face in his hands, and I could only perceive that a far more than ordinary wanness had overspread the emaciated fingers through which trickled many passionate tears.

The disease of the lady Madeline had long baffled the skill of her physicians. A settled apathy, a gradual wasting away of the person, and frequent although transient affections of a partially cataleptical character, were the unusual diagnosis. Hitherto she had steadily borne up against the pressure of her malady, and had not betaken herself finally to bed; but, on the closing in of the evening of my arrival at the house, she succumbed (as her brother told me at night with inexpressible agitation) to the prostrating power of the destroyer; and I learned that the glimpse I had obtained of her person would thus probably be the last I should obtain—that the lady, at least while living, would be seen by me no more.

For several days ensuing, her name was unmentioned by either Usher or myself: and during this period I was busied in earnest endeavours to alleviate the melancholy of my friend. We painted and read together; or I listened, as if in a dream, to the wild improvisations of his speaking guitar. And thus, as a closer and still closer intimacy admitted me more unreservedly into the recesses of his spirit, the more bitterly did I perceive the futility of all attempt at cheering a mind from which darkness, as if an inherent positive quality, poured forth upon all objects of the moral and physical universe, in one unceasing radiation of gloom.

I shall ever bear about me a memory of the many solemn hours I thus spent alone with the master of the House of Usher. Yet I should fail in any attempt to convey an idea of the exact character of the studies, or of the occupations, in which he involved me, or led me the way. An excited and highly distempered ideality threw a sulphurous lustre over all. His long improvised dirges will ring forever in my ears. Among other things, I hold painfully in mind a certain singular perversion and amplification of the wild air of the last waltz of Von Weber. From the paintings over which his elaborate fancy brooded, and which grew, touch by touch, into vaguenesses at which I shuddered the more thrillingly, because I shuddered knowing not why;—from these paintings (vivid as their images now are before me) I would in vain endeavour to educe more than a small portion which should lie within the compass of merely written words. By the utter simplicity, by the nakedness of his designs, he arrested and overawed attention. If ever mortal painted an idea, that mortal was Roderick Usher. For me at least—in the circumstances then surrounding me—there arose out of the pure abstractions which the hypochondriac contrived to throw upon his canvass, an intensity of intolerable awe, no shadow of which felt I ever yet in the contemplation of the certainly glowing yet too concrete reveries of Fuseli.

One of the phantasmagoric conceptions of my friend, partaking not so rigidly of the spirit of abstraction, may be shadowed forth, although feebly, in words. A small picture presented the interior of an immensely long and rectangular vault or tunnel, with low walls, smooth, white, and without interruption or device. Certain accessory points of the design served well to convey the idea that this excavation lay at an exceeding depth below the surface of the earth. No outlet was observed in any portion of its vast extent, and no torch, or other artificial source of light was discernible; yet a flood of intense rays rolled throughout, and bathed the whole in a ghastly and inappropriate splendour.

I have just spoken of that morbid condition of the auditory nerve which rendered all music intolerable to the sufferer, with the exception of certain effects of stringed instruments. It was, perhaps, the narrow limits to which he thus confined himself upon the guitar, which gave birth, in great measure, to the fantastic character of his performances. But the fervid *facility* of his *impromptus* could not be so accounted for. They must have been, and were, in the notes, as well as in the words of his wild fantasias (for he not unfrequently accompanied himself with rhymed verbal improvisations), the result of that intense mental collectedness and concentration to which I have previously alluded as observable only in particular moments of the highest artificial excitement. The words of one of these rhapsodies I have easily remembered. I was, perhaps, the more forcibly impressed with it, as he gave it, because, in the under or mystic current of its meaning, I fancied that I perceived, and for the first time, a full consciousness on the part of Usher, of the tottering of his lofty reason upon her throne. The verses, which were entitled "The Haunted Palace," ran very nearly, if not accurately, thus:

I.

In the greenest of our valleys,
   By good angels tenanted,
Once a fair and stately palace—
   Radiant palace—reared its head.
In the monarch Thought's dominion—
   It stood there!
Never seraph spread a pinion
   Over fabric half so fair.

II.

Banners yellow, glorious, golden,
   On its roof did float and flow;
(This—all this—was in the olden
   Time long ago)
And every gentle air that dallied,
   In that sweet day,
Along the ramparts plumed and pallid,
   A winged odour went away.

III.

Wanderers in that happy valley
   Through two luminous windows saw
Spirits moving musically
   To a lute's well-tunéd law,
Round about a throne, where sitting
   (Porphyrogene!)
In state his glory well befitting,
   The ruler of the realm was seen.

IV.

And all with pearl and ruby glowing
   Was the fair palace door,
Through which came flowing, flowing, flowing,
   And sparkling evermore,

A troop of Echoes whose sweet duty
   Was but to sing,
In voices of surpassing beauty,
   The wit and wisdom of their king.

V.

But evil things, in robes of sorrow,
   Assailed the monarch's high estate;
(Ah, let us mourn, for never morrow
   Shall dawn upon him, desolate!)
And, round about his home, the glory
   That blushed and bloomed
Is but a dim-remembered story
   Of the old time entombed.

VI.

And travellers now within that valley,
   Through the red-litten windows, see
Vast forms that move fantastically
   To a discordant melody;
While, like a rapid ghastly river,
   Through the pale door,
A hideous throng rush out forever,
   And laugh—but smile no more.

I well remember that suggestions arising from this ballad, led us into a train of thought wherein there became manifest an opinion of Usher's which I mention not so much on account of its novelty, (for other men[1] have thought thus,) as on account of the pertinacity with which he maintained it. This opinion, in its general form, was that of the sentience of all vegetable things. But, in his disordered fancy, the idea had assumed a more daring character, and trespassed, under certain conditions, upon the kingdom of inorganization. I lack words to express the full extent, or the earnest *abandon* of his persuasion. The belief, however, was connected (as I have previously hinted) with the grey stones of the home of his forefathers. The conditions of the sentience had been here, he imagined, fulfilled in the method of collocation of these stones—in the order of their arrangement, as well as in that of the many *fungi* which overspread them, and of the decayed trees which stood around—above all, in the long undisturbed endurance of this arrangement, and in its reduplication in the still waters of the tarn. Its evidence—the evidence of the sentience—was to be seen, he said, (and I here started as he spoke,) in the gradual yet certain condensation of an atmosphere of their own about the waters and the walls. The result was discoverable, he added, in that silent, yet importunate and terrible influence which for centuries had moulded the destinies of his family, and which made *him* what I now saw him—what he was. Such opinions need no comment, and I will make none.

Our books—the books which, for years, had formed no small portion of the mental existence of the invalid—were, as might be supposed, in strict keeping with this character of phantasm. We pored

---

1 Watson, Dr. Percival, Spallanzani, and especially the Bishop of Landaff. — See "Chemical Essays," vol v.

together over such works as the Ververt et Chartreuse of Gresset; the Belphegor of Machiavelli; the Heaven and Hell of Swedenborg; the Subterranean Voyage of Nicholas Klimm by Holberg; the Chiromancy of Robert Flud, of Jean D'Indaginé, and of De la Chambre; the Journey into the Blue Distance of Tieck; and the City of the Sun of Campanella. One favourite volume was a small octavo edition of the *Directorium Inquisitorum*, by the Dominican Eymeric de Gironne; and there were passages in Pomponius Mela, about the old African Satyrs and œgipans, over which Usher would sit dreaming for hours. His chief delight, however, was found in the perusal of an exceedingly rare and curious book in quarto Gothic—the manual of a forgotten church—the *Vigiliae Mortuorum secundum Chorum Ecclesiae Maguntinae*.

I could not help thinking of the wild ritual of this work, and of its probable influence upon the hypochondriac, when, one evening, having informed me abruptly that the lady Madeline was no more, he stated his intention of preserving her corpse for a fortnight, (previously to its final interment,) in one of the numerous vaults within the main walls of the building. The worldly reason, however, assigned for this singular proceeding, was one which I did not feel at liberty to dispute. The brother had been led to his resolution (so he told me) by consideration of the unusual character of the malady of the deceased, of certain obtrusive and eager inquiries on the part of her medical men, and of the remote and exposed situation of the burial-ground of the family. I will not deny that when I called to mind the sinister countenance of the person whom I met upon the staircase, on the day of my arrival at the house, I had no desire to oppose what I regarded as at best but a harmless, and by no means an unnatural, precaution.

At the request of Usher, I personally aided him in the arrangements for the temporary entombment. The body having been encoffined, we two alone bore it to its rest. The vault in which we placed it (and which had been so long unopened that our torches, half smothered in its oppressive atmosphere, gave us little opportunity for investigation) was small, damp, and entirely without means of admission for light; lying, at great depth, immediately beneath that portion of the building in which was my own sleeping apartment. It had been used, apparently, in remote feudal times, for the worst purposes of a donjon-keep, and, in later days, as a place of deposit for powder, or some other highly combustible substance, as a portion of its floor, and the whole interior of a long archway through which we reached it, were carefully sheathed with copper. The door, of massive iron, had been, also, similarly protected. Its immense weight caused an unusually sharp grating sound, as it moved upon its hinges.

Having deposited our mournful burden upon tressels within this region of horror, we partially turned aside the yet unscrewed lid of the coffin, and looked upon the face of the tenant. A striking similitude between the brother and sister now first arrested my attention; and Usher, divining, perhaps, my thoughts, murmured out some few words from which I learned that the deceased and himself had been twins, and that sympathies of a scarcely intelligible nature had always existed between them. Our glances, however, rested not long upon the dead—for we could not regard her unawed. The disease which had thus entombed the lady in the maturity of youth, had left, as usual in all maladies of a strictly cataleptical character, the mockery of a faint blush upon the bosom and the face, and that suspiciously lingering smile upon the lip which is so terrible in death. We replaced and screwed down the lid, and, having secured the door of iron, made our way, with toil, into the scarcely less gloomy apartments of the upper portion of the house.

And now, some days of bitter grief having elapsed, an observable change came over the features of the mental disorder of my friend.

His ordinary manner had vanished. His ordinary occupations were neglected or forgotten. He roamed from chamber to chamber with hurried, unequal, and objectless step. The pallor of his countenance had assumed, if possible, a more ghastly hue—but the luminousness of his eye had utterly gone out. The once occasional huskiness of his tone was heard no more; and a tremulous quaver, as if of extreme terror, habitually characterized his utterance. There were times, indeed, when I thought his unceasingly agitated mind was labouring with some oppressive secret, to divulge which he struggled for the necessary courage. At times, again, I was obliged to resolve all into the mere inexplicable vagaries of madness, for I beheld him gazing upon vacancy for long hours, in an attitude of the profoundest attention, as if listening to some imaginary sound. It was no wonder that his condition terrified—that it infected me. I felt creeping upon me, by slow yet certain degrees, the wild influences of his own fantastic yet impressive superstitions.

It was, especially, upon retiring to bed late in the night of the seventh or eighth day after the placing of the lady Madeline within the donjon, that I experienced the full power of such feelings. Sleep came not near my couch—while the hours waned and waned away. I struggled to reason off the nervousness which had dominion over me. I endeavoured to believe that much, if not all of what I felt, was due to the bewildering influence of the gloomy furniture of the room—of the dark and tattered draperies, which, tortured into motion by the breath of a rising tempest, swayed fitfully to and fro upon the walls, and rustled uneasily about the decorations of the bed. But my efforts were fruitless. An irrepressible tremor gradually pervaded my frame; and, at length, there sat upon my very heart an incubus of utterly causeless alarm. Shaking this off with a gasp and a struggle, I uplifted myself upon the pillows, and, peering earnestly within the intense darkness of the chamber, harkened—I know not why, except that an instinctive spirit prompted me—to certain low and indefinite sounds which came, through the pauses of the storm, at long intervals, I knew not whence. Overpowered by an intense sentiment of horror, unaccountable yet unendurable, I threw on my clothes with haste (for I felt that I should sleep no more during the night), and endeavoured to arouse myself from the pitiable condition into which I had fallen, by pacing rapidly to and fro through the apartment.

I had taken but few turns in this manner, when a light step on an adjoining staircase arrested my attention. I presently recognized it as that of Usher. In an instant afterward he rapped, with a gentle touch, at my door, and entered, bearing a lamp. His countenance was, as usual, cadaverously wan—but, moreover, there was a species of mad hilarity in his eyes—an evidently restrained *hysteria* in his whole demeanour. His air appalled me—but anything was preferable to the solitude which I had so long endured, and I even welcomed his presence as a relief.

"And you have not seen it?" he said abruptly, after having stared about him for some moments in silence—"you have not then seen it?—but, stay! you shall." Thus speaking, and having carefully shaded his lamp, he hurried to one of the casements, and threw it freely open to the storm.

The impetuous fury of the entering gust nearly lifted us from our feet. It was, indeed, a tempestuous yet sternly beautiful night, and one wildly singular in its terror and its beauty. A whirlwind had apparently collected its force in our vicinity; for there were frequent and violent alterations in the direction of the wind; and the exceeding density of the clouds (which hung so low as to press upon the turrets of the house) did not prevent our perceiving the life-like velocity with which they flew careering from all points against each other, without passing away into the distance. I say that even their exceeding density did not prevent our perceiving this—yet we had no glimpse of the moon or stars—nor was there any flashing forth of the lightning. But the under surfaces of the huge masses of agitated vapour, as well as all terrestrial objects immediately around us, were glowing in the unnatural light of a faintly luminous and distinctly visible gaseous exhalation which hung about and enshrouded the mansion.

"You must not—you shall not behold this!" said I, shudderingly, to Usher, as I led him, with a gentle violence, from the window to a seat. "These appearances, which bewilder you, are merely electrical phenomena not uncommon—or it may be that they have their ghastly origin in the rank miasma of the tarn. Let us close this casement;—the air is chilling and dangerous to your frame. Here is one of your favourite romances. I will read, and you shall listen;—and so we will pass away this terrible night together."

The antique volume which I had taken up was the "Mad Trist" of Sir Launcelot Canning; but I had called it a favourite of Usher's more in sad jest than in earnest; for, in truth, there is little in its uncouth and unimaginative prolixity which could have had interest for the lofty and spiritual ideality of my friend. It was, however, the only book immediately at hand; and I indulged a vague hope that the excitement which now agitated the hypochondriac, might find relief (for the history of mental disorder is full of similar anomalies) even in the extremeness of the folly which I should read. Could I have judged, indeed, by the wild overstrained air of vivacity with which he harkened, or apparently harkened, to the words of the tale, I might well have congratulated myself upon the success of my design.

I had arrived at that well-known portion of the story where Ethelred, the hero of the Trist, having sought in vain for peaceable admission into the dwelling of the hermit, proceeds to make good an entrance by force. Here, it will be remembered, the words of the narrative run thus:

"And Ethelred, who was by nature of a doughty heart, and who was now mighty withal, on account of the powerfulness of the wine which he had drunken, waited no longer to hold parley with the hermit, who, in sooth, was of an obstinate and maliceful turn, but, feeling the rain upon his shoulders, and fearing the rising of the tempest, uplifted his mace outright, and, with blows, made quickly room in the plankings of the door for his gauntleted hand; and now pulling therewith sturdily, he so cracked, and ripped, and tore all asunder, that the noise of the dry and hollow-sounding wood alarummed and reverberated throughout the forest."

At the termination of this sentence I started, and for a moment, paused; for it appeared to me (although I at once concluded that my excited fancy had deceived me)—it appeared to me that, from some very remote portion of the mansion, there came, indistinctly, to my ears, what might have been, in its exact similarity of character, the echo (but a stifled and dull one certainly) of the very cracking and ripping sound which Sir Launcelot had so particularly described. It was, beyond doubt, the coincidence alone which had arrested my attention; for, amid the rattling of the sashes of the casements, and the ordinary commingled noises of the still increasing storm, the sound, in itself, had nothing, surely, which should have interested or disturbed me. I continued the story:

"But the good champion Ethelred, now entering within the door, was sore enraged and amazed to perceive no signal of the maliceful hermit; but, in the stead thereof, a dragon of a scaly and prodigious demeanour, and of a fiery tongue, which sate in guard before a palace of gold, with a floor of silver; and upon the wall there hung a shield of shining brass with this legend enwritten—

> Who entereth herein, a conqueror hath bin;
> Who slayeth the dragon, the shield he shall win;

And Ethelred uplifted his mace, and struck upon the head of the dragon, which fell before him, and gave up his pesty breath, with a shriek so horrid and harsh, and withal so piercing, that Ethelred had fain to close his ears with his hands against the dreadful noise of it, the like whereof was never before heard."

Here again I paused abruptly, and now with a feeling of wild amazement—for there could be no doubt whatever that, in this instance, I did actually hear (although from what direction it proceeded I found it impossible to say) a low and apparently distant, but harsh, protracted, and most unusual screaming or grating sound—the exact counterpart of what my fancy had already conjured up for the dragon's unnatural shriek as described by the romancer.

Oppressed, as I certainly was, upon the occurrence of this second and most extraordinary coincidence, by a thousand conflicting sensations, in which wonder and extreme terror were predominant, I still retained sufficient presence of mind to avoid exciting, by any observation, the sensitive nervousness of my companion. I was by no means certain that he had noticed the sounds in question; although, assuredly, a strange alteration had, during the last few minutes, taken place in his demeanour. From a position fronting my own, he had gradually brought round his chair, so as to sit with his face to the door of the chamber; and thus I could but partially perceive his features, although I saw that his lips trembled as if he were murmuring inaudibly. His head had dropped upon his breast—yet I knew that he was not asleep, from the wide and rigid opening of the eye as I caught a glance of it in profile. The motion of his body, too, was at variance with this idea—for he rocked from side to side with a gentle yet constant and uniform sway. Having rapidly taken notice of all this, I resumed the narrative of Sir Launcelot, which thus proceeded:

"And now, the champion, having escaped from the terrible fury of the dragon, bethinking himself of the brazen shield, and of the breaking up of the enchantment which was upon it, removed the carcass from out of the way before him, and approached valorously over the silver pavement of the castle to where the shield was upon the wall; which in sooth tarried not for his full coming, but fell down at his feet upon the silver floor, with a mighty great and terrible ringing sound."

No sooner had these syllables passed my lips, than—as if a shield of brass had indeed, at the moment, fallen heavily upon a floor of silver—I became aware of a distinct, hollow, metallic, and clangorous, yet apparently muffled reverberation. Completely unnerved, I leaped to my feet; but the measured rocking movement of Usher was undisturbed. I rushed to the chair in which he sat. His eyes were bent fixedly before him, and throughout his whole countenance there reigned a stony rigidity. But, as I placed my hand upon his shoulder, there came a strong shudder over his whole person; a sickly smile quivered about his lips; and I saw that he spoke in a low, hurried, and gibbering murmur, as if unconscious of my presence. Bending closely over him, I at length drank in the hideous import of his words.

"Not hear it?—yes, I hear it, and *have* heard it. Long—long—long—many minutes, many hours, many days, have I heard it—yet I dared not—oh, pity me, miserable wretch that I am!—I dared not—I *dared* not speak! *We have put her living in the tomb!* Said I not that my senses were acute? I *now* tell you that I heard her first feeble movements in the hollow coffin. I heard them—many, many days ago—yet I dared not—*I dared not speak!* And now—tonight—Ethelred—ha! ha!—the breaking of the hermit's door, and the death-cry of the dragon, and the clangour of the shield!—say, rather, the rending of her coffin, and the grating of the iron hinges of her prison, and her struggles within the coppered archway of the vault! Oh whither shall I fly? Will she not be here anon? Is she not hurrying to upbraid me for my haste? Have I not heard her footstep on the stair? Do I not distinguish that heavy and horrible beating of her heart? Madman!"—here he sprang furiously to his feet, and shrieked out his syllables, as if in the effort he were giving up his soul—"*Madman! I tell you that she now stands without the door!*"

As if in the superhuman energy of his utterance there had been found the potency of a spell—the huge antique panels to which the speaker pointed, threw slowly back, upon the instant, their ponderous and ebony jaws. It was the work of the rushing gust—but then without those doors there *did* stand the lofty and enshrouded figure of the lady Madeline of Usher. There was blood upon her white robes, and the evidence of some bitter struggle upon every portion of her emaciated frame. For a moment she remained trembling and reeling to and fro upon the threshold—then, with a low moaning cry, fell heavily inward upon the person of her brother, and in her violent and now final death-agonies, bore him to the floor a corpse, and a victim to the terrors he had anticipated.

From that chamber, and from that mansion, I fled aghast. The storm was still abroad in all its wrath as I found myself crossing the old causeway. Suddenly there shot along the path a wild light, and I turned to see whence a gleam so unusual could have issued; for the vast house and its shadows were alone behind me. The radiance was that of the full, setting, and blood-red moon, which now shone vividly through that once barely-discernible fissure, of which I have before spoken as extending from the roof of the building, in a zigzag direction, to the base. While I gazed, this fissure rapidly widened—there came a fierce breath of the whirlwind—the entire orb of the satellite burst at once upon my sight—my brain reeled as I saw the mighty walls rushing asunder—there was a long tumultuous shouting sound like the voice of a thousand waters—and the deep and dank tarn at my feet closed sullenly and silently over the fragments of the "*House of Usher*."

1892

THE YELLOW WALL-PAPER

Charlotte Perkins Gilman

One of the greatest horror stories of all time, "The Yellow Wall-Paper", written in 1890, famously had its origins in the enforced bed-rest treatment Gilman was forced to endure for her postpartum depression. As she later remembered: "I went home and obeyed these directions for some three months, and came so near the border line of utter mental ruin that I could see over… [b]eing naturally moved to rejoicing by [my] narrow escape, I wrote The Yellow Wallpaper, with its embellishments and additions to carry out the ideal (I never had hallucinations or objected to my mural decorations) and sent a copy to the physician who so nearly drove me mad. He never acknowledged it." This harrowing tale, long celebrated as an early feminist allegory, admits of multiple interpretations. Is the horror supernatural in nature, or purely psychological? Critics remain divided. Despite fungi being only conceptual or metaphorical here (though I have heard it argued that the story is really about toxic mould), they contribute memorably to Gilman's delineation of her narrator's growing insanity.

It is very seldom that mere ordinary people like John and myself secure ancestral halls for the summer.

A colonial mansion, a hereditary estate, I would say a haunted house, and reach the height of romantic felicity—but that would be asking too much of fate!

Still I will proudly declare that there is something queer about it.

Else, why should it be let so cheaply? And why have stood so long untenanted?

John laughs at me, of course, but one expects that in marriage.

John is practical in the extreme. He has no patience with faith, an intense horror of superstition, and he scoffs openly at any talk of things not to be felt and seen and put down in figures.

John is a physician, and *perhaps*—(I would not say it to a living soul, of course, but this is dead paper and a great relief to my mind—) *perhaps* that is one reason I do not get well faster.

You see he does not believe I am sick!

And what can one do?

If a physician of high standing, and one's own husband, assures friends and relatives that there is really nothing the matter with one but temporary nervous depression—a slight hysterical tendency—what is one to do?

My brother is also a physician, and also of high standing, and he says the same thing.

So I take phosphates or phosphites—whichever it is, and tonics, and journeys, and air, and exercise, and am absolutely forbidden to "work" until I am well again.

Personally, I disagree with their ideas.

Personally, I believe that congenial work, with excitement and change, would do me good.

But what is one to do?

I did write for a while in spite of them; but it *does* exhaust me a good deal—having to be so sly about it, or else meet with heavy opposition.

I sometimes fancy that in my condition if I had less opposition and more society and stimulus—but John says the very worst thing I can do is to think about my condition, and I confess it always makes me feel bad.

So I will let it alone and talk about the house.

The most beautiful place! It is quite alone, standing well back from the road, quite three miles from the village. It makes me think of English places that you read about, for there are hedges and walls and gates that lock, and lots of separate little houses for the gardeners and people.

There is a *delicious* garden! I never saw such a garden—large and shady, full of box-bordered paths, and lined with long grape-covered arbours with seats under them.

There were greenhouses, too, but they are all broken now.

There was some legal trouble, I believe, something about the heirs and co-heirs; anyhow, the place has been empty for years.

That spoils my ghostliness, I am afraid, but I don't care—there is something strange about the house—I can feel it.

I even said so to John one moonlight evening, but he said what I felt was a *draught*, and shut the window.

I get unreasonably angry with John sometimes. I'm sure I never used to be so sensitive. I think it is due to this nervous condition.

But John says if I feel so, I shall neglect proper self-control; so I take pains to control myself—before him, at least, and that makes me very tired.

I don't like our room a bit. I wanted one downstairs that opened on the piazza and had roses all over the window, and such pretty old-fashioned chintz hangings! but John would not hear of it.

He said there was only one window and not room for two beds, and no near room for him if he took another.

He is very careful and loving, and hardly lets me stir without special direction.

I have a schedule prescription for each hour in the day; he takes all care from me, and so I feel basely ungrateful not to value it more.

He said we came here solely on my account, that I was to have perfect rest and all the air I could get. "Your exercise depends on your strength, my dear," said he, "and your food somewhat on your appetite; but air you can absorb all the time." So we took the nursery at the top of the house.

It is a big, airy room, the whole floor nearly, with windows that look all ways, and air and sunshine galore. It was nursery first and then playroom and gymnasium, I should judge; for the windows are barred for little children, and there are rings and things in the walls.

The paint and paper look as if a boys' school had used it. It is stripped off—the paper—in great patches all around the head of my bed, about as far as I can reach, and in a great place on the other side of the room low down. I never saw a worse paper in my life.

One of those sprawling flamboyant patterns committing every artistic sin.

It is dull enough to confuse the eye in following, pronounced enough to constantly irritate and provoke study, and when you follow the lame uncertain curves for a little distance they suddenly commit suicide—plunge off at outrageous angles, destroy themselves in unheard of contradictions.

The colour is repellant, almost revolting; a smouldering unclean yellow, strangely faded by the slow-turning sunlight.

It is a dull yet lurid orange in some places, a sickly sulphur tint in others.

No wonder the children hated it! I should hate it myself if I had to live in this room long.

There comes John, and I must put this away,—he hates to have me write a word.

We have been here two weeks, and I haven't felt like writing before, since that first day.

I am sitting by the window now, up in this atrocious nursery, and there is nothing to hinder my writing as much as I please, save lack of strength.

John is away all day, and even some nights when his cases are serious.

I am glad my case is not serious!

But these nervous troubles are dreadfully depressing.

John does not know how much I really suffer. He knows there is no *reason* to suffer, and that satisfies him.

Of course it is only nervousness. It does weigh on me so not to do my duty in any way!

I meant to be such a help to John, such a real rest and comfort, and here I am a comparative burden already!

Nobody would believe what an effort it is to do what little I am able,—to dress and entertain, and order things.

It is fortunate Mary is so good with the baby. Such a dear baby!

And yet I *cannot* be with him, it makes me so nervous.

I suppose John never was nervous in his life. He laughs at me so about this wall-paper!

At first he meant to repaper the room, but afterwards he said that I was letting it get the better of me, and that nothing was worse for a nervous patient than to give way to such fancies.

He said that after the wall-paper was changed it would be the heavy bedstead, and then the barred windows, and then that gate at the head of the stairs, and so on.

"You know the place is doing you good," he said, "and really, dear, I don't care to renovate the house just for a three months' rental."

"Then do let us go downstairs," I said, "there are such pretty rooms there."

Then he took me in his arms and called me a blessed little goose, and said he would go down cellar, if I wished, and have it whitewashed into the bargain.

But he is right enough about the beds and windows and things.

It is an airy and comfortable room as any one need wish, and, of course, I would not be so silly as to make him uncomfortable just for a whim.

I'm really getting quite fond of the big room, all but that horrid paper.

Out of one window I can see the garden, those mysterious deep-shaded arbours, the riotous old-fashioned flowers, and bushes and gnarly trees.

Out of another I get a lovely view of the bay and a little private wharf belonging to the estate. There is a beautiful shaded lane that runs down there from the house. I always fancy I see people walking in these numerous paths and arbours, but John has cautioned me not to give way to fancy in the least. He says that with my imaginative power and habit of story-making, a nervous weakness like mine is sure to lead to all manner of excited fancies, and that I ought to use my will and good sense to check the tendency. So I try.

I think sometimes that if I were only well enough to write a little it would relieve the press of ideas and rest me.

But I find I get pretty tired when I try.

It is so discouraging not to have any advice and companionship about my work. When I get really well, John says we will ask Cousin Henry and Julia down for a long visit; but he says he would as soon put fireworks in my pillow-case as to let me have those stimulating people about now.

I wish I could get well faster.

But I must not think about that. This paper looks to me as if it *knew* what a vicious influence it had!

There is a recurrent spot where the pattern lolls like a broken neck and two bulbous eyes stare at you upside down.

I get positively angry with the impertinence of it and the everlastingness. Up and down and sideways they crawl, and those absurd, unblinking eyes are everywhere. There is one place where two breaths didn't match, and the eyes go all up and down the line, one a little higher than the other.

I never saw so much expression in an inanimate thing before, and we all know how much expression they have! I used to lie awake as a child and get more entertainment and terror out of blank walls and plain furniture than most children could find in a toy-store.

I remember what a kindly wink the knobs of our big, old bureau used to have, and there was one chair that always seemed like a strong friend.

I used to feel that if any of the other things looked too fierce I could always hop into that chair and be safe.

The furniture in this room is no worse than inharmonious, however, for we had to bring it all from downstairs. I suppose when this was used as a playroom they had to take the nursery things out, and no wonder! I never saw such ravages as the children have made here.

The wall-paper, as I said before, is torn off in spots, and it sticketh closer than a brother—they must have had perseverance as well as hatred.

Then the floor is scratched and gouged and splintered, the plaster itself is dug out here and there, and this great heavy bed which is all we found in the room, looks as if it had been through the wars.

But I don't mind it a bit—only the paper.

There comes John's sister. Such a dear girl as she is, and so careful of me! I must not let her find me writing.

She is a perfect and enthusiastic housekeeper, and hopes for no better profession. I verily believe she thinks it is the writing which made me sick!

But I can write when she is out, and see her a long way off from these windows.

There is one that commands the road, a lovely shaded winding road, and one that just looks off over the country. A lovely country, too, full of great elms and velvet meadows.

This wall-paper has a kind of sub-pattern in a different shade, a particularly irritating one, for you can only see it in certain lights, and not clearly then.

But in the places where it isn't faded and where the sun is just so—I can see a strange, provoking, formless sort of figure, that seems to skulk about behind that silly and conspicuous front design.

There's sister on the stairs!

*

Well, the Fourth of July is over! The people are all gone and I am tired out. John thought it might do me good to see a little company, so we just had mother and Nellie and the children down for a week.

Of course I didn't do a thing. Jennie sees to everything now.

But it tired me all the same.

John says if I don't pick up faster he shall send me to Weir Mitchell in the fall.

But I don't want to go there at all. I had a friend who was in his hands once, and she says he is just like John and my brother, only more so!

Besides, it is such an undertaking to go so far.

I don't feel as if it was worth while to turn my hand over for anything, and I'm getting dreadfully fretful and querulous.

I cry at nothing, and cry most of the time.

Of course I don't when John is here, or anybody else, but when I am alone.

And I am alone a good deal just now. John is kept in town very often by serious cases, and Jennie is good and lets me alone when I want her to.

So I walk a little in the garden or down that lovely lane, sit on the porch under the roses, and lie down up here a good deal.

I'm getting really fond of the room in spite of the wall-paper. Perhaps *because* of the wall-paper.

It dwells in my mind so!

I lie here on this great immovable bed—it is nailed down, I believe—and follow that pattern about by the hour. It is as good as gymnastics, I assure you. I start, we'll say, at the bottom, down in the corner over there where it has not been touched, and I determine for the thousandth time that I *will* follow that pointless pattern to some sort of a conclusion.

I know a little of the principle of design, and I know this thing was not arranged on any laws of radiation, or alternation, or repetition, or symmetry, or anything else that I ever heard of.

It is repeated, of course, by the breadths, but not otherwise.

Looked at in one way each breadth stands alone, the bloated curves and flourishes—a kind of "debased Romanesque" with *delirium tremens*—go waddling up and down in isolated columns of fatuity.

But, on the other hand, they connect diagonally, and the sprawling outlines run off in great slanting waves of optic horror, like a lot of wallowing seaweeds in full chase.

The whole thing goes horizontally, too, at least it seems so, and I exhaust myself in trying to distinguish the order of its going in that direction.

They have used a horizontal breadth for a frieze, and that adds wonderfully to the confusion.

There is one end of the room where it is almost intact, and there, when the crosslights fade and the low sun shines directly upon it, I can almost fancy radiation after all,—the interminable grotesque seem to form around a common centre and rush off in headlong plunges of equal distraction.

It makes me tired to follow it. I will take a nap I guess.

I don't know why I should write this.

I don't want to.

I don't feel able.

And I know John would think it absurd. But I *must* say what I feel and think in some way—it is such a relief!

But the effort is getting to be greater than the relief.

Half the time now I am awfully lazy, and lie down ever so much.

John says I mustn't lose my strength, and has me take cod liver oil and lots of tonics and things, to say nothing of ale and wine and rare meat.

Dear John! He loves me very dearly, and hates to have me sick. I tried to have a real earnest reasonable talk with him the other day, and tell him how I wish he would let me go and make a visit to Cousin Henry and Julia.

But he said I wasn't able to go, nor able to stand it after I got there; and I did not make out a very good case for myself, for I was crying before I had finished.

It is getting to be a great effort for me to think straight. Just this nervous weakness I suppose.

And dear John gathered me up in his arms, and just carried me upstairs and laid me on the bed, and sat by me and read to me till it tired my head.

He said I was his darling and his comfort and all he had, and that I must take care of myself for his sake, and keep well.

He says no one but myself can help me out of it, that I must use my will and self-control and not let any silly fancies run away with me.

There's one comfort, the baby is well and happy, and does not have to occupy this nursery with the horrid wall-paper.

If we had not used it, that blessed child would have! What a fortunate escape! Why, I wouldn't have a child of mine, an impressionable little thing, live in such a room for worlds.

I never thought of it before, but it is lucky that John kept me here after all, I can stand it so much easier than a baby, you see.

Of course I never mention it to them any more—I am too wise,—but I keep watch of it all the same.

There are things in that paper that nobody knows but me, or ever will.

Behind that outside pattern the dim shapes get clearer every day.

It is always the same shape, only very numerous.

And it is like a woman stooping down and creeping about behind that pattern. I don't like it a bit. I wonder—I begin to think—I wish John would take me away from here!

It is so hard to talk with John about my case because he is so wise, and because he loves me so.

But I tried it last night.

It was moonlight. The moon shines in all around just as the sun does.

I hate to see it sometimes, it creeps so slowly, and always comes in by one window or another.

John was asleep and I hated to waken him, so I kept still and watched the moonlight on that undulating wall-paper till I felt creepy.

The faint figure behind seemed to shake the pattern, just as if she wanted to get out.

I got up softly and went to feel and see if the paper *did* move, and when I came back John was awake.

"What is it, little girl?" he said. "Don't go walking about like that—you'll get cold."

I thought it was a good time to talk, so I told him that I really was not gaining here, and that I wished he would take me away.

"Why, darling!" said he, "our lease will be up in three weeks, and I can't see how to leave before.

"The repairs are not done at home, and I cannot possibly leave town just now. Of course if you were in any danger, I could and would, but you really are better, dear, whether you can see it or not. I am a doctor, dear, and I know. You are gaining flesh and colour, your appetite is better, I feel really much easier about you."

"I don't weigh a bit more," said I, "nor as much; and my appetite may be better in the evening when you are here, but it is worse in the morning when you are away!"

"Bless her little heart!" said he with a big hug, "she shall be as sick as she pleases! But now let's improve the shining hours by going to sleep, and talk about it in the morning!"

"And you won't go away?" I asked gloomily.

"Why, how can I, dear? It is only three weeks more and then we will take a nice little trip of a few days while Jennie is getting the house ready. Really dear you are better!"

"Better in body perhaps—" I began, and stopped short, for he sat up straight and looked at me with such a stern, reproachful look that I could not say another word.

"My darling," said he, "I beg of you, for my sake and for our child's sake, as well as for your own, that you will never for one instant let that idea enter your mind! There is nothing so dangerous, so fascinating, to a temperament like yours. It is a false and foolish fancy. Can you not trust me as a physician when I tell you so?"

So of course I said no more on that score, and we went to sleep before long. He thought I was asleep first, but I wasn't, and lay there for hours trying to decide whether that front pattern and the back pattern really did move together or separately.

On a pattern like this, by daylight, there is a lack of sequence, a defiance of law, that is a constant irritant to a normal mind.

The colour is hideous enough, and unreliable enough, and infuriating enough, but the pattern is torturing.

You think you have mastered it, but just as you get well underway in following, it turns a back-somersault and there you are. It slaps you in the face, knocks you down, and tramples upon you. It is like a bad dream.

The outside pattern is a florid arabesque, reminding one of a fungus. If you can imagine a toadstool in joints, an interminable string of toadstools, budding and sprouting in endless convolutions—why, that is something like it.

That is, sometimes!

There is one marked peculiarity about this paper, a thing nobody seems to notice but myself, and that is that it changes as the light changes.

When the sun shoots in through the east window—I always watch for that first long, straight ray—it changes so quickly that I never can quite believe it.

That is why I watch it always.

By moonlight—the moon shines in all night when there is a moon—I wouldn't know it was the same paper.

At night in any kind of light, in twilight, candlelight, lamplight, and worst of all by moonlight, it becomes bars! The outside pattern I mean, and the woman behind it is as plain as can be.

I didn't realize for a long time what the thing was that showed behind, that dim sub-pattern, but now I am quite sure it is a woman.

By daylight she is subdued, quiet. I fancy it is the pattern that keeps her so still. It is so puzzling. It keeps me quiet by the hour.

I lie down ever so much now. John says it is good for me, and to sleep all I can.

Indeed he started the habit by making me lie down for an hour after each meal.

It is a very bad habit I am convinced, for you see I don't sleep. And that cultivates deceit, for I don't tell them I'm awake—O no!

The fact is I am getting a little afraid of John.

He seems very queer sometimes, and even Jennie has an inexplicable look.

It strikes me occasionally, just as a scientific hypothesis,—that perhaps it is the paper!

I have watched John when he did not know I was looking, and come into the room suddenly on the most innocent excuses, and I've caught him several times *looking at the paper*! And Jennie too. I caught Jennie with her hand on it once.

She didn't know I was in the room, and when I asked her in a quiet, a very quiet voice, with the most restrained manner possible, what she was doing with the paper—she turned around as if she had been caught stealing, and looked quite angry—asked me why I should frighten her so!

Then she said that the paper stained everything it touched, that she had found yellow smooches on all my clothes and John's, and she wished we would be more careful!

Did not that sound innocent? But I know she was studying that pattern, and I am determined that nobody shall find it out but myself!

Life is very much more exciting now than it used to be. You see I have something more to expect, to look forward to, to watch. I really do eat better, and am more quiet than I was.

John is so pleased to see me improve! He laughed a little the other day, and said I seemed to be flourishing in spite of my wall-paper.

I turned it off with a laugh. I had no intention of telling him it was *because* of the wall-paper—he would make fun of me. He might even want to take me away.

I don't want to leave now until I have found it out. There is a week more, and I think that will be enough.

I'm feeling ever so much better! I don't sleep much at night, for it is so interesting to watch developments; but I sleep a good deal in the daytime.

In the daytime it is tiresome and perplexing.

There are always new shoots on the fungus, and new shades of yellow all over it. I cannot keep count of them, though I have tried conscientiously.

It is the strangest yellow, that wall-paper! It makes me think of all the yellow things I ever saw—not beautiful ones like buttercups, but old foul, bad yellow things.

But there is something else about that paper—the smell! I noticed it the moment we came into the room, but with so much air and sun it was not bad. Now we have had a week of fog and rain, and whether the windows are open or not, the smell is here.

It creeps all over the house.

I find it hovering in the dining-room, skulking in the parlour, hiding in the hall, lying in wait for me on the stairs.

It gets into my hair.

Even when I go to ride, if I turn my head suddenly and surprise it—there is that smell!

Such a peculiar odour, too! I have spent hours in trying to analyse it, to find what it smelled like.

It is not bad—at first, and very gentle, but quite the subtlest, most enduring odour I ever met.

In this damp weather it is awful, I wake up in the night and find it hanging over me.

It used to disturb me at first. I thought seriously of burning the house—to reach the smell.

But now I am used to it. The only thing I can think of that it is like is the *colour* of the paper! A yellow smell.

There is a very funny mark on this wall, low down, near the mopboard. A streak that runs round the room. It goes behind every piece of furniture, except the bed, a long, straight, even *smooch*, as if it had been rubbed over and over.

I wonder how it was done and who did it, and what they did it for. Round and round and round—round and round and round—it makes me dizzy!

I really have discovered something at last.

Through watching so much at night, when it changes so, I have finally found out.

The front pattern *does* move—and no wonder! The woman behind shakes it!

Sometimes I think there are a great many women behind, and sometimes only one, and she crawls around fast, and her crawling shakes it all over.

Then in the very bright spots she keeps still, and in the very shady spots she just takes hold of the bars and shakes them hard.

And she is all the time trying to climb through. But nobody could climb through that pattern—it strangles so; I think that is why it has so many heads.

They get through, and then the pattern strangles them off and turns them upside down, and makes their eyes white!

If those heads were covered or taken off it would not be half so bad.

I think that woman gets out in the daytime!

And I'll tell you why—privately—I've seen her!

I can see her out of every one of my windows!

It is the same woman, I know, for she is always creeping, and most women do not creep by daylight.

I see her in that long shaded lane, creeping up and down. I see her in those dark grape arbours, creeping all around the garden.

I see her on that long road under the trees, creeping along, and when a carriage comes she hides under the blackberry vines.

I don't blame her a bit. It must be very humiliating to be caught creeping by daylight!

I always lock the door when I creep by daylight. I can't do it at night, for I know John would suspect something at once.

And John is so queer now, that I don't want to irritate him. I wish he would take another room! Besides, I don't want anybody to get that woman out at night but myself.

I often wonder if I could see her out of all the windows at once.

But, turn as fast as I can, I can only see out of one at one time.

And though I always see her, she *may* be able to creep faster than I can turn!

I have watched her sometimes away off in the open country, creeping as fast as a cloud shadow in a high wind.

If only that top pattern could be gotten off from the under one! I mean to try it, little by little.

I have found out another funny thing, but I shan't tell it this time! It does not do to trust people too much.

There are only two more days to get this paper off, and I believe John is beginning to notice. I don't like the look in his eyes.

And I heard him ask Jennie a lot of professional questions about me. She had a very good report to give.

She said I slept a good deal in the daytime.

John knows I don't sleep very well at night, for all I'm so quiet!

He asked me all sorts of questions, too, and pretended to be very loving and kind.

As if I couldn't see through him!

Still, I don't wonder he acts so, sleeping under this paper for three months.

It only interests me, but I feel sure John and Jennie are secretly affected by it. Hurrah! This is the last day, but it is enough. John to stay in town over night, and won't be out until this evening.

Jennie wanted to sleep with me—the sly thing! but I told her I should undoubtedly rest better for a night all alone.

That was clever, for really I wasn't alone a bit! As soon as it was moonlight and that poor thing began to crawl and shake the pattern, I got up and ran to help her.

I pulled and she shook, I shook and she pulled, and before morning we had peeled off yards of that paper.

A strip about as high as my head and half around the room.

And then when the sun came and that awful pattern began to laugh at me, I declared I would finish it today!

We go away tomorrow, and they are moving all my furniture down again to leave things as they were before.

Jennie looked at the wall in amazement, but I told her merrily that I did it out of pure spite at the vicious thing.

She laughed and said she wouldn't mind doing it herself, but I must not get tired.

How she betrayed herself that time!

But I am here, and no person touches this paper but me,—not *alive*!

She tried to get me out of the room—it was too patent! But I said it was so quiet and empty and clean now that I believed I would lie down again and sleep all I could; and not to wake me even for dinner—I would call when I woke.

So now she is gone, and the servants are gone, and the things are gone, and there is nothing left but that great bedstead nailed down, with the canvas mattress we found on it.

We shall sleep downstairs tonight, and take the boat home tomorrow.

I quite enjoy the room, now it is bare again.

How those children did tear about here!

This bedstead is fairly gnawed!

But I must get to work.

I have locked the door and thrown the key down into the front path.

I don't want to go out, and I don't want to have anybody come in, till John comes.

I want to astonish him.

I've got a rope up here that even Jennie did not find. If that woman does get out, and tries to get away, I can tie her!

But I forgot I could not reach far without anything to stand on!

This bed will *not* move!

I tried to lift and push it until I was lame, and then I got so angry I bit off a little piece at one corner—but it hurt my teeth.

Then I peeled off all the paper I could reach standing on the floor. It sticks horribly and the pattern just enjoys it! All those strangled heads and bulbous eyes and waddling fungus growths just shriek with derision!

I am getting angry enough to do something desperate. To jump out of the window would be admirable exercise, but the bars are too strong even to try.

Besides I wouldn't do it. Of course not. I know well enough that a step like that is improper and might be misconstrued.

I don't like to *look* out of the windows even—there are so many of those creeping women, and they creep so fast.

I wonder if they all come out of that wall-paper as I did?

But I am securely fastened now by my well-hidden rope—you don't get *me* out in the road there!

I suppose I shall have to get back behind the pattern when it comes night, and that is hard!

It is so pleasant to be out in this great room and creep around as I please!

I don't want to go outside. I won't, even if Jennie asks me to.

For outside you have to creep on the ground, and everything is green instead of yellow.

But here I can creep smoothly on the floor, and my shoulder just fits in that long smooch around the wall, so I cannot lose my way.

Why there's John at the door!

It is no use, young man, you can't open it!

How he does call and pound!

Now he's crying for an axe.

It would be a shame to break down that beautiful door!

"John dear!" said I in the gentlest voice, "the key is down by the front steps, under a plantain leaf!"

That silenced him for a few moments.

Then he said—very quietly indeed, "Open the door, my darling!"

"I can't," said I. "The key is down by the front door under a plantain leaf!"

And then I said it again, several times, very gently and slowly, and said it so often that he had to go and see, and he got it of course, and came in. He stopped short by the door.

"What is the matter?" he cried. "For God's sake, what are you doing!"

I kept on creeping just the same, but I looked at him over my shoulder.

"I've got out at last," said I, "in spite of you and Jane? And I've pulled off most of the paper, so you can't put me back!"

Now why should that man have fainted? But he did, and right across my path by the wall, so that I had to creep over him every time!

1937

THE SHUNNED HOUSE

H. P. Lovecraft

Among his other claims as an innovator in the development of modern horror fiction, one might call genre titan H. P. Lovecraft (1890–1937) an early practitioner of the fungal weird: he envisioned a race of extraterrestrial fungoid lifeforms, the Mi-Go, who hail from Pluto ("Yuggoth" in the Lovecraftian cosmos); they feature prominently in the novella "The Whisperer in Darkness" and seem to be referenced in the title of his sonnet sequence *Fungi from Yuggoth*. There are "fungous moon-beasts" (as well as "grotesque", "obscene" fungi and "rotting mould" galore) in *The Dream-Quest of Unknown Kadath*, and "fungous, flabby beasts" in the hair-raising "The Rats in the Walls". Post-Lovecraft authors who have taken the fungal theme to new extremes include Brian Lumley, Ramsey Campbell, Marc Laidlaw, Caitlín R. Kiernan, and Jeff VanderMeer (though he, I think, would disavow the connection). But perhaps the most consistently mycologically-inflected story by Lovecraft himself is the following tale, written in 1924 (but published in *Weird Tales* magazine in October 1937) and based on an actual house in his native Providence, Rhode Island. It's at 135 Benefit Street, in case you are planning a pilgrimage there—but here's a protip: bring your flamethrower, and plenty of sulphuric acid.

I.

From even the greatest of horrors irony is seldom absent. Sometimes it enters directly into the composition of the events, while sometimes it relates only to their fortuitous position among persons and places. The latter sort is splendidly exemplified by a case in the ancient city of Providence, where in the late forties Edgar Allan Poe used to sojourn often during his unsuccessful wooing of the gifted poetess, Mrs. Whitman. Poe generally stopped at the Mansion House in Benefit Street—the renamed Golden Ball Inn whose roof has sheltered Washington, Jefferson, and Lafayette—and his favourite walk led northward along the same street to Mrs. Whitman's home and the neighbouring hillside churchyard of St. John's, whose hidden expanse of eighteenth-century gravestones had for him a peculiar fascination.

Now the irony is this. In this walk, so many times repeated, the world's greatest master of the terrible and the bizarre was obliged to pass a particular house on the eastern side of the street; a dingy, antiquated structure perched on the abruptly rising side-hill, with a great unkempt yard dating from a time when the region was partly open country. It does not appear that he ever wrote or spoke of it, nor is there any evidence that he even noticed it. And yet that house, to the two persons in possession of certain information, equals or outranks in horror the wildest phantasy of the genius who so often passed it unknowingly, and stands starkly leering as a symbol of all that is unutterably hideous.

The house was—and for that matter still is—of a kind to attract the attention of the curious. Originally a farm or semi-farm building, it followed the average New England colonial lines of the middle eighteenth century—the prosperous peaked-roof sort, with two storeys and dormerless attic, and with the Georgian doorway and interior panelling dictated by the progress of taste at that time. It faced south, with one gable end buried to the lower windows in the eastward rising hill, and the other exposed to the foundations toward the street. Its construction, over a century and a half ago, had followed the grading and straightening of the road in that especial vicinity; for Benefit Street—at first called Back Street—was laid out as a lane winding amongst the graveyards of the first settlers, and straightened only when the removal of the bodies to the North Burial Ground made it decently possible to cut through the old family plots.

At the start, the western wall had lain some twenty feet up a precipitous lawn from the roadway; but a widening of the street at about the time of the Revolution sheared off most of the intervening space, exposing the foundations so that a brick basement wall had to be made, giving the deep cellar a street frontage with door and two windows above ground, close to the new line of public travel. When the sidewalk was laid out a century ago the last of the intervening space was removed; and Poe in his walks must have seen only a sheer ascent of dull grey brick flush with the sidewalk and surmounted at a height of ten feet by the antique shingled bulk of the house proper.

The farm-like grounds extended back very deeply up the hill, almost to Wheaton Street. The space south of the house, abutting on Benefit Street, was of course greatly above the existing sidewalk level, forming a terrace bounded by a high bank wall of damp, mossy stone pierced by a steep flight of narrow steps which led inward between canyon-like surfaces to the upper region of mangy lawn, rheumy brick walls, and neglected gardens whose dismantled cement urns, rusted kettles fallen from tripods of knotty sticks, and similar paraphernalia set off the weather-beaten front door with its broken fanlight, rotting Ionic pilasters, and wormy triangular pediment.

What I heard in my youth about the shunned house was merely that people died there in alarmingly great numbers. That, I was told, was why the original owners had moved out some twenty years after building the place. It was plainly unhealthy, perhaps because of the dampness and fungous growth in the cellar, the general sickish smell, the draughts of the hallways, or the quality of the well and pump water. These things were bad enough, and these were all that gained belief among the persons whom I knew. Only the notebooks of my antiquarian uncle, Dr. Elihu Whipple, revealed to me at length the darker, vaguer surmises which formed an undercurrent of folklore among old-time servants and humble folk; surmises which never travelled far, and which were largely forgotten when Providence grew to be a metropolis with a shifting modern population.

The general fact is, that the house was never regarded by the solid part of the community as in any real sense "haunted". There were no widespread tales of rattling chains, cold currents of air, extinguished lights, or faces at the window. Extremists sometimes said the house was "unlucky", but that is as far as even they went. What was really beyond dispute is that a frightful proportion of persons died there; or more accurately, *had* died there, since after some peculiar happenings over sixty years ago the building had become deserted through the sheer impossibility of renting it. These persons were not all cut off suddenly by any one cause; rather did it seem that their vitality was insidiously sapped, so that each one died the sooner from whatever tendency to weakness he may have naturally had. And those who did not die displayed in varying degree a type of anaemia or consumption, and sometimes a decline of the mental faculties, which spoke ill for the salubriousness of the building. Neighbouring houses, it must be added, seemed entirely free from the noxious quality.

This much I knew before my insistent questioning led my uncle to shew me the notes which finally embarked us both on our hideous investigation. In my childhood the shunned house was vacant, with barren, gnarled, and terrible old trees, long, queerly pale grass, and nightmarishly misshapen weeds in the high terraced yard where birds never lingered. We boys used to overrun the place, and I can still recall my youthful terror not only at the morbid strangeness of this sinister vegetation, but at the eldritch atmosphere and odour of the dilapidated house, whose unlocked front door was often entered in quest of shudders. The small-paned windows were largely broken, and a nameless air of desolation hung round the precarious panelling, shaky interior shutters, peeling wall-paper, falling plaster, rickety staircases, and such fragments of battered furniture as still remained. The dust and cobwebs added their touch of the fearful; and brave indeed was the boy who would voluntarily ascend the ladder to the attic, a vast raftered length lighted only by small blinking windows in the gable ends, and filled with a massed wreckage of chests, chairs, and spinning-wheels which infinite years of deposit had shrouded and festooned into monstrous and hellish shapes.

But after all, the attic was not the most terrible part of the house. It was the dank, humid cellar which somehow exerted the strongest repulsion on us, even though it was wholly above ground on the street side, with only a thin door and window-pierced brick wall to separate it from the busy sidewalk. We scarcely knew whether to haunt it in spectral fascination, or to shun it for the sake of our souls and our sanity. For one thing, the bad odour of the house was strongest there; and for another thing, we did not like the white fungous growths which occasionally sprang up in rainy summer weather from the hard earth floor. Those fungi, grotesquely like the vegetation in the yard outside, were truly horrible in their outlines; detestable parodies of toadstools and Indian pipes, whose like we had never seen in any other situation. They rotted quickly, and at one stage became slightly phosphorescent; so that nocturnal passers-by sometimes spoke of witch-fires glowing behind the broken panes of the foetor-spreading windows.

We never—even in our wildest Hallowe'en moods—visited this cellar by night, but in some of our daytime visits could detect the phosphorescence, especially when the day was dark and wet. There was also a subtler thing we often thought we detected—a very strange thing which was, however, merely suggestive at most. I refer to a sort of cloudy whitish pattern on the dirt floor—a vague, shifting deposit of mould or nitre which we sometimes thought we could trace amidst the sparse fungous growths near the huge fireplace of the basement kitchen. Once in a while it struck us that this patch bore an uncanny resemblance to a doubled-up human figure, though generally no such kinship existed, and often there was no whitish deposit whatever. On a certain rainy afternoon when this illusion seemed phenomenally strong, and when, in addition, I had fancied I glimpsed a kind of thin, yellowish, shimmering exhalation rising from the nitrous pattern toward the yawning fireplace, I spoke to my uncle about the matter. He smiled at this odd conceit, but it seemed that his smile was tinged with reminiscence. Later I heard that a similar notion entered into some of the wild ancient tales of the common folk—a notion likewise alluding to ghoulish, wolfish shapes taken by smoke from the great chimney, and queer contours assumed by certain of the sinuous tree-roots that thrust their way into the cellar through the loose foundation-stones.

II.

Not till my adult years did my uncle set before me the notes and data which he had collected concerning the shunned house. Dr. Whipple was a sane, conservative physician of the old school, and for all his interest in the place was not eager to encourage young thoughts toward the abnormal. His own view, postulating simply a building and location of markedly unsanitary qualities, had nothing to do with abnormality; but he realized that the very picturesqueness which aroused his own interest would in a boy's fanciful mind take on all manner of gruesome imaginative associations.

The doctor was a bachelor; a white-haired, clean-shaven, old-fashioned gentleman, and a local historian of note, who had often broken a lance with such controversial guardians of tradition as Sidney S. Rider and Thomas W. Bicknell. He lived with one manservant in a Georgian homestead with knocker and iron-railed steps, balanced eerily on the steep ascent of North Court Street beside the ancient brick court and colony house where his grandfather—a cousin of that celebrated privateersman, Capt. Whipple, who burnt His Majesty's armed schooner *Gaspee* in 1772—had voted in the legislature on May 4, 1776, for the independence of the Rhode-Island Colony. Around him in the damp, low-ceiled library with the musty white panelling, heavy carved overmantel, and small-paned, vine-shaded windows, were the relics and records of his ancient family, among which were many dubious allusions to the shunned house in Benefit Street. That pest spot lies not far distant—for Benefit runs ledgewise just above the court-house along the precipitous hill up which the first settlement climbed.

When, in the end, my insistent pestering and maturing years evoked from my uncle the hoarded lore I sought, there lay before me a strange enough chronicle. Long-winded, statistical, and drearily genealogical as some of the matter was, there ran through it a continuous thread of brooding, tenacious horror and preternatural malevolence which impressed me even more than it had impressed the good doctor. Separate events fitted together uncannily, and seemingly irrelevant details held mines of hideous possibilities. A new and burning curiosity grew in me, compared to which my boyish curiosity was feeble and inchoate. The first revelation led to an exhaustive research, and finally to that shuddering quest which proved so disastrous to myself and mine. For at last my uncle insisted on joining the search I had commenced, and after a certain night in that house he did not come away with me. I am lonely without that gentle soul whose long years were filled only with honour, virtue, good taste, benevolence, and learning. I have reared a marble urn to his memory in St. John's churchyard—the place that Poe loved—the hidden grove of giant willows on the hill, where tombs and headstones huddle quietly between the hoary bulk of the church and the houses and bank walls of Benefit Street.

The history of the house, opening amidst a maze of dates, revealed no trace of the sinister either about its construction or about the prosperous and honourable family who built it. Yet from the first a taint of calamity, soon increased to boding significance, was apparent. My uncle's carefully compiled record began with the building of the structure in 1763, and followed the theme with an unusual amount of detail. The shunned house, it seems, was first inhabited by William Harris and his wife Rhoby Dexter, with their children, Elkanah, born in 1755, Abigail, born in 1757, William, Jr., born in 1759, and Ruth, born in 1761. Harris was a substantial merchant and seaman in the West India trade, connected with the firm of Obadiah Brown and his nephews. After Brown's death in 1761, the new firm of Nicholas

Brown & Co. made him master of the brig *Prudence*, Providence-built, of 120 tons, thus enabling him to erect the new homestead he had desired ever since his marriage.

The site he had chosen—a recently straightened part of the new and fashionable Back Street, which ran along the side of the hill above crowded Cheapside—was all that could be wished, and the building did justice to the location. It was the best that moderate means could afford, and Harris hastened to move in before the birth of a fifth child which the family expected. That child, a boy, came in December; but was still-born. Nor was any child to be born alive in that house for a century and a half.

The next April sickness occurred among the children, and Abigail and Ruth died before the month was over. Dr. Job Ives diagnosed the trouble as some infantile fever, though others declared it was more of a mere wasting-away or decline. It seemed, in any event, to be contagious; for Hannah Bowen, one of the two servants, died of it in the following June. Eli Liddeason, the other servant, constantly complained of weakness; and would have returned to his father's farm in Rehoboth but for a sudden attachment for Mehitabel Pierce, who was hired to succeed Hannah. He died the next year—a sad year indeed, since it marked the death of William Harris himself, enfeebled as he was by the climate of Martinique, where his occupation had kept him for considerable periods during the preceding decade.

The widowed Rhoby Harris never recovered from the shock of her husband's death, and the passing of her first-born Elkanah two years later was the final blow to her reason. In 1768 she fell victim to a mild form of insanity, and was thereafter confined to the upper part of the house; her elder maiden sister, Mercy Dexter, having moved in to take charge of the family. Mercy was a plain, raw-boned woman of great strength; but her health visibly declined from the time of her advent. She was greatly devoted to her unfortunate sister, and had an especial affection for her only surviving nephew William, who from a sturdy infant had become a sickly, spindling lad. In this year the servant Mehitabel died, and the other servant, Preserved Smith, left without coherent explanation—or at least, with only some wild tales and a complaint that he disliked the smell of the place. For a time Mercy could secure no more help, since the seven deaths and case of madness, all occurring within five years' space, had begun to set in motion the body of fireside rumour which later became so bizarre. Ultimately, however, she obtained new servants from out of town; Ann White, a morose woman from that part of North Kingstown now set off as the township of Exeter, and a capable Boston man named Zenas Low.

It was Ann White who first gave definite shape to the sinister idle talk. Mercy should have known better than to hire anyone from the Nooseneck Hill country, for that remote bit of backwoods was then, as now, a seat of the most uncomfortable superstitions. As lately as 1892 an Exeter community exhumed a dead body and ceremoniously burnt its heart in order to prevent certain alleged visitations injurious to the public health and peace, and one may imagine the point of view of the same section in 1768. Ann's tongue was perniciously active, and within a few months Mercy discharged her, filling her place with a faithful and amiable Amazon from Newport, Maria Robbins.

Meanwhile poor Rhoby Harris, in her madness, gave voice to dreams and imaginings of the most hideous sort. At times her screams became insupportable, and for long periods she would utter shrieking horrors which necessitated her son's temporary residence with his cousin, Peleg Harris, in Presbyterian Lane near the new college building. The boy would seem to improve after these visits, and had Mercy been as wise as she was well-meaning, she would have let him live permanently with Peleg. Just what Mrs. Harris cried out in her fits of violence, tradition hesitates to say; or rather, presents such extravagant accounts that they nullify themselves through sheer absurdity. Certainly it sounds absurd to hear that a woman educated only in the rudiments of French often shouted for hours in a coarse and idiomatic form of that language, or that the same person, alone and guarded, complained wildly of a staring thing which bit and chewed at her. In 1772 the servant Zenas died, and when Mrs. Harris heard of it she laughed with a shocking delight utterly foreign to her. The next year she herself died, and was laid to rest in the North Burial Ground beside her husband.

Upon the outbreak of trouble with Great Britain in 1775, William Harris, despite his scant sixteen years and feeble constitution, managed to enlist in the Army of Observation under General Greene; and from that time on enjoyed a steady rise in health and prestige. In 1780, as a Captain in Rhode Island forces in New Jersey under Colonel Angell, he met and married Phebe Hetfield of Elizabethtown, whom he brought to Providence upon his honourable discharge in the following year.

The young soldier's return was not a thing of unmitigated happiness. The house, it is true, was still in good condition; and the street had been widened and changed in name from Back Street to Benefit Street. But Mercy Dexter's once robust frame had undergone a sad and curious decay, so that she was now a stooped and pathetic figure with hollow voice and disconcerting pallor—qualities shared to a singular degree by the one remaining servant Maria. In the autumn of 1782 Phebe Harris gave birth to a still-born daughter, and on the fifteenth of the next May Mercy Dexter took leave of a useful, austere, and virtuous life.

William Harris, at last thoroughly convinced of the radically unhealthful nature of his abode, now took steps toward quitting it and closing it for ever. Securing temporary quarters for himself and his wife at the newly opened Golden Ball Inn, he arranged for the building of a new and finer house in Westminster Street, in the growing part of the town across the Great Bridge. There, in 1785, his son Dutee was born; and there the family dwelt till the encroachments of commerce drove them back across the river and over the hill to Angell Street, in the newer East Side residence district, where the late Archer Harris built his sumptuous but hideous French-roofed mansion in 1876. William and Phebe both succumbed to the yellow fever epidemic of 1797, but Dutee was brought up by his cousin Rathbone Harris, Peleg's son.

Rathbone was a practical man, and rented the Benefit Street house despite William's wish to keep it vacant. He considered it an obligation to his ward to make the most of all the boy's property, nor did he concern himself with the deaths and illnesses which caused so many changes of tenants, or the steadily growing aversion with which the house was generally regarded. It is likely that he felt only vexation when, in 1804, the town council ordered him to fumigate the place with sulphur, tar, and gum camphor on account of the much-discussed deaths of four persons, presumably caused by the then diminishing fever epidemic. They said the place had a febrile smell.

Dutee himself thought little of the house, for he grew up to be a privateersman, and served with distinction on the *Vigilant* under Capt. Cahoone in the War of 1812. He returned unharmed, married in 1814, and became a father on that memorable night of September 23, 1815, when a great gale drove the waters of the bay over half the town, and floated a tall sloop well up Westminster Street so that its masts almost tapped the Harris windows in symbolic affirmation that the new boy, Welcome, was a seaman's son.

Welcome did not survive his father, but lived to perish gloriously at Fredericksburg in 1862. Neither he nor his son Archer knew of the shunned house as other than a nuisance almost impossible to rent—perhaps on account of the mustiness and sickly odour of unkempt old age. Indeed, it never was rented after a series of deaths culminating in 1861, which the excitement of the war tended to throw into obscurity. Carrington Harris, last of the male line, knew it only as a deserted and somewhat picturesque centre of legend until I told him my experience. He had meant to tear it down and build an apartment house on the site, but after my account decided to let it stand, install plumbing, and rent it. Nor has he yet had any difficulty in obtaining tenants. The horror has gone.

III.

It may well be imagined how powerfully I was affected by the annals of the Harrises. In this continuous record there seemed to me to brood a persistent evil beyond anything in Nature as I had known it; an evil clearly connected with the house and not with the family. This impression was confirmed by my uncle's less systematic array of miscellaneous data—legends transcribed from servant gossip, cuttings from the papers, copies of death-certificates by fellow-physicians, and the like. All of this material I cannot hope to give, for my uncle was a tireless antiquarian and very deeply interested in the shunned house; but I may refer to several dominant points which earn notice by their recurrence through many reports from diverse sources. For example, the servant gossip was practically unanimous in attributing to the fungous and malodorous *cellar* of the house a vast supremacy in evil influence. There had been servants—Ann White especially—who would not use the cellar kitchen, and at least three well-defined legends bore upon the queer quasi-human or diabolic outlines assumed by tree-roots and patches of mould in that region. These latter narratives interested me profoundly, on account of what I had seen in my boyhood, but I felt that most of the significance had in each case been largely obscured by additions from the common stock of local ghost lore.

Ann White, with her Exeter superstition, had promulgated the most extravagant and at the same time most consistent tale; alleging that there must lie buried beneath the house one of those vampires—the dead who retain their bodily form and live on the blood or breath of the living—whose hideous legions send their preying shapes or spirits abroad by night. To destroy a vampire one must, the grandmothers say, exhume it and burn its heart, or at least drive a stake through that organ; and Ann's dogged insistence on a search under the cellar had been prominent in bringing about her discharge.

Her tales, however, commanded a wide audience, and were the more readily accepted because the house indeed stood on land once used for burial purposes. To me their interest depended less on this circumstance than on the peculiarly appropriate way in which they dovetailed with certain other things—the complaint of the departing servant Preserved Smith, who had preceded Ann and never heard of her, that something "sucked his breath" at night; the death-certificates of fever victims of 1804, issued by Dr. Chad Hopkins, and shewing the four deceased persons all unaccountably lacking in blood; and the obscure passages of poor Rhoby Harris's ravings, where she complained of the sharp teeth of a glassy-eyed, half-visible presence.

Free from unwarranted superstition though I am, these things produced in me an odd sensation, which was intensified by a pair of widely separated newspaper cuttings relating to deaths in the shunned house—one from the *Providence Gazette and Country-Journal* of April 12, 1815, and the other from the *Daily Transcript and Chronicle* of October 27, 1845—each of which detailed an appallingly grisly circumstance whose duplication was remarkable. It seems that in both instances the dying person, in 1815 a gentle old lady named Stafford and in 1845 a school-teacher of middle age named Eleazar Durfee, became transfigured in a horrible way; glaring glassily and attempting to bite the throat of the attending physician. Even more puzzling, though, was the final case which put an end to the renting of the house—a series of anaemia deaths preceded by progressive madnesses wherein the patient would craftily attempt the lives of his relatives by incisions in the neck or wrist.

This was in 1860 and 1861, when my uncle had just begun his medical practice; and before leaving for the front he heard much of it from his elder professional colleagues. The really inexplicable thing was the way in which the victims—ignorant people, for the ill-smelling and widely shunned house could now be rented to no others—would babble maledictions in French, a language they could not possibly have studied to any extent. It made one think of poor Rhoby Harris nearly a century before, and so moved my uncle that he commenced collecting historical data on the house after listening, some time subsequent to his return from the war, to the first-hand account of Drs. Chase and Whitmarsh. Indeed, I could see that my uncle had thought deeply on the subject, and that he was glad of my own interest—an open-minded and sympathetic interest which enabled him to discuss with me matters at which others would merely have laughed. His fancy had not gone so far as mine, but he felt that the place was rare in its imaginative potentialities, and worthy of note as an inspiration in the field of the grotesque and macabre.

For my part, I was disposed to take the whole subject with profound seriousness, and began at once not only to review the evidence, but to accumulate as much more as I could. I talked with the elderly Archer Harris, then owner of the house, many times before his death in 1916; and obtained from him and his still surviving maiden sister Alice an authentic corroboration of all the family data my uncle had collected. When, however, I asked them what connexion with France or its language the house could have, they confessed themselves as frankly baffled and ignorant as I. Archer knew nothing, and all that Miss Harris could say was that an old allusion her grandfather, Dutee Harris, had heard of might have shed a little light. The old seaman, who had survived his son Welcome's death in battle by two years, had not himself known the legend; but recalled that his earliest nurse, the ancient Maria Robbins, seemed darkly aware of something that might have lent a weird significance to the French ravings of Rhoby Harris, which she had so often heard during the last days of that hapless woman. Maria had been at the shunned house from 1769 till the removal of the family in 1783, and had seen Mercy Dexter die. Once she hinted to the child Dutee of a somewhat peculiar circumstance in Mercy's last moments, but he had soon forgotten all about it save that it was something peculiar. The granddaughter, moreover, recalled even this much with difficulty. She and her brother were not so much interested in the house as was Archer's son Carrington, the present owner, with whom I talked after my experience.

Having exhausted the Harris family of all the information it could furnish, I turned my attention to early town records and deeds with a zeal more penetrating than that which my uncle had occasionally shewn in the same work. What I wished was a comprehensive history of the site from its very settlement in 1636—or even before, if any Narragansett Indian legend could be unearthed to supply the data. I found, at the start, that the land had been part of the long strip of home lot granted originally to John Throckmorton; one of many similar strips beginning at the Town Street beside the river and extending up over the hill to a line roughly corresponding with the modern Hope Street. The Throckmorton lot had later, of course, been much subdivided; and I became very assiduous in tracing that section through which Back or Benefit Street was later run. It had, a rumour indeed said, been the Throckmorton graveyard; but as I examined the records more carefully, I found that the graves had all been transferred at an early date to the North Burial Ground on the Pawtucket West Road.

Then suddenly I came—by a rare piece of chance, since it was not in the main body of records and might easily have been missed—upon something which aroused my keenest eagerness, fitting in as it did with several of the queerest phases of the affair. It was the record of a lease, in 1697, of a small tract of ground to an Etienne Roulet and wife. At last the French element had appeared—that, and another deeper element of horror which the name conjured up from the darkest recesses of my weird and heterogeneous reading—and I feverishly studied the platting of the locality as it had been before the cutting through and partial straightening of Back Street between 1747 and 1758. I found what I had half expected, that where the shunned house now stood the Roulets had laid out their graveyard behind a one-storey and attic cottage, and that no record of any transfer of graves existed. The document, indeed, ended in much confusion; and I was forced to ransack both the Rhode Island Historical Society and Shepley Library before I could find a local door which the name Etienne Roulet would unlock. In the end I did find something; something of such vague but monstrous import that I set about at once to examine the cellar of the shunned house itself with a new and excited minuteness.

The Roulets, it seemed, had come in 1696 from East Greenwich, down the west shore of Narragansett Bay. They were Huguenots from Caude, and had encountered much opposition before the Providence selectmen allowed them to settle in the town. Unpopularity had dogged them in East Greenwich, whither they had come in 1686, after the revocation of the Edict of Nantes, and rumour said that the cause of dislike extended beyond mere racial and national prejudice, or the land disputes which involved other French settlers with the English in rivalries which not even Governor Andros could quell. But their ardent Protestantism—too ardent, some whispered—and their evident distress when virtually driven from the village down the bay, had moved the sympathy of the town fathers. Here the strangers had been granted a haven; and the swarthy Etienne Roulet, less apt at agriculture than at reading queer books and drawing queer diagrams, was given a clerical post in the warehouse at Pardon Tillinghast's wharf, far south in Town Street. There had, however, been a riot of some sort later on—perhaps forty years later, after old Roulet's death—and no one seemed to hear of the family after that.

For a century and more, it appeared, the Roulets had been well remembered and frequently discussed as vivid incidents in the quiet life of a New England seaport. Etienne's son Paul, a surly fellow whose erratic conduct had probably provoked the riot which wiped out the family, was particularly a source of speculation; and though Providence never shared the witchcraft panics of her Puritan neighbours, it was freely intimated by old wives that his prayers were neither uttered at the proper time nor directed toward the proper object. All this had undoubtedly formed the basis of the legend known by old Maria Robbins. What relation it had to the French ravings of Rhoby Harris and other inhabitants of the shunned house, imagination or future discovery alone could determine. I wondered how many of those who had known the legends realized that additional link with the terrible which my wider reading had given me; that ominous item in the annals of morbid horror which tells of the creature *Jacques Roulet, of Caude,* who in 1598 was condemned to death as a daemoniac but afterward saved from the stake by the Paris parliament and shut in a madhouse. He had been found covered with blood and shreds of flesh in a wood, shortly after the killing and rending of a boy by a pair of wolves. One wolf was seen to lope away unhurt. Surely a pretty hearthside tale, with a queer significance as to name and place; but I decided that the Providence gossips could not have generally known of it. Had they known, the coincidence of names would have brought some drastic and frightened action—indeed, might not its limited whispering have precipitated the final riot which erased the Roulets from the town?

I now visited the accursed place with increased frequency; studying the unwholesome vegetation of the garden, examining all the walls of the building, and poring over every inch of the earthen cellar floor. Finally, with Carrington Harris's permission, I fitted a key to the disused door opening from the cellar directly upon Benefit Street, preferring to have a more immediate access to the outside world than the dark stairs, ground-floor hall, and front door could give. There, where morbidity lurked most thickly, I searched and poked during long afternoons when the sunlight filtered in through the cobwebbed above-ground windows, and a sense of security glowed from the unlocked door which placed me only a few feet from the placid sidewalk outside. Nothing new rewarded my efforts—only the same depressing mustiness and faint suggestions of noxious odours and nitrous outlines on the floor—and I fancy that many pedestrians must have watched me curiously through the broken panes.

At length, upon a suggestion of my uncle's, I decided to try the spot nocturnally; and one stormy midnight ran the beams of an electric torch over the mouldy floor with its uncanny shapes and distorted, half-phosphorescent fungi. The place had dispirited me curiously that evening, and I was almost prepared when I saw—or thought I saw—amidst the whitish deposits a particularly sharp definition of the "huddled form" I had suspected from boyhood. Its clearness was astonishing and unprecedented—and as I watched I seemed to see again the thin, yellowish, shimmering exhalation which had startled me on that rainy afternoon so many years before.

Above the anthropomorphic patch of mould by the fireplace it rose; a subtle, sickish, almost luminous vapour which as it hung trembling in the dampness seemed to develop vague and shocking suggestions of form, gradually trailing off into nebulous decay and passing up into the blackness of the great chimney with a foetor in its wake. It was truly horrible, and the more so to me because of what I knew of the spot. Refusing to flee, I watched it fade—and as I watched I felt that it was in turn watching me greedily with eyes more imaginable than visible. When I told my uncle about it he was greatly aroused; and after a tense hour of reflection, arrived at a definite and drastic decision. Weighing in his mind the importance of the matter, and the significance of our relation to it, he insisted that we both test—and if possible destroy—the horror of the house by a joint night or nights of aggressive vigil in that musty and fungus-cursed cellar.

IV.

On Wednesday, June 25, 1919, after a proper notification of Carrington Harris which did not include surmises as to what we expected to find, my uncle and I conveyed to the shunned house two camp chairs and a folding camp cot, together with some scientific mechanism of greater weight and intricacy. These we placed in the cellar during the day, screening the windows with paper and planning to return in the evening for our first vigil. We had locked the door from the cellar to the ground floor; and having a key to the outside cellar door, we were prepared to leave our expensive and delicate apparatus—which we had obtained secretly and at great cost—as many days as our vigils might need to be protracted. It was our design to sit up together till very late, and then watch singly till dawn in two-hour stretches, myself first and then my companion; the inactive member resting on the cot.

The natural leadership with which my uncle procured the instruments from the laboratories of Brown University and the Cranston Street Armoury, and instinctively assumed direction of our venture, was a marvellous commentary on the potential vitality and resilience of a man of eighty-one. Elihu Whipple had lived according to the hygienic laws he had preached as a physician, and but for what happened later would be here in full vigour today. Only two persons suspect what did happen—Carrington Harris and myself. I had to tell Harris because he owned the house and deserved to know what had gone out of it. Then too, we had spoken to him in advance of our quest; and I felt after my uncle's going that he would understand and assist me in some vitally necessary public explanations. He turned very pale, but agreed to help me, and decided that it would now be safe to rent the house.

To declare that we were not nervous on that rainy night of watching would be an exaggeration both gross and ridiculous. We were not, as I have said, in any sense childishly superstitious, but scientific study and reflection had taught us that the known universe of three dimensions embraces the merest fraction of the whole cosmos of substance and energy. In this case an overwhelming preponderance of evidence from numerous authentic sources pointed to the tenacious existence of certain forces of great power and, so far as the human point of view is concerned, exceptional malignancy. To say that we actually believed in vampires or werewolves would be a carelessly inclusive statement. Rather must it be said that we were not prepared to deny the possibility of certain unfamiliar and unclassified modifications of vital force and attenuated matter; existing very infrequently in three-dimensional space because of its more intimate connexion with other spatial units, yet close enough to the boundary of our own to furnish us occasional manifestations which we, for lack of a proper vantage-point, may never hope to understand.

In short, it seemed to my uncle and me that an incontrovertible array of facts pointed to some lingering influence in the shunned house; traceable to one or another of the ill-favoured French settlers of two centuries before, and still operative through rare and unknown laws of atomic and electronic motion. That the family of Roulet had possessed an abnormal affinity for outer circles of entity—dark spheres which for normal folk hold only repulsion and terror—their recorded history seemed to prove. Had not, then, the riots of those bygone seventeen-thirties set moving certain kinetic patterns in the morbid brain of one or more of them—notably the sinister Paul Roulet—which obscurely survived the bodies murdered and buried by the mob, and continued to function in some multiple-dimensioned space along the original lines of force determined by a frantic hatred of the encroaching community?

Such a thing was surely not a physical or biochemical impossibility in the light of a newer science which includes the theories of relativity and intra-atomic action. One might easily imagine an alien nucleus of substance or energy, formless or otherwise, kept alive by imperceptible or immaterial subtractions from the life-force or bodily tissues and fluids of other and more palpably living things into which it penetrates and with whose fabric it sometimes completely merges itself. It might be actively hostile, or it might be dictated merely by blind motives of self-preservation. In any case such a monster must of necessity be in our scheme of things an anomaly and an intruder, whose extirpation forms a primary duty with every man not an enemy to the world's life, health, and sanity.

What baffled us was our utter ignorance of the aspect in which we might encounter the thing. No sane person had even seen it, and few had ever felt it definitely. It might be pure energy—a form ethereal and outside the realm of substance—or it might be partly material; some unknown and equivocal mass of plasticity, capable of changing at will to nebulous approximations of the solid, liquid, gaseous, or tenuously unparticled states. The anthropomorphic patch of mould on the floor, the form of the yellowish vapour, and the curvature of the tree-roots in some of the old tales, all argued at least a remote and reminiscent connexion with the human shape; but how representative or permanent that similarity might be, none could say with any kind of certainty.

We had devised two weapons to fight it; a large and specially fitted Crookes tube operated by powerful storage batteries and provided with peculiar screens and reflectors, in case it proved intangible and opposable only by vigorously destructive ether radiations, and a pair of military flamethrowers of the sort used in the world-war, in case it proved partly material and susceptible of mechanical destruction—for like the superstitious Exeter rustics, we were prepared to burn the thing's heart out if heart existed to burn. All this aggressive mechanism we set in the cellar in positions carefully arranged with reference to the cot and chairs, and to the spot before the fireplace where the mould had taken strange shapes. That suggestive patch, by the way, was only faintly visible when we placed our furniture and instruments, and when we returned that evening for the actual vigil. For a moment I half doubted that I had ever seen it in the more definitely limned form—but then I thought of the legends.

Our cellar vigil began at 10 p.m., daylight saving time, and as it continued we found no promise of pertinent developments. A weak, filtered glow from the rain-harassed street-lamps outside, and a feeble phosphorescence from the detestable fungi within, shewed the dripping stone of the walls, from which all traces of whitewash had vanished; the dank, foetid, and mildew-tainted hard earth floor with its obscene fungi; the rotting remains of what had been stools, chairs, and tables, and other more shapeless furniture; the heavy planks and massive beams of the ground floor overhead; the decrepit plank door leading to bins and chambers beneath other parts of the house; the crumbling stone staircase with ruined wooden hand-rail; and the crude and cavernous fireplace of blackened brick where rusted iron fragments revealed the past presence of hooks, andirons, spit, crane, and a door to the Dutch oven—these things, and our austere cot and camp chairs, and the heavy and intricate destructive machinery we had brought.

We had, as in my own former explorations, left the door to the street unlocked; so that a direct and practical path of escape might lie open in case of manifestations beyond our power to deal with. It was our idea that our continued nocturnal presence would call forth whatever malign entity lurked there; and that being prepared, we could dispose of the thing with one or the other of our provided means as soon as we had recognized and observed it sufficiently. How long it might require to evoke and extinguish the thing, we had no notion. It occurred to us, too, that our venture was far from safe; for in what strength the thing might appear no one could tell. But we deemed the game worth the hazard, and embarked on it alone and unhesitatingly; conscious that the seeking of outside aid would only expose us to ridicule and perhaps defeat our entire purpose. Such was our frame of mind as we talked—far into the night, till my uncle's growing drowsiness made me remind him to lie down for his two-hour sleep.

Something like fear chilled me as I sat there in the small hours alone—I say alone, for one who sits by a sleeper is indeed alone; perhaps more alone than he can realize. My uncle breathed heavily, his deep inhalations and exhalations accompanied by the rain outside, and punctuated by another nerve-racking sound of distant dripping water within—for the house was repulsively damp even in dry weather, and in this storm positively swamp-like. I studied the loose, antique masonry of the walls in the fungus-light and the feeble rays which stole in from the street through the screened windows; and once, when the noisome atmosphere of the place seemed about to sicken me, I opened the door and looked up and down the street, feasting my eyes on familiar sights and my nostrils on wholesome air. Still nothing occurred to reward my watching; and I yawned repeatedly, fatigue getting the better of apprehension.

Then the stirring of my uncle in his sleep attracted my notice. He had turned restlessly on the cot several times during the latter half of the first hour, but now he was breathing with unusual irregularity, occasionally heaving a sigh which held more than a few of the qualities of a choking moan. I turned my electric flashlight on him and found his face averted, so rising and crossing to the other side of the cot, I again flashed the light to see if he seemed in any pain. What I saw unnerved me most surprisingly, considering its relative triviality. It must have been merely the association of any odd circumstance with the sinister nature of our location and mission, for surely the circumstance was not in itself frightful or unnatural. It was merely that my uncle's facial expression, disturbed no doubt by the strange dreams which our situation prompted, betrayed considerable agitation, and seemed not at all characteristic of him. His habitual expression was one of kindly and well-bred calm, whereas now a variety of emotions seemed struggling within him. I think, on the whole, that it was this *variety* which chiefly disturbed me. My uncle, as he gasped and tossed in increasing perturbation and with eyes that had now started open, seemed not one but many men, and suggested a curious quality of alienage from himself.

All at once he commenced to mutter, and I did not like the look of his mouth and teeth as he spoke. The words were at first indistinguishable, and then—with a tremendous start—I recognized something about them which filled me with icy fear till I recalled the breadth of my uncle's education and the interminable translations he had made from anthropological and antiquarian articles in the *Revue des Deux Mondes*. For the venerable Elihu Whipple was muttering *in French*, and the few phrases I could distinguish seemed connected with the darkest myths he had ever adapted from the famous Paris magazine.

Suddenly a perspiration broke out on the sleeper's forehead, and he leaped abruptly up, half awake. The jumble of French changed to a cry in English, and the hoarse voice shouted excitedly, "My breath, my breath!" Then the awakening became complete, and with a subsidence of facial expression to the normal state my uncle seized my hand and began to relate a dream whose nucleus of significance I could only surmise with a kind of awe.

He had, he said, floated off from a very ordinary series of dream-pictures into a scene whose strangeness was related to nothing he had ever read. It was of this world, and yet not of it—a shadowy geometrical confusion in which could be seen elements of familiar things in most unfamiliar and perturbing combinations. There was a suggestion of queerly disordered pictures superimposed one upon another; an arrangement in which the essentials of time as well as of space seemed dissolved and mixed in the most illogical fashion. In this kaleidoscopic vortex of phantasmal images were occasional snapshots, if one might use the term, of singular clearness but unaccountable heterogeneity.

Once my uncle thought he lay in a carelessly dug open pit, with a crowd of angry faces framed by straggling locks and three-cornered hats frowning down on him. Again he seemed to be in the interior of a house—an old house, apparently—but the details and inhabitants were constantly changing, and he could never be certain of the faces or the furniture, or even of the room itself, since doors and windows seemed in just as great a state of flux as the more presumably mobile objects. It was queer—damnably queer—and my uncle spoke almost sheepishly, as if half expecting not to be believed, when he declared that of the strange faces many had unmistakably borne the features of the Harris family. And all the while there was a personal sensation of choking, as if some pervasive presence had spread itself through his body and sought to possess itself of his vital processes. I shuddered at the thought of those vital processes, worn as they were by eighty-one years of continuous functioning, in conflict with unknown forces of which the youngest and strongest system might well be afraid; but in another moment reflected that dreams are only dreams, and that these uncomfortable visions could be, at most, no more than my uncle's reaction to the investigations and expectations which had lately filled our minds to the exclusion of all else.

Conversation, also, soon tended to dispel my sense of strangeness; and in time I yielded to my yawns and took my turn at slumber. My uncle seemed now very wakeful, and welcomed his period of watching even though the nightmare had aroused him far ahead of his allotted two hours. Sleep seized me quickly, and I was at once haunted with dreams of the most disturbing kind. I felt, in my visions, a cosmic and abysmal loneness; with hostility surging from all sides upon some prison where I lay confined. I seemed bound and gagged, and taunted by the echoing yells of distant multitudes who thirsted for my blood. My uncle's face came to me with less pleasant associations than in waking hours, and I recall many futile struggles and attempts to scream. It was not a pleasant sleep, and for a second I was not sorry for the echoing shriek which clove through the barriers of dream and flung me to a sharp and startled awakeness in which every actual object before my eyes stood out with more than natural clearness and reality.

v.

I had been lying with my face away from my uncle's chair, so that in this sudden flash of awakening I saw only the door to the street, the more northerly window, and the wall and floor and ceiling toward the north of the room, all photographed with morbid vividness on my brain in a light brighter than the glow of the fungi or the rays from the street outside. It was not a strong or even a fairly strong light; certainly not nearly strong enough to read an average book by. But it cast a shadow of myself and the cot on the floor, and had a yellowish, penetrating force that hinted at things more potent than luminosity. This I perceived with unhealthy sharpness despite the fact that two of my other senses were violently assailed. For on my ears rang the reverberations of that shocking scream, while my nostrils revolted at the stench which filled the place. My mind, as alert as my senses, recognized the gravely unusual; and almost automatically I leaped up and turned about to grasp the destructive instruments which we had left trained on the mouldy spot before the fireplace. As I turned,

I dreaded what I was to see; for the scream had been in my uncle's voice, and I knew not against what menace I should have to defend him and myself.

Yet after all, the sight was worse than I had dreaded. There are horrors beyond horrors, and this was one of those nuclei of all dreamable hideousness which the cosmos saves to blast an accursed and unhappy few. Out of the fungus-ridden earth steamed up a vaporous corpse-light, yellow and diseased, which bubbled and lapped to a gigantic height in vague outlines half human and half monstrous, through which I could see the chimney and fireplace beyond. It was all eyes—wolfish and mocking—and the rugose insect-like head dissolved at the top to a thin stream of mist which curled putridly about and finally vanished up the chimney. I say that I saw this thing, but it is only in conscious retrospection that I ever definitely traced its damnable approach to form. At the time it was to me only a seething, dimly phosphorescent cloud of fungous loathsomeness, enveloping and dissolving to an abhorrent plasticity the one object to which all my attention was focussed. That object was my uncle—the venerable Elihu Whipple—who with blackening and decaying features leered and gibbered at me, and reached out dripping claws to rend me in the fury which this horror had brought.

It was a sense of routine which kept me from going mad. I had drilled myself in preparation for the crucial moment, and blind training saved me. Recognizing the bubbling evil as no substance reachable by matter or material chemistry, and therefore ignoring the flame-thrower which loomed on my left, I threw on the current of the Crookes tube apparatus, and focussed toward that scene of immortal blasphemousness the strongest ether radiations which man's art can arouse from the spaces and fluids of Nature. There was a bluish haze and a frenzied sputtering, and the yellowish phosphorescence grew dimmer to my eyes. But I saw the dimness was only that of contrast, and that the waves from the machine had no effect whatever.

Then, in the midst of that daemoniac spectacle, I saw a fresh horror which brought cries to my lips and sent me fumbling and staggering toward that unlocked door to the quiet street, careless of what abnormal terrors I loosed upon the world, or what thoughts or judgments of men I brought down upon my head. In that dim blend of blue and yellow the form of my uncle had commenced a nauseous liquefaction whose essence eludes all description, and in which there played across his vanishing face such changes of identity as only madness can conceive. He was at once a devil and a multitude, a charnel-house and a pageant. Lit by the mixed and uncertain beams, that gelatinous face assumed a dozen—a score—a hundred—aspects; grinning, as it sank to the ground on a body that melted like tallow, in the caricatured likeness of legions strange and yet not strange.

I saw the features of the Harris line, masculine and feminine, adult and infantile, and other features old and young, coarse and refined, familiar and unfamiliar. For a second there flashed a degraded counterfeit of a miniature of poor mad Rhoby Harris that I had seen in the School of Design Museum, and another time I thought I caught the raw-boned image of Mercy Dexter as I recalled her from a painting in Carrington Harris's house. It was frightful beyond conception; toward the last, when a curious blend of servant and baby visages flickered close to the fungous floor where a pool of greenish grease was spreading, it seemed as though the shifting features fought against themselves, and strove to form contours like those of my uncle's kindly face. I like to think that he existed at that moment, and that he tried to bid me farewell. It seems to me I hiccoughed a farewell from my own parched throat as I lurched out into the street; a thin stream of grease following me through the door to the rain-drenched sidewalk.

The rest is shadowy and monstrous. There was no one in the soaking street, and in all the world there was no one I dared tell. I walked aimlessly south past College Hill and the Athenaeum, down Hopkins Street, and over the bridge to the business section where tall buildings seemed to guard me as modern material things guard the world from ancient and unwholesome wonder. Then grey dawn unfolded wetly from the east, silhouetting the archaic hill and its venerable steeples, and beckoning me to the place where my terrible work was still unfinished. And in the end I went, wet, hatless, and dazed in the morning light, and entered that awful door in Benefit Street which I had left ajar, and which still swung cryptically in full sight of the early householders to whom I dared not speak.

The grease was gone, for the mouldy floor was porous. And in front of the fireplace was no vestige of the giant doubled-up form in nitre. I looked at the cot, the chairs, the instruments, my neglected hat, and the yellowed straw hat of my uncle. Dazedness was uppermost, and I could scarcely recall what was dream and what was reality. Then thought trickled back, and I knew that I had witnessed things more horrible than I had dreamed. Sitting down, I tried to conjecture as nearly as sanity would let me just what had happened, and how I might end the horror, if indeed it had been real. Matter it seemed not to be, nor ether, nor anything else conceivable by mortal mind. What, then, but some exotic *emanation*; some vampirish vapour such as Exeter rustics tell of as lurking over certain churchyards? This I felt was the clue, and again I looked at the floor before the fireplace where the mould and nitre had taken strange forms. In ten minutes my mind was made up, and taking my hat I set out for home, where I bathed, ate, and gave by telephone an order for a pickaxe, a spade, a military gas-mask, and six carboys of sulphuric acid, all to be delivered the next morning at the cellar door of the shunned house in Benefit

Street. After that I tried to sleep; and failing, passed the hours in reading and in the composition of inane verses to counteract my mood.

At 11 a.m. the next day I commenced digging. It was sunny weather, and I was glad of that. I was still alone, for as much as I feared the unknown horror I sought, there was more fear in the thought of telling anybody. Later I told Harris only through sheer necessity, and because he had heard odd tales from old people which disposed him ever so little toward belief. As I turned up the stinking black earth in front of the fireplace, my spade causing a viscous yellow ichor to ooze from the white fungi which it severed, I trembled at the dubious thoughts of what I might uncover. Some secrets of inner earth are not good for mankind, and this seemed to me one of them.

My hand shook perceptibly, but still I delved; after a while standing in the large hole I had made. With the deepening of the hole, which was about six feet square, the evil smell increased; and I lost all doubt of my imminent contact with the hellish thing whose emanations had cursed the house for over a century and a half. I wondered what it would look like—what its form and substance would be, and how big it might have waxed through long ages of life-sucking. At length I climbed out of the hole and dispersed the heaped-up dirt, then arranging the great carboys of acid around and near two sides, so that when necessary I might empty them all down the aperture in quick succession. After that I dumped earth only along the other two sides; working more slowly and donning my gas-mask as the smell grew. I was nearly unnerved at my proximity to a nameless thing at the bottom of a pit.

Suddenly my spade struck something softer than earth. I shuddered, and made a motion as if to climb out of the hole, which was now as deep as my neck. Then courage returned, and I scraped away more dirt in the light of the electric torch I had provided. The surface

I uncovered was fishy and glassy—a kind of semi-putrid congealed jelly with suggestions of translucency. I scraped further, and saw that it had form. There was a rift where a part of the substance was folded over. The exposed area was huge and roughly cylindrical; like a mammoth soft blue-white stovepipe doubled in two, its largest part some two feet in diameter. Still more I scraped, and then abruptly I leaped out of the hole and away from the filthy thing; frantically unstopping and tilting the heavy carboys, and precipitating their corrosive contents one after another down that charnel gulf and upon the unthinkable abnormality whose titan *elbow* I had seen.

The blinding maelstrom of greenish-yellow vapour which surged tempestuously up from that hole as the floods of acid descended, will never leave my memory. All along the hill people tell of the yellow day, when virulent and horrible fumes arose from the factory waste dumped in the Providence River, but I know how mistaken they are as to the source. They tell, too, of the hideous roar which at the same time came from some disordered water-pipe or gas main underground—but again I could correct them if I dared. It was unspeakably shocking, and I do not see how I lived through it. I did faint after emptying the fourth carboy, which I had to handle after the fumes had begun to penetrate my mask; but when I recovered I saw that the hole was emitting no fresh vapours.

The two remaining carboys I emptied down without particular result, and after a time I felt it safe to shovel the earth back into the pit. It was twilight before I was done, but fear had gone out of the place. The dampness was less foetid, and all the strange fungi had withered to a kind of harmless greyish powder which blew ash-like along the floor. One of earth's nethermost terrors had perished for ever; and if there be a hell, it had received at last the daemon soul of an unhallowed thing. And as I patted down the last spadeful of mould,

I shed the first of the many tears with which I have paid unaffected tribute to my beloved uncle's memory.

The next spring no more pale grass and strange weeds came up in the shunned house's terraced garden, and shortly afterward Carrington Harris rented the place. It is still spectral, but its strangeness fascinates me, and I shall find mixed with my relief a queer regret when it is torn down to make way for a tawdry shop or vulgar apartment building. The barren old trees in the yard have begun to bear small, sweet apples, and last year the birds nested in their gnarled boughs.

1896

THE PURPLE PILAEUS

H. G. Wells

The boy who would grow up to be the author of such pioneering scientific romances as *The Time Machine*, *The Island of Doctor Moreau*, *The Invisible Man*, and *The War of the Worlds* was born in 1866 in Bromley, Kent, where his father, like Mr. Coombes in "The Purple Pilaeus", was a less-than-successful small shopkeeper. After two years of a hellish apprenticeship at Hyde's Drapery Emporium in Southsea, young "Bertie" Wells was able to enrol in the Normal School of Science, with the intention of becoming a science teacher (I cannot help imagining that he would excel as a YouTube "science communicator" today). When his poor health made it impossible for him to continue teaching, he turned to writing, winning immediate and widespread fame for the stream of gripping and thought-provoking novels that poured from his pen. At the same time he was producing short stories as well, many of which remain classics of the emergent genre of speculative fiction which he was helping to shape and define. "The Purple Pilaeus", first published in 1896 in the magazine *Black and White*, was included in his landmark collection *Thirty Strange Stories* the following year. Wells was also to use the conceit of the intoxicating fungus in his wonderful imperial satire *The First Men in the Moon* (1901), in which one of the protagonists, Bedford, drunk on the "fleshy red [and] monstrous coralline growths", fantasizes about extending Queen Victoria's empire into space, becoming a Cecil

Rhodes of the heavens: "We must annex this moon... There must be no shilly-shally. This is part of the White Man's Burthen." Coombes's transformation is even more alarming than Bedford's; indeed, the reader may well agree with me that "The Purple Pilaeus", despite its predominating comic tone, is rather a dark little story.

Mr. Coombes was sick of life. He walked away from his unhappy home, and, sick not only of his own existence, but of everybody else's, turned aside down Gaswork Lane to avoid the town, and, crossing the wooden bridge that goes over the canal to Starling's Cottages, was presently alone in the damp pinewoods and out of sight and sound of human habitation. He would stand it no longer. He repeated aloud with blasphemies unusual to him that he would stand it no longer.

He was a pale-faced little man, with dark eyes and a fine and very black moustache. He had a very stiff, upright collar slightly frayed, that gave him an illusory double chin, and his overcoat (albeit shabby) was trimmed with astrachan. His gloves were a bright brown with black stripes over the knuckles, and split at the finger-ends. His appearance, his wife had said once in the dear, dead days beyond recall,—before he married her, that is,—was military. But now she called him—It seems a dreadful thing to tell of between husband and wife, but she called him "a little grub." It wasn't the only thing she had called him, either.

The row had arisen about that beastly Jennie again. Jennie was his wife's friend, and, by no invitation of Mr. Coombes, she came in every blessed Sunday to dinner, and made a shindy all the afternoon. She was a big, noisy girl, with a taste for loud colours and a strident laugh; and this Sunday she had outdone all her previous intrusions by bringing in a fellow with her, a chap as showy as herself. And Mr. Coombes, in a starchy, clean collar and his Sunday frock-coat, had sat dumb and wrathful at his own table, while his wife and her guests talked foolishly and undesirably, and laughed aloud. Well, he stood that, and after dinner (which, "as usual," was late), what must Miss Jennie do but go to the piano and play banjo tunes, for all the world as if it were a week-day! Flesh and blood could not endure such goings-on. They would hear next door; they would hear in the road; it was a public announcement of their disrepute. He had to speak.

He had felt himself go pale, and a kind of rigour had affected his respiration as he delivered himself. He had been sitting on one of the chairs by the window—the new guest had taken possession of the arm-chair. He turned his head. "Sun Day!" he said over the collar, in the voice of one who warns. "Sun Day!" What people call a "nasty" tone it was.

Jennie had kept on playing; but his wife, who was looking through some music that was piled on the top of the piano, had stared at him. "What's wrong now?" she said; "can't people enjoy themselves?"

"I don't mind rational 'njoyment, at all," said little Coombes; "but I ain't a-going to have week-day tunes playing on a Sunday in this house."

"What's wrong with my playing now?" said Jennie, stopping and twirling round on the music-stool with a monstrous rustle of flounces.

Coombes saw it was going to be a row, and opened too vigorously, as is common with your timid, nervous men all the world over. "Steady on with that music-stool!" said he; "it ain't made for 'eavy weights."

"Never you mind about weights," said Jennie, incensed. "What was you saying behind my back about my playing?"

"Surely you don't 'old with not having a bit of music on a Sunday, Mr. Coombes?" said the new guest, leaning back in the arm-chair, blowing a cloud of cigarette smoke and smiling in a kind of pitying way. And simultaneously his wife said something to Jennie about "Never mind 'im. You go on, Jinny."

"I do," said Mr. Coombes, addressing the new guest.

"May I arst why?" said the new guest, evidently enjoying both his cigarette and the prospect of an argument. He was, by-the-by, a lank young man, very stylishly dressed in bright drab, with a white cravat and a pearl and silver pin. It had been better taste to come in a black coat, Mr. Coombes thought.

"Because," began Mr. Coombes, "it don't suit me. I'm a business man. I 'ave to study my connection. Rational 'njoyment—"

"His connection!" said Mrs. Coombes, scornfully. "That's what he's always a-saying. We got to do this, and we got to do that—"

"If you don't mean to study my connection," said Mr. Coombes, "what did you marry me for?"

"I wonder," said Jennie, and turned back to the piano.

"I never saw such a man as you," said Mrs. Coombes. "You've altered all round since we were married. Before—"

Then Jennie began at the tum, tum, tum again.

"Look here!" said Mr. Coombes, driven at last to revolt, standing up and raising his voice. "I tell you I won't have that." The frock-coat heaved with his indignation.

"No vi'lence, now," said the long young man in drab, sitting up.

"Who the juice are you?" said Mr. Coombes, fiercely.

Whereupon they all began talking at once. The new guest said he was Jennie's "intended," and meant to protect her, and Mr. Coombes said he was welcome to do so anywhere but in his (Mr. Coombes') house; and Mrs. Coombes said he ought to be ashamed of insulting his guests, and (as I have already mentioned) that he was getting a regular little grub; and the end was, that Mr. Coombes ordered his visitors out of the house, and they wouldn't go, and so he said he would go himself. With his face burning and tears of excitement in his eyes, he went into the passage, and as he struggled with his overcoat—his frock-coat sleeves got concertinaed up his arm—and gave a brush at his silk hat, Jennie began again at the piano, and strummed him insultingly out of the house. Tum, tum, tum. He slammed the shop-door so that the house quivered. That, briefly, was the immediate making of his mood. You will perhaps begin to understand his disgust with existence.

As he walked along the muddy path under the firs,—it was late October, and the ditches and heaps of fir-needles were gorgeous with clumps of fungi,—he recapitulated the melancholy history of his marriage. It was brief and commonplace enough. He now perceived with sufficient clearness that his wife had married him out of a natural curiosity and in order to escape from her worrying, laborious, and uncertain life in the workroom; and, like the majority of her class, she was far too stupid to realize that it was her duty to co-operate with him in his business. She was greedy of enjoyment, loquacious, and socially-minded, and evidently disappointed to find the restraints of poverty still hanging about her. His worries exasperated her, and the slightest attempt to control her proceedings resulted in a charge of "grumbling." Why couldn't he be nice—as he used to be? And Coombes was such a harmless little man, too, nourished mentally on "Self-Help," and with a meagre ambition of self-denial and competition, that was to end in a "sufficiency." Then Jennie came in as a female Mephistopheles, a gabbling chronicle of "fellers," and was always wanting his wife to go to theatres, and "all that." And in addition were aunts of his wife, and cousins (male and female), to eat up capital, insult him personally, upset business arrangements, annoy good customers, and generally blight his life. It was not the first occasion by many that Mr. Coombes had fled his home in wrath and indignation, and something like fear, vowing furiously and even aloud that he wouldn't stand it, and so frothing away his energy along the line of least resistance. But never before had he been quite so sick of life as on this particular Sunday afternoon. The Sunday dinner may have had its share in his despair—and the greyness of the sky. Perhaps, too, he was beginning to realize his unendurable frustration as a business man as the consequence of his marriage. Presently bankruptcy, and after that—Perhaps she might have reason to repent when it was too late. And destiny, as I have already intimated, had planted the path through the wood with evil-smelling fungi, thickly and variously planted it, not only on the right side, but on the left.

A small shopman is in such a melancholy position, if his wife turns out a disloyal partner. His capital is all tied up in his business, and to leave her, means to join the unemployed in some strange part of the earth. The luxuries of divorce are beyond him altogether. So that the good old tradition of marriage for better or worse holds inexorably for him, and things work up to tragic culminations. Bricklayers kick their wives to death, and dukes betray theirs; but it is among the small clerks and shopkeepers nowadays that it comes most often to a cutting of throats. Under the circumstances it is not so very remarkable—and you must take it as charitably as you can—that the mind of Mr. Coombes ran for awhile on some such glorious close to his disappointed hopes, and that he thought of razors, pistols, bread-knives, and touching letters to the coroner denouncing his enemies by name, and praying piously for forgiveness. After a time his fierceness gave way to melancholia. He had been married in this very overcoat, in his first and only frock-coat that was buttoned up beneath it. He began to recall their courting along this very walk, his years of penurious saving to get capital, and the bright hopefulness of his marrying days. For it all to work out like this! Was there no sympathetic ruler anywhere in the world? He reverted to death as a topic.

He thought of the canal he had just crossed, and doubted whether he shouldn't stand with his head out, even in the middle, and it was while drowning was in his mind that the purple pileus caught his eye. He looked at it mechanically for a moment, and stopped and stooped towards it to pick it up, under the impression that it was some such small leather object as a purse. Then he saw that it was the purple top of a fungus, a peculiarly poisonous-looking purple: slimy, shiny, and emitting a sour odour. He hesitated with his hand an inch or so from it, and the thought of poison crossed his mind. With that he picked the thing, and stood up again with it in his hand.

The odour was certainly strong—acrid, but by no means disgusting. He broke off a piece, and the fresh surface was a creamy white, that changed like magic in the space of ten seconds to a yellowish-green colour. It was even an inviting-looking change. He broke off two other pieces to see it repeated. They were wonderful things, these fungi, thought Mr. Coombes, and all of them the deadliest poisons, as his father had often told him. Deadly poisons!

There is no time like the present for a rash resolve. Why not here and now? thought Mr. Coombes. He tasted a little piece, a very little piece indeed—a mere crumb. It was so pungent that he almost spat it out again, then merely hot and full-flavoured,—a kind of German mustard with a touch of horse-radish and—well, mushroom. He swallowed it in the excitement of the moment. Did he like it or did he not? His mind was curiously careless. He would try another bit. It really wasn't bad—it was good. He forgot his troubles in the interest of the immediate moment. Playing with death it was. He took another bite, and then deliberately finished a mouthful. A curious tingling sensation began in his finger-tips and toes. His pulse began to move faster. The blood in his ears sounded like a mill-race. "Try bi' more," said Mr. Coombes. He turned and looked about him, and found his feet unsteady. He saw and struggled towards a little patch of purple a dozen yards away. "Jol' goo' stuff," said Mr. Coombes. "E—lomore ye'." He pitched forward and fell on his face, his hands outstretched towards the cluster of pilei. But he did not eat any more of them. He forgot forthwith.

He rolled over and sat up with a look of astonishment on his face. His carefully brushed silk hat had rolled away towards the ditch. He pressed his hand to his brow. Something had happened, but he could not rightly determine what it was. Anyhow, he was no longer dull—he felt bright, cheerful. And his throat was afire. He laughed in the sudden gaiety of his heart. Had he been dull? He did not know; but at any rate he would be dull no longer. He got up and stood unsteadily, regarding the universe with an agreeable smile. He began to remember. He could not remember very well, because of a steam roundabout that was beginning in his head. And he knew he had been disagreeable at home, just because they wanted to be happy. They were quite right; life should be as gay as possible. He would go home and make it up, and reassure them. And why not take some of this delightful toadstool with him, for them to eat? A hatful, no less. Some of those red ones with white spots as well, and a few yellow. He had been a dull dog, an enemy to merriment; he would make up for it. It would be gay to turn his coat-sleeves inside out, and stick some yellow gorse into his waistcoat pockets. Then home—singing—for a jolly evening.

After the departure of Mr. Coombes, Jennie discontinued playing, and turned round on the music-stool again. "What a fuss about nothing," said Jennie.

"You see, Mr. Clarence, what I've got to put up with," said Mrs. Coombes.

"He is a bit hasty," said Mr. Clarence, judicially.

"He ain't got the slightest sense of our position," said Mrs. Coombes; "that's what I complain of. He cares for nothing but his old shop; and if I have a bit of company, or buy anything to keep myself decent, or get any little thing I want out of the housekeeping money, there's disagreeables. 'Economy,' he says; 'struggle for life,' and all that. He lies awake of nights about it, worrying how he can screw me out of a shilling. He wanted us to eat Dorset butter once. If once I was to give in to him—there!"

"Of course," said Jennie.

"If a man values a woman," said Mr. Clarence, lounging back in the arm-chair, "he must be prepared to make sacrifices for her. For my own part," said Mr. Clarence, with his eye on Jennie, "I shouldn't think of marrying till I was in a position to do the thing in style. It's downright selfishness. A man ought to go through the rough-and-tumble by himself, and not drag her—"

"I don't agree altogether with that," said Jennie. "I don't see why a man shouldn't have a woman's help, provided he doesn't treat her meanly, you know. It's meanness—"

"You wouldn't believe," said Mrs. Coombes. "But I was a fool to 'ave 'im. I might 'ave known. If it 'adn't been for my father, we shouldn't have had not a carriage to our wedding."

"Lord! he didn't stick out at that?" said Mr. Clarence, quite shocked.

"Said he wanted the money for his stock, or some such rubbish. Why, he wouldn't have a woman in to help me once a week if it wasn't for my standing out plucky. And the fusses he makes about money—comes to me, well, pretty near crying, with sheets of paper and figgers.

'If only we can tide over this year,' he says, 'the business is bound to go.' 'If only we can tide over this year,' I says; 'then it'll be, if only we can tide over next year. I know you,' I says. 'And you don't catch me screwing myself lean and ugly. Why didn't you marry a slavey,' I says, 'if you wanted one—instead of a respectable girl?' I says."

So Mrs. Coombes. But we will not follow this unedifying conversation further. Suffice it that Mr. Coombes was very satisfactorily disposed of, and they had a snug little time round the fire. Then Mrs. Coombes went to get the tea, and Jennie sat coquettishly on the arm of Mr. Clarence's chair until the tea-things clattered outside. "What was that I heard?" asked Mrs. Coombes, playfully, as she entered, and there was badinage about kissing. They were just sitting down to the little circular table when the first intimation of Mr. Coombes' return was heard.

This was a fumbling at the latch of the front door.

"'Ere's my lord," said Mrs. Coombes. "Went out like a lion and comes back like a lamb, I'll lay."

Something fell over in the shop: a chair, it sounded like. Then there was a sound as of some complicated step exercise in the passage. Then the door opened and Coombes appeared. But it was Coombes transfigured. The immaculate collar had been torn carelessly from his throat. His carefully-brushed silk hat, half-full of a crush of fungi, was under one arm; his coat was inside out, and his waistcoat adorned with bunches of yellow-blossomed furze. These little eccentricities of Sunday costume, however, were quite overshadowed by the change in his face; it was livid white, his eyes were unnaturally large and bright, and his pale blue lips were drawn back in a cheerless grin. "Merry!" he said. He had stopped dancing to open the door. "Rational 'njoyment. Dance." He made three fantastic steps into the room, and stood bowing.

"Jim!" shrieked Mrs. Coombes, and Mr. Clarence sat petrified, with a dropping lower jaw.

"Tea," said Mr. Coombes. "Jol' thing, tea. Tose-stools, too. Brosher."

"He's drunk," said Jennie, in a weak voice. Never before had she seen this intense pallor in a drunken man, or such shining, dilated eyes.

Mr. Coombes held out a handful of scarlet agaric to Mr. Clarence. "Jo' stuff," said he; "ta' some."

At that moment he was genial. Then at the sight of their startled faces he changed, with the swift transition of insanity, into overbearing fury. And it seemed as if he had suddenly recalled the quarrel of his departure. In such a huge voice as Mrs. Coombes had never heard before, he shouted, "My house. I'm master 'ere. Eat what I give yer!" He bawled this, as it seemed, without an effort, without a violent gesture, standing there as motionless as one who whispers, holding out a handful of fungus.

Clarence approved himself a coward. He could not meet the mad fury in Coombes' eyes; he rose to his feet, pushing back his chair, and turned, stooping. At that Coombes rushed at him. Jennie saw her opportunity, and, with the ghost of a shriek, made for the door. Mrs. Coombes followed her. Clarence tried to dodge. Over went the tea-table with a smash as Coombes clutched him by the collar and tried to thrust the fungus into his mouth. Clarence was content to leave his collar behind him, and shot out into the passage with red patches of fly agaric still adherent to his face. "Shut 'im in!" cried Mrs. Coombes, and would have closed the door, but her supports deserted her; Jennie saw the shop-door open, and vanished thereby, locking it behind her, while Clarence went on hastily into the kitchen. Mr. Coombes came heavily against the door, and Mrs. Coombes, finding the key was inside, fled upstairs and locked herself in the spare bedroom.

So the new convert to *joie de vivre* emerged upon the passage, his decorations a little scattered, but that respectable hatful of fungi still under his arm. He hesitated at the three ways, and decided on the kitchen. Whereupon Clarence, who was fumbling with the key, gave up the attempt to imprison his host, and fled into the scullery, only to be captured before he could open the door into the yard. Mr. Clarence is singularly reticent of the details of what occurred. It seems that Mr. Coombes' transitory irritation had vanished again, and he was once more a genial playfellow. And as there were knives and meat-choppers about, Clarence very generously resolved to humour him and so avoid anything tragic. It is beyond dispute that Mr. Coombes played with Mr. Clarence to his heart's content; they could not have been more playful and familiar if they had known each other for years. He insisted gaily on Clarence trying the fungi, and after a friendly tussle, was smitten with remorse at the mess he was making of his guest's face. It also appears that Clarence was dragged under the sink and his face scrubbed with the blacking-brush,—he being still resolved to humour the lunatic at any cost,—and that finally, in a somewhat dishevelled, chipped, and discoloured condition, he was assisted to his coat and shown out by the back door, the shopway being barred by Jennie. Mr. Coombes' wandering thoughts then turned to Jennie. Jennie had been unable to unfasten the shop-door, but she shot the bolts against Mr. Coombes' latch-key, and remained in possession of the shop for the rest of the evening.

It would appear that Mr. Coombes then returned to the kitchen, still in pursuit of gaiety, and, albeit a strict Good Templar, drank (or spilt down the front of the first and only frock-coat) no less than five bottles of the stout Mrs. Coombes insisted upon having for her health's sake. He made cheerful noises by breaking off the necks of the bottles with several of his wife's wedding-present dinner-plates, and during the earlier part of this great drunk he sang divers merry ballads. He cut his finger rather badly with one of the bottles,—the only bloodshed in this story,—and what with that, and the systematic convulsion of his inexperienced physiology by the liquorish brand of Mrs. Coombes' stout, it may be the evil of the fungus poison was somehow allayed. But we prefer to draw a veil over the concluding incidents of this Sunday afternoon. They ended in the coal cellar, in a deep and healing sleep.

An interval of five years elapsed. Again it was a Sunday afternoon in October, and again Mr. Coombes walked through the pinewood beyond the canal. He was still the same dark-eyed, black-moustached little man that he was at the outset of the story, but his double chin was now scarcely so illusory as it had been. His overcoat was new, with a velvet lapel, and a stylish collar with turndown corners, free of any coarse starchiness, had replaced the original all-round article. His hat was glossy, his gloves newish—though one finger had split and been carefully mended. And a casual observer would have noticed about him a certain rectitude of bearing, a certain erectness of head that marks the man who thinks well of himself. He was a master now, with three assistants. Beside him walked a larger sunburnt parody of himself, his brother Tom, just back from Australia. They were recapitulating their early struggles, and Mr. Coombes had just been making a financial statement.

"It's a very nice little business, Jim," said brother Tom. "In these days of competition you're jolly lucky to have worked it up so. And you're jolly lucky, too, to have a wife who's willing to help like yours does."

"Between ourselves," said Mr. Coombes, "it wasn't always so. It wasn't always like this. To begin with, the missus was a bit giddy. Girls are funny creatures."

"Dear me!"

"Yes. You'd hardly think it, but she was downright extravagant, and always having slaps at me. I was a bit too easy and loving, and all that, and she thought the whole blessed show was run for her. Turned the 'ouse into a regular caravansary, always having her relations and girls from business in, and their chaps. Comic songs a' Sunday, it was getting to, and driving trade away. And she was making eyes at the chaps, too! I tell you, Tom, the place wasn't my own."

"Shouldn't 'a' thought it."

"It was so. Well—I reasoned with her. I said, 'I ain't a duke, to keep a wife like a pet animal. I married you for 'elp and company.' I said, 'You got to 'elp and pull the business through.' She wouldn't 'ear of it. 'Very well,' I says; 'I'm a mild man till I'm roused,' I says, 'and it's getting to that.' But she wouldn't 'ear of no warnings."

"Well?"

"It's the way with women. She didn't think I 'ad it in me to be roused. Women of her sort (between ourselves, Tom) don't respect a man until they're a bit afraid of him. So I just broke out to show her. In comes a girl named Jennie, that used to work with her, and her chap. We 'ad a bit of a row, and I came out 'ere—it was just such another day as this—and I thought it all out. Then I went back and pitched into them."

"You did?"

"I did. I was mad, I can tell you. I wasn't going to 'it 'er, if I could 'elp it, so I went back and licked into this chap, just to show 'er what I could do. 'E was a big chap, too. Well, I chucked him, and smashed things about, and gave 'er a scaring, and she ran up and locked 'erself into the spare room."

"Well?"

"That's all. I says to 'er the next morning, 'Now you know,' I says, 'what I'm like when I'm roused.' And I didn't 'ave to say anything more."

"And you've been happy ever after, eh?"

"So to speak. There's nothing like putting your foot down with them. If it 'adn't been for that afternoon I should 'a' been tramping the roads now, and she'd 'a' been grumbling at me, and all her family grumbling for bringing her to poverty—I know their little ways. But we're all right now. And it's a very decent little business, as you say."

They proceed on their way meditatively. "Women are funny creatures," said brother Tom.

"They want a firm hand," says Coombes.

"What a lot of these funguses there are about here!" remarked brother Tom, presently. "I can't see what use they are in the world."

Mr. Coombes looked. "I dessay they're sent for some wise purpose," said Mr. Coombes.

And that was as much thanks as the purple pileus ever got for maddening this absurd little man to the pitch of decisive action, and so altering the whole course of his life.

1873

THE FIDDLER IN THE FAIRY RING

Julia Horatia Ewing

Once greatly respected and loved as a writer of stories for the young—she numbered among her admirers Rudyard Kipling, Edith Nesbit, and Roger Lancelyn Green—Julia Horatia Ewing (1841–1885) today merits little more than a footnote in histories of children's literature. Born in Ecclesfield, South Yorkshire, Ewing was the daughter of Alfred Gatty, a vicar with vaguely high-church leanings, and Margaret Gatty, who wrote both children's stories and works of natural history. (She had a particular obsession with seaweed; for her book *The Fairy Godmothers* the publisher George Bell paid her in works of marine botany.) Storytelling apparently ran in the blood, and young Julia soon emerged as the dominant voice whenever the (rather large) family circle gathered together to spin yarns. As the one "who held the post of nursery story-teller", as she put it, she was given the nickname "Aunt Judy", which her mother used when founding the highly successful children's periodical *Aunt Judy's Magazine* (Lewis Carroll and Hans Christian Andersen appeared in its pages, and a young A. A. Milne devoured it eagerly). Most of Ewing's own stories were published in the family-run monthly, including "The Fiddler in the Fairy Ring" in 1873 (it was subsequently included in her collection *Old-Fashioned Fairy Tales*, published in 1882 by the Society for the Promotion of Christian Knowledge). The basic story derives from Celtic folk tales (and can be found in several Victorian collections), but Ewing's rendition has some original touches. We are told that in her youth she tried her hand at Gothic fiction only once; perhaps she should have written more in a dark vein.

As Merlin Sheldrake writes in *Entangled Life* (2020), "The mycelium of some fungal species grows into 'fairy rings' that stretch across hundreds of metres, reach hundreds of years in age, and then somehow produce a circle of mushrooms in a synchronized flush." The fairy ring champignon or Scotch bonnet—*Marasmius oreades*—is one such species, but it is far from the only one, and while some, like *M. oreades*, are edible, others, such as *Chlorophyllum molybdites*, are extremely poisonous, so beware. Beware, too, the unseen figures who may dance within the ring; remember, you enter at your peril.

Generations ago, there once lived a farmer's son, who had no great harm in him, and no great good either. He always meant well, but he had a poor spirit, and was too fond of idle company.

One day his father sent him to market with some sheep for sale, and when business was over for the day, the rest of the country-folk made ready to go home, and more than one of them offered the lad a lift in his cart.

"Thank you kindly, all the same," said he, "but I am going back across the downs with Limping Tim."

Then out spoke a steady old farmer and bade the lad go home with the rest, and by the main road. For Limping Tim was an idle, graceless kind of fellow, who fiddled for his livelihood, but what else he did to earn the money he squandered, no one knew. And as to the sheep path over the downs, it stands to reason that the highway is better travelling after sunset, for the other is no such very short cut; and has a big fairy ring so near it, that a butter-woman might brush it with the edge of her market cloak, as she turned the brow of the hill.

But the farmer's son would go his own way, and that was with Limping Tim, and across the downs.

So they started, and the fiddler had his fiddle in his hand, and a bundle of marketings under his arm, and he sang snatches of strange

THE FIDDLER IN THE FAIRY RING

songs, the like of which the lad had never heard before. And the moon drew out their shadows over the short grass till they were as long as the great stones of Stonehenge.

At last they turned the hill, and the fairy ring looked dark under the moon, and the farmer's son blessed himself that they were passing it quietly, when Limping Tim suddenly pulled his cloak from his back, and handing it to his companion, cried, "Hold this for a moment, will you? I'm wanted. They're calling for me."

"I hear nothing," said the farmer's son. But before he had got the words out of his mouth, the fiddler had completely disappeared. He shouted aloud, but in vain, and had begun to think of proceeding on his way, when the fiddler's voice cried, "Catch!" and there came, flying at him from the direction of the fairy ring, the bundle of marketings which the fiddler had been carrying.

"It's in my way," he then heard the fiddler cry. "Ah, this is dancing! Come in, my lad, come in!"

But the farmer's son was not totally without prudence, and he took good care to keep at a safe distance from the fairy ring.

"Come back, Tim! Come back!" he shouted, and, receiving no answer, he adjured his friend to break the bonds that withheld him, and return to the right way, as wisely as one man can counsel another.

After talking for some time to no purpose, he again heard his friend's voice, crying, "Take care of it for me! The money dances out of my pocket." And therewith the fiddler's purse was hurled to his feet, where it fell with a heavy chinking of gold within.

He picked it up, and renewed his warnings and entreaties, but in vain; and, after waiting for a long time, he made the best of his way home alone, hoping that the fiddler would follow, and come to reclaim his property.

The fiddler never came. And when at last there was a fuss about his disappearance, the farmer's son, who had but a poor spirit, began to be afraid to tell the truth of the matter. "Who knows but they may accuse me of theft?" said he. So he hid the cloak, and the bundle, and the money-bag in the garden.

But when three months passed, and still the fiddler did not return, it was whispered that the farmer's son had been his last companion; and the place was searched, and they found the cloak, and the bundle, and the money-bag and the lad was taken to prison.

Now, when it was too late, he plucked up a spirit, and told the truth; but no one believed him, and it was said that he had murdered the fiddler for the sake of his money and goods. And he was taken before the judge, found guilty, and sentenced to death.

Fortunately, his old mother was a Wise Woman. And when she heard that he was condemned, she said, "Only follow my directions, and we may save you yet; for I guess how it is."

So she went to the judge, and begged for her son three favours before his death.

"I will grant them," said the judge, "if you do not ask for his life."

"The first," said the old woman, "is, that he may choose the place where the gallows shall be erected; the second, that he may fix the hour of his execution; and the third favour is, that you will not fail to be present."

"I grant all three," said the judge. But when he learned that the criminal had chosen a certain hill on the downs for the place of execution, and an hour before midnight for the time, he sent to beg the sheriff to bear him company on this important occasion.

The sheriff placed himself at the judge's disposal, but he commanded the attendance of the gaoler as some sort of protection; and the gaoler, for his part, implored his reverence the chaplain to be of the party, as the hill was not in good spiritual repute. So, when the time came, the four started together, and the hangman and the farmer's son went before them to the foot of the gallows.

Just as the rope was being prepared, the farmer's son called to the judge, and said, "If your Honour will walk twenty paces down the hill, to where you will see a bit of paper, you will learn the fate of the fiddler."

"That is, no doubt, a copy of the poor man's last confession," thought the judge.

"Murder will out, Mr. Sheriff," said he; and in the interests of truth and justice he hastened to pick up the paper.

But the farmer's son had dropped it as he came along, by his mother's direction, in such a place that the judge could not pick it up without putting his foot on the edge of the fairy ring. No sooner had he done so than he perceived an innumerable company of little people dressed in green cloaks and hoods, who were dancing round in a circle as wide as the ring itself.

They were all about two feet high, and had aged faces, brown and withered, like the knots on gnarled trees in hedge bottoms, and they squinted horribly; but, in spite of their seeming age, they flew round and round like children.

"Mr. Sheriff! Mr. Sheriff!" cried the judge, "come and see the dancing. And hear the music, too, which is so lively that it makes the soles of my feet tickle."

"There is no music, my Lord Judge," said the sheriff, running down the hill. "It is the wind whistling over the grass that your lordship hears."

But when the sheriff had put his foot by the judge's foot, he saw and heard the same, and he cried out, "Quick, Gaoler, and come down! I should like you to be witness to this matter. And you may take my arm, Gaoler, for the music makes me feel unsteady."

"There is no music, sir," said the gaoler; "but your worship doubtless hears the creaking of the gallows."

But no sooner had the gaoler's feet touched the fairy ring, than he saw and heard like the rest, and he called lustily to the chaplain to come and stop the unhallowed measure.

"It is a delusion of the Evil One," said the parson; "there is not a sound in the air but the distant croaking of some frogs." But when he too touched the ring, he perceived his mistake.

At this moment the moon shone out, and in the middle of the ring they saw Limping Tim the fiddler, playing till great drops stood out on his forehead, and dancing as madly as he played.

"Ah, you rascal!" cried the judge. "Is this where you've been all the time, and a better man than you as good as hanged for you? But you shall come home now."

Saying which, he ran in, and seized the fiddler by the arm, but Limping Tim resisted so stoutly that the sheriff had to go to the judge's assistance, and even then the fairies so pinched and hindered them that the sheriff was obliged to call upon the gaoler to put his arms about his waist, who persuaded the chaplain to add his strength to the string. But as ill luck would have it, just as they were getting off, one of the fairies picked up Limping Tim's fiddle, which had fallen in the scuffle, and began to play. And as he began to play, every one began to dance—the fiddler, and the judge, and the sheriff, and the gaoler, and even the chaplain.

"Hangman! hangman!" screamed the judge, as he lifted first one leg and then the other to the tune, "come down, and catch hold of his reverence the chaplain. The prisoner is pardoned, and he can lay hold too."

The hangman knew the judge's voice, and ran towards it; but as they were now quite within the ring he could see nothing, either of him or his companions.

The farmer's son followed, and warning the hangman not to touch the ring, he directed him to stretch his hands forwards in hopes of catching hold of some one. In a few minutes the wind blew the chaplain's cassock against the hangman's fingers, and he caught the parson round the waist. The farmer's son then seized him in like fashion, and each holding firmly by the other, the fiddler, the judge, the sheriff, the gaoler, the parson, the hangman, and the farmer's son all got safely out of the charmed circle.

"Oh, you scoundrel!" cried the judge to the fiddler; "I have a very good mind to hang you up on the gallows without further ado."

But the fiddler only looked like one possessed, and upbraided the farmer's son for not having the patience to wait three minutes for him.

"Three minutes!" cried he; "why, you've been here three months and a day."

This the fiddler would not believe, and as he seemed in every way beside himself, they led him home, still upbraiding his companion, and crying continually for his fiddle.

His neighbours watched him closely, but one day he escaped from their care and wandered away over the hills to seek his fiddle, and came back no more.

His dead body was found upon the downs, face downwards, with the fiddle in his arms. Some said he had really found the fiddle where he had left it, and had been lost in a mist, and died of exposure. But others held that he had perished differently, and laid his death at the door of the fairy dancers.

As to the farmer's son, it is said that thenceforward he went home from market by the high-road, and spoke the truth straight out, and was more careful of his company.

1911

HOW FEAR DEPARTED FROM THE LONG GALLERY

E. F. Benson

The father of this story's author (Edward White Benson, Archbishop of Canterbury from 1883–1896) might be called the father as well, in a sense, of one of the greatest ghost stories in the world, having related to Henry James a tale of two spectral servants who "corrupt and deprave" the children formerly in their care—a premise James recorded in his notebook as a promisingly "gruesome" one. In his student days, Benson Senior had also been the co-founder of the Cambridge Ghost Society or "Ghostlie Guild". Perhaps it is not all that surprising, then, that all three of Benson's sons would themselves become writers of horror fiction. The most talented and prolific of these was Edward Frederic (1867–1940), who was present when another James, the peerless Monty, read his first stories aloud, and whose own tales of ghosts, vampires, and creatures less generic (the giant slug in "Negotium Perambulans" is particularly memorable) appeared in four collections: *The Room in the Tower* (1912), *Visible and Invisible* (1923), *Spook Stories* (1928), and *More Spook Stories* (1934). (Mike Ashley has excavated a number of additional Benson stories which can be found in the British Library's volume *The Outcast and Other Dark Tales*.) "How Fear Departed from the Long Gallery" first appeared in *The Windsor Magazine* in 1911, and was included in *The Room in the Tower*.

Church-Peveril is a house so beset and frequented by spectres, both visible and audible, that none of the family which it shelters under its acre and a half of green copper roofs takes psychical phenomena with any seriousness. For to the Peverils the appearance of a ghost is a matter of hardly greater significance than is the appearance of the post to those who live in more ordinary houses. It arrives, that is to say, practically every day, it knocks—or makes other noises—it is observed coming up the drive, or in other places. I myself, when staying there, have seen the present Mrs. Peveril, who is rather short-sighted, peer into the dusk, while we were taking our coffee on the terrace after dinner, and say to her daughter—

"My dear, was not that the Blue Lady who has just gone into the shrubbery? I hope she won't frighten Flo. Whistle for Flo, dear." Flo, it may be remarked, is the youngest and most precious of many dachshunds.

Blanche Peveril gave a cursory whistle and crunched the sugar left unmelted at the bottom of her coffee cup between her very white teeth.

"Oh, darling Flo isn't so silly as to mind," she said. "Poor blue Aunt Barbara is such a bore! Whenever I meet her she always looks as if she wanted to speak to me; but when I say, 'What is it, Aunt Barbara?' she never utters, but only points somewhere towards the house, which is so vague. I believe there was something she wanted to confess about two hundred years ago, but she has forgotten what it is."

Here Flo gave two short, phased barks, and came out of the shrubbery wagging her tail and capering round what appeared to me to be a perfectly empty space on the lawn.

"There, Flo has made friends with her," said Mrs. Peveril. "What a darling! I wonder why she dresses in that very stupid shade of blue."

From this it may be gathered that even with regard to psychical phenomena there is some truth in the proverb that speaks of familiarity. But the Peverils do not exactly treat their ghosts with contempt, since none of that delightful family ever despised anybody except such people as avowedly did not care for hunting or shooting or golf or skating. And as all of their ghosts are of their family, it seems reasonable to suppose that they all, even the poor Blue Lady, excelled at one time in field sports. So far, then, they harbour no such unkindness or contempt, but only pity. Of one Peveril, indeed, who broke his neck in vainly attempting to ride up the main staircase on a thoroughbred mare, after some monstrous and violent deed in the back garden, they are very fond, and Blanche comes downstairs in the morning with an eye unusually bright when she can announce that Master Anthony was "very loud" last night. He—apart from the fact of his having been so foul a ruffian—was a tremendous fellow across country, and they like these indications of the continuance of his superb vitality. In fact, it is supposed to be a compliment, when you go to stay at Church-Peveril, to be assigned a bedroom which is frequented by defunct members of the family. It means that you are worthy to look on the august and villainous dead, and you will find yourself shown into some vaulted or tapestried chamber, without benefit of electric light, and are told that Great-great-grandmamma Bridget occasionally has vague business by the fireplace, but it is better not to talk to her, and that you will hear Master Anthony "awfully well" if he attempts the front staircase any time before morning. There you are left for your night's repose, and, having quakingly undressed, begin reluctantly to put out your candles. It is draughty in these great chambers, and the solemn tapestry swings and bellows and subsides, and the firelight dances on the forms of huntsmen and warriors and stern pursuits. Then you climb up into your bed—a bed so huge that you feel us if the desert of Sahara was spread for you—and pray, like the mariners who sailed with St. Paul, for day. And all the time you are aware that Freddy and Harry and Blanche, and possibly even Mrs. Peveril, are quite capable of dressing up and making disquieting tappings outside your door, so that, when you open it, some inconjecturable horror fronts you. For myself, I stick steadily to the assertion that I have an obscure valvular disease of the heart, and so sleep undisturbed in the new wing of the house, where Aunt Barbara and Great-great-grandmamma Bridget and Master Anthony never penetrate. I forget the details of Great-great-grandmamma Bridget, but she certainly cut the throat of some distant relation before she disembowelled herself with the axe that had been used at Agincourt. Before that she had led a very sultry life, crammed with amazing incident.

But there is one ghost at Church-Peveril at which the family never laugh, in which they feel no friendly and amused interest, and of which they only speak just as much as is necessary for the safety of their guests. More properly it should be described as two ghosts, for the "haunt" in question is that of two very young children who were twins. These, not without reason, the family take very seriously indeed. The story of them, as told me by Mrs. Peveril, is as follows:—

In the year 1602, the same being the last of Queen Elizabeth's reign, a certain Dick Peveril was greatly in favour at Court. He was brother to Master Joseph Peveril, then owner of the family house and lands, who, two years previously, became father of twin boys, first-born of his progeny. It is known that the royal and ancient virgin had said to Handsome Dick, who was nearly forty years his brother's junior, "'Tis pity that you are not master of Church-Peveril," and these words probably suggested to him a sinister design. Be that as it may, Handsome Dick, who very adequately sustained the family reputation for wickedness, set off to ride down to Yorkshire, and found that, very conveniently, his brother Joseph had just been seized with an apoplexy, which appeared to be the result of a continued spell of hot weather combined with the necessity of quenching his thirst with an augmented amount of sack, and had actually died while Handsome Dick, with Heaven knows what thoughts in his mind, was journeying northwards.

Thus it came about that he arrived at Church-Peveril just in time for his brother's funeral. It was with great propriety that he attended the obsequies, and returned to spend a sympathetic day or two of mourning with his widowed sister-in-law, who was but a faint-hearted dame, little fit to be mated with such hawks as these.

On the second night of his stay he did that which the Peverils regret to this day. He entered the room where the twins slept with their nurse, and quietly strangled the latter as she slept. Then he took the twins and put them into the fire which warms the Long Gallery. The weather, which up to the day of Joseph's death had been so hot, had changed suddenly to bitter cold, and the fire was heaped high with burning logs and was exultant with flame. In the core of this conflagration he struck out a cremation chamber, and into that he threw the two children, stamping them down with his riding-boots. They could just walk, but they could not walk out of that ardent place. It is said that he laughed as he added more logs. Thus he became master of Church-Peveril.

The crime was never brought home to him, but he lived no longer than a year in the enjoyment of his bloodstained inheritance. When he lay a-dying, he made his confession to the priest who attended him, but his spirit struggled forth from its fleshly coil before absolution could be given him. On that very night there began in Church-Peveril the haunting which to this day is but seldom spoken of by the family, and then only in low tones and with serious mien. For only an hour or two after Handsome Dick's death, one of the servants, passing the door of the Long Gallery, heard from within peals of the loud laughter, so jovial and yet so sinister, which he had thought would never be heard in the house again. In a moment of that cold courage which is so nearly akin to mortal terror, he opened the door and entered, expecting to see he knew not what manifestation of him who lay dead in the room below. Instead he saw two little white-robed figures toddling towards him hand in hand across the moon-lit floor.

The watchers in the room below ran upstairs, startled by the crash of his fallen body, and found him lying in the grip of some dread convulsion. Just before morning he regained consciousness and told his tale. Then, pointing with trembling and ash-grey finger towards the door, he screamed aloud and so fell back dead.

During the next fifty years this strange and terrible legend of the twin babies became fixed and consolidated. Their appearance, luckily for those who inhabited the house, was exceedingly rare, and during these years they seem to have been seen four or five times only. On each occasion they appeared at night, between sunset and sunrise, always in the same Long Gallery, and always as two toddling children scarcely able to walk. And on each occasion the luckless individual who saw them died either speedily or terribly, or with both speed and terror, after the accursed vision had appeared to him. Sometimes he might live for a few months; he was lucky if he died, as did the servant who first saw them, in a few hours. Vastly more awful was the fate of a certain Mrs. Canning, who had the ill-luck to see them in the middle of the next century, or, to be quite accurate, in the year 1760. By this time the hours and the place of their appearance was well known, and, as to this day, visitors were warned not to go between sunset and sunrise into the Long Gallery.

But Mrs. Canning, a brilliantly clever and beautiful woman, admirer also and friend of the notorious sceptic M. Voltaire, wilfully went and sat night after night, in spite of all protestations, in the haunted place. For four evenings she saw nothing, but on the fifth she had her will, for the door in the middle of the gallery opened, and there came toddling towards her the ill-omened innocent little pair. It seemed that even then she was not frightened, but she thought good, poor wretch, to mock at them, telling them it was time for them to get back into the fire. They gave no word in answer, but turned away from her, crying and sobbing. Immediately after they disappeared from her vision, and she rustled downstairs to where the family and guests in the house were waiting for her, with the triumphant announcement that she had seen them both, and must needs write to M. Voltaire, saying that she had spoken to spirits made manifest. It would make him laugh. But when some months later the whole news reached him, he did not laugh at all.

Mrs. Canning was one of the great beauties of her day, and in the year 1760 she was at the height and zenith of her blossoming. Her chief beauty, if it is possible to single out one point where all was so exquisite, lay in the dazzling colour and incomparable brilliance of her complexion. She was now just thirty years of age, but, in spite of the excesses of her life, retained the snow and roses of girlhood, and she courted the bright light of day, which other women shunned, for it but showed to greater advantage the splendour of her skin. In consequence, she was very considerably dismayed one morning, about a fortnight after her strange experience in the Long Gallery, to observe on her left cheek, an inch or two below her turquoise-coloured eyes, a little greyish patch of skin about as big as a threepenny piece. It was in vain that she applied her accustomed washes and unguents; vain, too, were the arts of her *fardeuse* and of her medical adviser. For a week she kept herself secluded, martyring herself with solitude and unaccustomed physics, and for result, at the end of the week, she had no amelioration to comfort herself with—instead, this woeful grey patch had doubled itself in size. Thereafter the nameless disease, whatever it was, developed in new and terrible ways. From the centre of the discoloured place there sprouted forth little lichen-like tendrils of greenish-grey and another patch appeared on her lower lip. This, too, soon vegetated, and one morning, on opening her eyes to the horror of a new day, she found that her vision was strangely blurred. She rushed to her looking-glass, and what she saw caused her to shriek aloud with horror. From under her upper eyelid a fresh growth had sprung up mushroom-like in the night, and its filaments extended downwards, screening the pupil of her eye. Soon after her tongue and throat were attacked, the air passages became obstructed, and death by suffocation was merciful after such suffering.

More terrible yet was the case of a certain Colonel Blantyre, who fired at the children with his revolver. What he went through is not to be recorded here.

It is this haunting, then, that the Peverils take quite seriously, and every guest on his arrival in the house is told that the Long Gallery must not be entered after nightfall on any pretext whatever. By day, however, it is a delightful room, and intrinsically merits description, apart from the fact that the due understanding of its geography is necessary for the account that here follows. It is full eighty feet in length, and is lit by a row of six tall windows looking over the gardens at the back of the house. A door communicates with the landing at the top of the main staircase, and about half-way down the gallery, in the wall facing the windows, is another door communicating with the back staircase and servants' quarters, and thus the gallery forms a constant place of passage for them in going to the rooms on the first landing. It was through this door that the baby figures came when they appeared to Mrs. Canning, and on several other occasions they have been known to make their entry here, for the room out of which Handsome Dick took them lies just beyond at the top of the back stairs. Further on again in the gallery is the fireplace into which he thrust them, and at the far end a large bow-window looks straight down the avenue. Above this fireplace there hangs with grim significance a portrait of Handsome Dick, in the insolent beauty of early manhood, attributed to Holbein, and a dozen other portraits of great merit face the windows. During the day this is the most frequented sitting-room in the house, for its other visitors never appear there then, nor does it then ever resound with the harsh, jovial laugh of Handsome Dick, which sometimes, after dark has fallen, is heard by passers-by on the landing outside. But Blanche does not grow bright-eyed when she hears it; she shuts her ears and hastens to put a greater distance between her and the sound of that atrocious mirth.

But during the day the Long Gallery is frequented by many occupants, and much laughter in no wise sinister or saturnine is heard there. When summer lies hot over the land, these occupants lounge in the deep window-seats, and when winter spreads his icy fingers and blows shrilly between his frozen palms, congregate round the fireplace at the far end, and perch in companies of cheerful chatterers upon sofa and chair and chair-back and floor. Often have I sat there on long August evenings up till dressing-time, but never have I been there when anyone has seemed disposed to linger over-late without hearing the warning: "It is close on sunset. Shall we go?" Later on, in the shorter autumn days, they often have tea laid there; and sometimes it has happened that even while merriment was most uproarious, Mrs. Peveril has suddenly looked out of the window and said: "My dears, it is getting so late; let us finish our nonsense downstairs in the hall." And then for a moment a curious hush always falls on loquacious family and guests alike, and, as if some bad news had just been made known, we all make our silent way out of the place. But the spirits of the Peverils—of the living ones, that is to say—are the most mercurial imaginable, and the blight which the thought of Handsome Dick and his doings casts over them passes away again with amazing rapidity.

A typical party, large, young, and peculiarly cheerful, was staying at Church-Peveril shortly after Christmas last year, and as usual, on December 31, Mrs. Peveril was giving her annual New Year's Eve ball. The house was quite full, and she had commandeered as well the greater part of "The Peveril Arms" to provide sleeping quarters for the overflow from the house. For some days past a black and windless frost had stopped all hunting; but it is an ill windlessness that blows no good—if so mixed a metaphor may be forgiven—and the lake below the house had for the last day or two been covered with an adequate and admirable sheet of ice. Everyone in the house had been occupied all the morning of that day in performing swift and violent manœuvres on the elusive surface, and as soon as lunch was over, we all, with one exception, hurried out again. This one exception was Madge Dalrymple, who had had the misfortune to fall rather badly earlier in the day, but hoped, by resting her injured knee, instead of joining the skaters again, to be able to dance that evening. The hope, it is true, was of the most sanguine sort, for she could but hobble ignobly back to the house, but with the breezy optimism which characterizes the

Peverils—she is Blanche's first cousin—she remarked that it would be but tepid enjoyment that she could in her present state derive from further skating, and thus she sacrificed little but might gain much.

Accordingly, after a rapid cup of coffee, which was served in the Long Gallery, we left Madge comfortably reclined on the big sofa at right-angles to the fireplace, with an attractive book to beguile the tedium till tea. Being of the family, she knew all about Handsome Dick and the babies, and the fate of Mrs. Canning and Colonel Blantyre, but as we went out, I heard Blanche say to her, "Don't run it too fine, dear," and Madge had replied, "No, I'll go away well before sunset." And so we left her alone in the Long Gallery.

Madge read her attractive book for some minutes, but, failing to get absorbed in it, put it down and limped across to the window. Though it was still but little after two, it was but a dim and uncertain light that entered, for the crystalline brightness of the morning had given place to a veiled obscurity produced by flocks of thick clouds which were coming sluggishly up from the northeast. Already the whole sky was overcast with them, and occasionally a few snowflakes fluttered waveringly down past the long windows. From the darkness and bitter cold of the afternoon it seemed to her that there was like to be a heavy snowfall before long, and these outward signs were echoed inwardly in her by that muffled drowsiness of the brain which, to those who are sensitive to the pressures and lightnesses of weather, portends storm. Madge was peculiarly the prey of such external influences. To her a brisk morning gave an ineffable brightness and gaiety of spirit, and correspondingly the approach of heavy weather produced a somnolence in sensation that both drowsed and depressed her.

It was in such mood as this that she limped back again to the sofa beside the log fire. The whole house was comfortably heated by water-pipes, and though the fire of logs and peat, an adorable mixture, had been allowed to burn low, the room was very warm. Idly she watched the dwindling flames, not opening her book again, but lying on the sofa with face towards the fireplace, intending drowsily and not immediately to go to her own room and spend the hours, until the return of the skaters made gaiety in the house again, in writing one or two neglected letters. Still drowsily she began thinking over what she had to communicate. One letter, several days overdue, should go to her mother, who was immensely interested in the psychical affairs of the family. She would tell her how Master Anthony had been prodigiously active on the staircase a night or two ago, and how the Blue Lady, regardless of the severity of the weather, had been seen by Mrs. Peveril that morning strolling about. It was rather interesting. The Blue Lady had gone down the laurel walk, and had been seen by her to enter the stables, where at the moment Freddy Peveril was inspecting the frost-bound hunters. Identically then a sudden panic had spread through the stables, and the horses had whinnied and kicked and shied and sweated. Of the fatal twins nothing had been seen for many years past, but, as her mother knew, the Peverils never used the Long Gallery after dark.

Then for a moment she sat up, remembering that she was in the Long Gallery now. But it was still but a little after half-past two, and if she went to her room in half an hour, she would have ample time to write this and another letter before tea. Till then she would read her book. But she found she had left it on the window-sill, and it seemed scarcely worth while to get it. She felt exceedingly drowsy.

The sofa where she lay had been lately re-covered in a greyish-green shade of velvet somewhat the colour of lichen. It was of very thick, soft texture, and she luxuriously stretched her arms out, one on each side of her body, and pressed her fingers into the nap. How horrible that story of Mrs. Canning was! The growth on her face was of the colour of lichen... And then, without further transition or blurring of thought, Madge fell asleep.

She dreamed. She dreamed that she awoke and found herself exactly where she had gone to sleep, and in exactly the same attitude. The flames from the logs had burned up again, and leaped on the walls, fitfully illuminating the picture of Handsome Dick above the fireplace. In her dream she knew exactly what she had done today, and for what reason she was lying here now instead of being out with the rest of the skaters. She remembered also—still dreaming—that she was going to write a letter or two before tea, and prepared to get up in order to go to her room. As she half rose, she caught sight of her own arms lying out on each side of her on the grey velvet sofa. But she could not see where her hands ended and where the grey velvet began; her fingers seemed to have melted into the stuff. She could see her wrists quite clearly, and a blue vein on the backs of her hands, and here and there a knuckle. Then in her dream she remembered the last thought which had been in her mind before she fell asleep—namely, the growth of the lichen-coloured vegetation on the face and the eyes and the throat of Mrs. Canning. At that thought the strangling terror of real nightmare began. She knew that she was being transformed into this grey stuff, and she was absolutely unable to move. Soon the grey would spread up her arms and over her face. When they came in from skating, they would find here nothing but a huge misshapen cushion of lichen-coloured velvet, and that would be she. The horror grew more acute, and then by a violent effort she shook herself free of the clutches of this very evil dream, and awoke.

For a minute or two she lay there, conscious only of the tremendous relief at finding herself awake. She felt again with her fingers the pleasant touch of the velvet, and drew them backwards and forwards, assuring herself that she was not, as her dream had suggested, melting into greyness and softness. But she was still, in spite of the violence of her awaking, very sleepy, and lay there till, looking down, she was aware that she could not see her hands at all; it was very nearly dark.

At that moment a sudden flicker of flame came from the dying fire, and a flare of burning gas from the peat flooded the room. The portrait of Handsome Dick looked evilly down on her, and her hands were visible again. And then a panic worse than the panic of her dreams seized her. Daylight had altogether faded, and she knew that she was alone in the dark in the terrible gallery. This panic was of the nature of nightmare, for she felt unable to move for terror. But it was worse than nightmare, because she knew she was awake. And then the full cause of this frozen fear dawned on her—she knew with the certainty of absolute conviction that she was about to see the twin babies.

She felt a sudden moisture break out on her face, and within her mouth her tongue and throat went suddenly dry, and she felt her tongue grate along the inner surface of her teeth. All power of movement had slipped from her limbs, leaving them dead and inert, and she stared with wide eyes into the blackness. The spurt of flame from the peat had burned itself out again, and darkness encompassed her.

Then on the wall opposite her, facing the windows, there grew a faint light of dusky crimson. For a moment she thought it but heralded the approach of the awful vision; then hope revived in her heart, and she remembered that thick clouds had overcast the sky before she went to sleep, and guessed that this light came from the sun, not yet quite sunk and set. This sudden revival of hope gave her the necessary stimulus, and she sprang off the sofa where she lay. She looked out of the window and saw the dull glow on the horizon. But before she could take a step forward, it was obscured again. A tiny sparkle of light came from the hearth, which did no more than illuminate the tiles of the fireplace, and snow falling heavily signalled at the window-panes. There was neither light nor sound except these.

But the courage that had come to her, giving her the power of movement, had not quite deserted her, and she began feeling her way down the gallery. And then she found that she was lost. She stumbled against a chair, and, recovering herself, stumbled against another. Then a table barred her way, and, turning swiftly aside, she found herself up against the back of a sofa. Once more she turned and saw the dim gleam of the firelight on the side opposite to that on which she expected it. In her blind gropings she must have reversed her direction. But which way was she to go now? She seemed blocked in by furniture. And all the time insistent and imminent was the fact that the two innocent terrible ghosts were about to appear to her.

Then she began to pray. "Lighten our darkness, O Lord!" she said to herself. But she could not remember how the prayer continued, and she had sore need of it. There was something about the perils of the night... All this time she felt about her with groping, fluttering hands. The fire glimmer, which should have been on her left, was on her right again, therefore she must turn herself round once more. "Lighten our darkness," she whispered, and then aloud she repeated, "Lighten our darkness!"

She stumbled up against a screen, and could not remember the existence of any such screen. Hastily she felt beside it with blind hands, and touched something soft and velvety. Was it the sofa on which she had lain? If so, where was the head of it? It had a head and a back and feet... it was like a person all covered with grey lichen... then she lost her head completely. All that remained to her was to pray. She was lost, lost in this awful place, where no one came in the dark except the babies that cried. And she heard her voice rising from whisper to speech, and speech to scream. She shrieked out the holy words, she yelled them as if blaspheming, as she groped among tables and chairs and the pleasant things of ordinary life which had become so terrible.

Then came a sudden and an awful answer to her screamed prayer. Once more a pocket of inflammable gas in the peat on the hearth was reached by the smouldering embers, and the room started into light. She saw the evil eyes of Handsome Dick, she saw the little ghostly snowflakes falling thickly outside, and she saw where she was—just opposite the door through which the terrible twins made their entrance. Then the flame went out again, and left her in blackness once more. But she had gained something, for she had her geography now. The centre of the room was bare of furniture, and one swift dart would take her to the door of the landing above the main staircase and into safety. In that gleam she had been able to see the handle of the door, bright-brassed, luminous like a star. She would go straight for it; it was but a matter of a few seconds now.

She took a long breath, partly of relief, partly to satisfy the demands of her galloping heart. But the breath was only half taken when she was stricken once more into the immobility of nightmare.

There came a little whisper—it was no more than that—from the door opposite which she stood, and through which the twin babies entered. It was not quite dark outside, for she could see that the door was opening. And there stood in the opening two little white figures, side by side. They came towards her slowly, shufflingly. She could not see face or form at all distinctly, but the two little white figures were advancing. She knew them to be the ghosts of terror, innocent of the awful doom they were bound to bring, even as she was innocent. With the inconceivable rapidity of thought, she made up her mind what to do. She had not hurt them or laughed at them, and they—they were but babies when the wicked and bloody deed had sent them to their burning death. Surely the spirits of these children would not be inaccessible to the cry of one who was of the same blood as they, who had committed no fault that merited the doom they brought. If she entreated them, they might have mercy, they might forbear to bring the curse on her, they might allow her to pass out of the place without blight, without the sentence of death or the shadow of things worse than death upon her.

It was but for the space of a moment that she hesitated: then she sank down on to her knees and stretched out her hands towards them.

"Oh, my dears," she said, "I only fell asleep! I have done no more wrong than that—"

She paused a moment, and her tender girl's heart thought no more of herself, but only of them, those little innocent spirits on whom so awful a doom was laid that they should bring death where other children bring laughter, and doom for delight. But all those who had seen them before had dreaded and feared them, or had mocked at them.

Then as the enlightenment of pity dawned on her, her fear fell from her like the wrinkled sheath that holds the sweet folded buds of spring.

"Dears, I am so sorry for you," she said. "It is not your fault that you must bring me what you must bring, but I am not afraid any longer. I am only sorry for you. God bless you, you poor darlings!"

She raised her head and looked at them. Though it was so dark, she could now see their faces, though all was dim and wavering, like the light of pale flames shaken by a draught. But the faces were not miserable or fierce: they smiled at her with shy little baby smiles. And as she looked, they grew faint, fading slowly away like wreaths of vapour in frosty air.

Madge did not at once move when they had vanished, for instead of fear there was wrapped round her a wonderful sense of peace, so happy and serene that she would not willingly stir and so perhaps disturb it. But before long she got up, and feeling her way, but without any sense of nightmare pressing her on, or frenzy of fear to spur her, she went out of the Long Gallery, to find Blanche just coming upstairs whistling and swinging her skates.

"How's the leg, dear?" she asked. "You're not limping any more."

Till that moment Madge had not thought of it.

"I think it must be all right," she said. "I had forgotten it, anyhow. Blanche, dear, you won't be frightened for me, will you, but—but I have seen the twins!"

For a moment Blanche's face whitened with terror.

"What?" she said in a whisper.

"Yes, I saw them just now. But they were kind, they smiled at me, and I was so sorry for them, and somehow I am sure I have nothing to fear."

It seems that Madge was right, for nothing untoward has come to her. Something—her attitude to them, we must suppose, her pity, her sympathy—touched and dissolved and annihilated the curse. Indeed, I was at Church-Peveril only last week, arriving there after dark. Just as I passed the gallery door. Blanche came out.

"Ah, there you are!" she said. "I've just been seeing the twins. They looked too sweet, and stopped nearly ten minutes. Let us have tea at once."

1932

THE VAULTS OF YOH-VOMBIS

Clark Ashton Smith

With H. P. Lovecraft and Robert E. Howard (of "Conan the Barbarian" fame) one of the "Big Three" of *Weird Tales* in its heyday, Clark Ashton Smith was an entirely different kind of writer from either of these—different, indeed, from any pulpsmith who ever lived. A poet and sculptor as well as the author of tales of fantasy, science fiction, and horror ("The Vaults of Yoh-Vombis" blends all three), Smith (1893–1961) was a Californian who spent much of his life making strange art, in various media, by himself in a remote cabin. Smith's elaborate style (somewhat reined in here) makes him one of those "love him or hate him" authors; for those in the former category, as Brian Stableford puts it, "[h]is highly ornamented prose [is] directed to the purpose of building phantasmagoric dream-worlds stranger than had ever been described before." With such evocative titles as "The Abominations of Yondo", "The Tale of Satampra Zeiros", "Ubbo-Sathla", and "The Garden of Adomtha", even the table of contents of one of Smith's collections can leave one feeling surfeited. Fungi, and hybrid entities partaking of the fungous, abound in Smith's fantastical worlds, in such tales as "The Immortals of Mercury", "The Seed from the Sepulchre", and this one (first published in *Weird Tales* in May 1932).

If the doctors are correct in their prognostication, I have only a few Martian hours of life remaining to me. In those hours I shall endeavour to relate, as a warning to others who might follow in our footsteps, the singular and frightful happenings that terminated our researches among the ruins of Yoh-Vombis. If my story will only serve to prevent future explorations, the telling will not have been in vain.

There were eight of us, professional archaeologists with more or less terrene and interplanetary experience, who set forth with native guides from Ignarh, the commercial metropolis of Mars, to inspect that ancient, eon-deserted city. Allan Octave, our official leader, held his primacy by knowing more about Martian archaeology than any other Terrestrial on the planet; and others of the party, such as William Harper and Jonas Halgren, had been associated with him in many of his previous researches. I, Rodney Severn, was more of a newcomer, having spent but a few months on Mars; and the greater part of my own ultra-terrene delvings had been confined to Venus.

The nude, spongy-chested Aihais had spoken deterringly of vast deserts filled with ever-swirling sandstorms, through which we must pass to reach Yoh-Vombis; and in spite of our munificent offers of payment, it had been difficult to secure guides for the journey. Therefore we were surprised as well as pleased when we came to the ruins after seven hours of plodding across the flat, treeless, orange-yellow desolation to the southwest of Ignarh.

We beheld our destination, for the first time, in the setting of the small, remote sun. For a little, we thought that the domeless, three-angled towers and broken-down monoliths were those of some unlegended city, other than the one we sought. But the disposition of the ruins, which lay in a sort of arc for almost the entire extent of a low, gneissic, league-long elevation of bare, eroded stone, together with the type of architecture, soon convinced us that we had found our goal. No other ancient city on Mars had been laid out in that manner; and the strange, many-terraced buttresses, like the stairways of forgotten Anakim, were peculiar to the prehistoric race that had built Yoh-Vombis.

I have seen the hoary, sky-confronting walls of Machu Pichu amid the desolate Andes; and the frozen, giant-built battlements of Uogam on the glacial tundras of the nightward hemisphere of Venus. But these were as things of yesteryear compared to the walls upon which we gazed. The whole region was far from the lifegiving canals beyond whose environs even the more noxious flora and fauna are seldom found; and we had seen no living thing since our departure from Ignarh. But here, in this place of petrified sterility, of eternal bareness and solitude, it seemed that life could never have been.

I think we all received the same impression as we stood staring in silence while the pale, sanies-like sunset fell on the dark and megalithic ruins. I remember gasping a little, in an air that seemed to have been touched by the irrespirable chill of death; and I heard the same sharp, laborious intake of breath from others of our party.

"That place is deader than an Egyptian morgue," observed Harper.

"Certainly it is far more ancient," Octave assented. "According to the most reliable legends, the Yorhis, who built Yoh-Vombis, were wiped out by the present ruling race at least forty thousand years ago."

"There's a story, isn't there," said Harper, "that the last remnant of the Yorhis was destroyed by some unknown agency—something too horrible and outré to be mentioned even in a myth?"

"Of course, I've heard that legend," agreed Octave. "Maybe we'll find evidence among the ruins to prove or disprove it. The Yorhis may have been cleaned out by some terrible epidemic, such as the Yashta pestilence, which was a kind of green mould that ate all the bones of the body, starting with the teeth. But we needn't be afraid of getting it, if there are any mummies in Yoh-Vombis—the bacteria will all be dead as their victims, after so many cycles of planetary desiccation."

The sun had gone down with uncanny swiftness, as if it had disappeared through some sort of prestidigitation rather that the normal process of setting. We felt the instant chill of the blue-green twilight; and the ether above us was like a huge, transparent dome of sunless ice, shot with a million bleak sparklings that were the stars. We donned the coats and helmets of Martian fur, which must always be worn at night; and going on to westward of the walls, we established our camp in their lee, so that we might be sheltered a little from the *jaar*, that cruel desert wind that always blows from the east before dawn. Then, lighting the alcohol lamps that had been brought along for cooking purposes, we huddled around them while the evening meal was prepared and eaten.

Afterward, for comfort rather than because of weariness, we retired early to our sleeping-bags; and the two Aihais, our guides, wrapped themselves in the cerement-like folds of *bassa*-cloth which are all the protection their leathery skins appear to require even in sub-zero temperatures.

Even in my thick, double-lined bag, I still felt the rigour of the night air; and I am sure it was this, rather than anything else, which kept me awake for a long while and rendered my eventual slumber somewhat restless and broken. At any rate, I was not troubled by even the least presentiment of alarm or danger; and I should have laughed at the idea that anything of peril could lurk in Yoh-Vombis, amid whose undreamable and stupefying antiquities the very phantoms of its dead must long since have faded into nothingness.

I must have drowsed again and again, with starts of semi-wakefulness. At last, in one of these, I knew vaguely that the small twin moons, Phobos and Deimos, had risen and were making huge and far-flung shadows with the domeless towers; shadows that almost touched the glimmering, shrouded forms of my companions.

The whole scene was locked in a petrific stillness; and none of the sleepers stirred. Then, as my lids were about to close, I received an impression of movement in the frozen gloom; and it seemed to me that a portion of the foremost shadow had detached itself and was crawling toward Octave, who lay nearer to the ruins than we others.

Even through my heavy lethargy, I was disturbed by a warning of something unnatural and perhaps ominous. I started to sit up; and even as I moved, the shadowy object, whatever it was, drew back and became merged once more in the greater shadow. Its vanishment startled me into full wakefulness; and yet I could not be sure that I had actually seen the thing. In that brief, final glimpse, it had seemed like a roughly circular piece of cloth or leather, dark and crumpled, and twelve or fourteen inches in diameter, that ran along the ground with the doubling movement of an inch-worm, causing it to fold and unfold in a startling manner as it went.

I did not go to sleep again for nearly an hour; and if it had not been for the extreme cold, I should doubtless have gotten up to investigate and make sure whether I had really beheld an object of such bizarre nature or had merely dreamt it. But more and more I began to convince myself that the thing was too unlikely and fantastical to have been anything but the figment of a dream. And at last I nodded off into light slumber.

The chill, demoniac sighing of the *jaar* across the jagged walls awoke me, and I saw that the faint moonlight had received the hueless accession of early dawn. We all arose, and prepared our breakfast with fingers that grew numb in spite of the spirit-lamps.

My queer visual experience during the night had taken on more than ever a fantasmagoric unreality; and I gave it no more than a passing thought and did not speak of it to the others. We were all eager to begin our explorations; and shortly after sunrise we started on a preliminary tour of examination.

Strangely, as it seemed, the two Martians refused to accompany us. Stolid and taciturn, they gave no explicit reason; but evidently nothing would induce them to enter Yoh-Vombis. Whether or not they were afraid of the ruins, we were unable to determine: their enigmatic faces, with the small oblique eyes and huge, flaring nostrils, betrayed neither fear nor any other emotion intelligible to man. In reply to our questions, they merely said that no Aihai had set foot among the ruins for ages. Apparently there was some mysterious taboo in connection with the place.

For equipment in that preliminary tour we took along only our electric torches and a crowbar. Our other tools, and some cartridges of high explosives, we left at our camp, to be used later if necessary, after we had surveyed the ground. One or two of us owned automatics; but these also were left behind; for it seemed absurd to imagine that any form of life would be encountered among the ruins.

Octave was visibly excited as we began our inspection, and maintained a running fire of exclamatory comment. The rest of us were subdued and silent: it was impossible to shake off the sombre awe and wonder that fell upon us from those megalithic stones.

We went on for some distance among the triangular, terraced buildings, following the zigzag streets that conformed to this peculiar architecture. Most of the towers were more or less dilapidated; and everywhere we saw the deep erosion wrought by cycles of blowing wind and sand, which, in many cases, had worn into roundness the sharp angles of the mighty walls. We entered some of the towers, but found utter emptiness within. Whatever they had contained in the way of furnishings must long ago have crumbled into dust; and the dust had been blown away by the searching desert gales.

At length we came to the wall of a vast terrace, hewn from the plateau itself. On this terrace, the central buildings were grouped like a sort of acropolis. A flight of time-eaten steps, designed for longer limbs than those of men or even the gangling modern Martians, afforded access to the hewn summit.

Pausing, we decided to defer our investigation of the higher buildings, which, being more exposed than the others, were doubly ruinous and dilapidated, and in all likelihood would offer little for our trouble. Octave had begun to voice his disappointment over our failure to find anything in the nature of artefacts or carvings that would throw light on the history of Yoh-Vombis.

Then, a little to the right of the stairway, we perceived an entrance in the main wall, half choked with ancient debris. Behind the heap of detritus, we found the beginning of a downward flight of steps. Darkness poured from the opening, noisome and musty with primordial stagnancies of decay; and we could see nothing below the first steps, which gave the appearance of being suspended over a black gulf.

Throwing his torch-beam into the abyss, Octave began to descend the stairs. His eager voice called us to follow.

At the bottom of the high, awkward steps, we found ourselves in a long and roomy vault, like a subterranean hallway. Its floor was deep with siftings of immemorial dust. The air was singularly heavy, as if the lees of an ancient atmosphere, less tenuous than that of Mars today, had settled down and remained in that stagnant darkness. It was harder to breathe than the outer air: it was filled with unknown effluvia; and the light dust arose before us at every step, diffusing a faintness of bygone corruption, like the dust of powdered mummies.

At the end of the vault, before a strait and lofty doorway, our torches revealed an immense shallow urn or pan, supported on short cube-shaped legs, and wrought from a dull, blackish-green material. In its bottom, we perceived a deposit of dark and cinder-like fragments, which gave off a slight but disagreeable pungence, like the phantom of some more powerful odour. Octave, bending over the rim, began to cough and sneeze as he inhaled it.

"That stuff, whatever it was, must have been a pretty strong fumigant," he observed. "The people of Yoh-Vombis may have used it to disinfect the vaults."

The doorway beyond the shallow urn admitted us to a larger chamber, whose floor was comparatively free of dust. We found that the dark stone beneath our feet was marked off in multiform geometric patterns, traced with ochreous ore, amid which, as in Egyptian cartouches, hieroglyphics and highly formalized drawings were enclosed. We could make little from most of them; but the figures in many were doubtless designed to represent the Yorhis themselves. Like the Aihais, they were tall and angular, with great, bellows-like chests. The ears and nostrils, as far as we could judge, were not so huge and flaring as those of the modern Martians. All of these Yorhis were depicted as being nude; but in one of the cartouches, done in a far hastier style than the others, we perceived two figures whose high, conical craniums were wrapped in what seemed to be a sort of turban, which they were about to remove or adjust. The artist seemed to have laid a peculiar emphasis on the odd gesture with which the sinuous, four-jointed fingers were plucking at these head-dresses; and the whole posture was unexplainably contorted.

From the second vault, passages ramified in all directions, leading to a veritable warren of catacombs. Here, enormous pot-bellied urns of the same material as the fumigating-pan, but taller than a man's head and fitted with angular-handled stoppers, were ranged in solemn rows along the walls, leaving scant room for two of us to walk abreast. When we succeeded in removing one of the huge stoppers, we saw that the jar was filled to the rim with ashes and charred fragments of bone. Doubtless (as is still the Martian custom) the Yorhis had stored the cremated remains of whole families in single urns.

Even Octave became silent as we went on; and a sort of meditative awe seemed to replace his former excitement. We others, I think, were utterly weighed down to a man by the solid gloom of a concept-defying antiquity, into which it seemed that we were going farther and farther at every step.

The shadows fluttered before us like the monstrous and misshapen wings of phantom bats. There was nothing anywhere but the atom-like dust of ages, and the jars that held the ashes of a long-extinct people. But, clinging to the high roof in one of the farther vaults, I saw a dark and corrugated patch of circular form, like a withered fungus. It was impossible to reach the thing; and we went on after peering at it with many futile conjectures. Oddly enough, I failed to remember at that moment the crumpled, shadowy object I had seen or dreamt of the night before.

I have no idea how far we had gone, when we came to the last vault; but it seemed that we had been wandering for ages in that forgotten underworld. The air was growing fouler and more irrespirable, with a thick, sodden quality, as if from a sediment of material rottenness; and we had about decided to turn back. Then, without warning, at the end of a long, urn-lined catacomb, we found ourselves confronted by a blank wall.

Here we came upon one of the strangest and most mystifying of our discoveries—a mummified and incredibly desiccated figure, standing erect against the wall. It was more than seven feet in height, of a brown, bituminous colour, and was wholly nude except for a sort of black cowl that covered the upper head and drooped down at the sides in wrinkled folds. From the size and general contour, it was plainly one of the ancient Yorhis—perhaps the sole member of this race whose body had remained intact.

We all felt an inexpressible thrill at the sheer age of this shrivelled thing, which, in the dry air of the vault, had endured through all the historic and geologic vicissitudes of the planet, to provide a visible link with lost cycles.

Then, as we peered closer with our torches, we saw *why* the mummy had maintained an upright position. At ankles, knees, waist, shoulders and neck it was shackled to the wall by heavy metal bands, so deeply eaten and embrowned with a sort of rust that we had failed to distinguish them at first sight in the shadow. The strange cowl on the head, when closelier studied, continued to baffle us. It was covered with a fine, mould-like pile, unclean and dusty as ancient cobwebs. Something about it, I know not what, was abhorrent and revolting.

"By Jove! this is a real find!" ejaculated Octave, as he thrust his torch into the mummified face, where shadows moved like living things in the pit-deep hollows of the eyes and the huge triple nostrils and wide ears that flared upward beneath the cowl.

Still lifting the torch, he put out his free hand and touched the body very lightly. Tentative as the touch had been, the lower part of the barrel-like torso, the legs, the hands and forearms all seemed to dissolve into powder, leaving the head and upper body and arms still hanging in their metal fetters. The progress of decay had been queerly unequal, for the remnant portions gave no sign of disintegration.

Octave cried out in dismay, and then began to cough and sneeze, as the cloud of brown powder, floating with airy lightness, enveloped him. We others all stepped back to avoid the powder. Then, above the spreading cloud, I saw an unbelievable thing. The black cowl on the mummy's head began to curl and twitch upward at the corners, it writhed with a verminous motion, it fell from the withered cranium, seeming to fold and unfold convulsively in midair as it fell. Then it dropped on the bare head of Octave who, in his disconcertment at the crumbling of the mummy, had remained standing close to the wall. At that instant, in a start of profound terror, I remembered the thing that had inched itself from the shadows of Yoh-Vombis in the light of the twin moons, and had drawn back like a figment of slumber at my first waking movement.

Cleaving closely as a tightened cloth, the thing enfolded Octave's hair and brow and eyes, and he shrieked wildly, with incoherent pleas for help, and tore with frantic fingers at the cowl, but failed to loosen it. Then his cries began to mount in a mad crescendo of agony, as if beneath some instrument of infernal torture; and he danced and capered blindly about the vault, eluding us with strange celerity as we all sprang forward in an effort to reach him and release him from his weird incumbrance. The whole happening was mysterious as a nightmare; but the thing that had fallen on his head was plainly some unclassified form of Martian life, which, contrary to all the known laws of science, had survived in those primordial catacombs. We must rescue him from its clutches if we could.

We tried to close in on the frenzied figure of our chief—which, in the far from roomy space between the last urns and the wall, should have been an easy matter. But, darting away, in a manner doubly incomprehensible because of his blindfolded condition, he circled about us and ran past, to disappear among the urns toward the outer labyrinth of intersecting catacombs.

"My God! What has happened to him?" cried Harper. "The man acts as if he were possessed."

There was obviously no time for a discussion of the enigma, and we all followed Octave as speedily as our astonishment would permit. We had lost sight of him in the darkness; and when we came to the first division of the vaults, we were doubtful as to which passage he had taken, till we heard a shrill scream, several times repeated, in a catacomb on the extreme left. There was a shrill, unearthly quality in those screams, which may have been due to the long-stagnant air or the peculiar acoustics of the ramifying caverns. But somehow I could not imagine them as issuing from human lips—at least not from those of a living man. They seemed to contain a soulless, mechanical agony, as if they had been wrung from a devil-driven corpse.

Thrusting our torches before us into the lurching, fleeing shadows, we raced along between rows of mighty urns. The screaming had died away in sepulchral silence; but far off we heard the light and muffled thud of running feet. We followed in headlong pursuit; but, gasping painfully in the vitiated, miasmal air, we were soon compelled to slacken our pace without coming in sight of Octave. Very faintly, and farther away than ever, like the tomb-swallowed steps of a phantom, we heard his vanishing footfalls. Then they ceased; and we heard nothing, except our own convulsive breathing, and the blood that throbbed in our temple-veins like steadily beaten drums of alarm.

We went on, dividing our party into three contingents when we came to a triple branching of the caverns. Harper and Halgren and I took the middle passage, and after we had gone on for an endless interval without finding any trace of Octave, and had threaded our way through recesses piled to the roof with colossal urns that must have held the ashes of a hundred generations, we came out in the huge chamber with the geometric floor-designs. Here, very shortly, we were joined by the others, who had likewise failed to locate our missing leader.

It would be useless to detail our renewed and hour-long search of the myriad vaults, many of which we had not hitherto explored. All were empty, as far as any sign of life was concerned. I remember passing once more through the vault in which I had seen the dark, rounded patch on the ceiling, and noting with a shudder that the patch was gone. It was a miracle that we did not lose ourselves in that underworld maze; but at last we came back again to the final catacomb, in which we had found the shackled mummy.

We heard a measured and recurrent clangour as we neared the place—a most alarming and mystifying sound under the circumstances. It was like the hammering of ghouls on some forgotten mausoleum. When we drew nearer, the beams of our torches revealed a sight that was no less unexplainable than unexpected. A human figure, with its back toward us and the head concealed by a swollen black object that had the size and form of a sofa cushion, was standing near the remains of the mummy and was striking at the wall with a pointed metal bar. How long Octave had been there, and where he had found the bar, we could not know. But the blank wall had crumbled away beneath his furious blows, leaving on the floor a pile of comet-like fragments; and a small, narrow door, of the same ambiguous material as the cinerary urns and the fumigating-pan, had been laid bare.

Amazed, uncertain, inexpressibly bewildered, we were all incapable of action or volition at that moment. The whole business was too fantastic and too horrifying, and it was plain that Octave had been overcome by some sort of madness. I, for one, felt the violent upsurge of sudden nausea when I had identified the loathsomely bloated thing that clung to Octave's head and drooped in obscene tumescence on his neck. I did not dare to surmise the causation of its bloating.

Before any of us could recover our faculties, Octave flung aside the metal bar and began to fumble for something in the wall. It must have been a hidden spring; though how he could have known its location or existence is beyond all legitimate conjecture. With a dull, hideous grating, the uncovered door swung inward, thick and ponderous as a mausolean slab, leaving an aperture from which the nether midnight seemed to well like a flood of eon-buried foulness. Somehow, at that instant, our electric torches appeared to flicker and grow dim; and we all breathed a suffocating fetor, like a draught from inner worlds of immemorial putrescence.

Octave had turned toward us now, and he stood in an idle posture before the open door, like one who has finished some ordained task. I was the first of our party to throw off the paralysing spell; and pulling out a clasp-knife—the only semblance of a weapon which I carried—I ran over to him. He moved back, but not quickly enough to evade me, when I stabbed with the four-inch blade at the black, turgescent mass that enveloped his whole upper head and hung down upon his eyes.

What the thing was, I should prefer not to imagine—if it were possible to imagine. It was formless as a great slug, with neither head nor tail nor apparent organs—an unclean, puffy, leathery thing, covered with that fine, mould-like fur of which I have spoken. The knife tore into it as if through rotten parchment, making a long gash, and the horror appeared to collapse like a broken bladder. Out of it there gushed a sickening torrent of human blood, mingled with dark, filiated masses that may have been half-dissolved hair, and floating gelatinous lumps like molten bone, and shreds of a curdy white substance. At the same time, Octave began to stagger, and went down at full length on the floor. Disturbed by his fall, the mummy-dust arose about him in a curling cloud, beneath which he lay mortally still.

Conquering my revulsion, and choking with the dust, I bent over him and tore the flaccid, oozing horror from his head. It came with unexpected ease, as if I had removed a limp rag: but I wish to God that I had let it remain. Beneath, there was no longer a human cranium, for all had been eaten away, even to the eyebrows, and the half-devoured brain was laid bare as I lifted the cowl-like object. I dropped the unnamable thing from fingers that had grown suddenly nerveless, and it turned over as it fell, revealing on the nether side many rows of pinkish suckers, arranged in circles about a pallid disk that was covered with nerve-like filaments, suggesting a sort of plexus.

My companions had pressed forward behind me; but, for an appreciable interval, no one spoke.

"How long do you suppose he has been dead?" It was Halgren who whispered the awful question, which we had all been asking ourselves. Apparently no one felt able or willing to answer it; and we could only stare in horrible, timeless fascination at Octave.

At length I made an effort to avert my gaze; and turning at random, I saw the remnants of the shackled mummy, and noted for the first time, with mechanical, unreal horror, the half-eaten condition of the withered head. From this, my gaze was diverted to the newly opened door at one side, without perceiving for a moment what had drawn my attention. Then, startled, I beheld beneath my torch, far down beyond the door, as if in some nether pit, a seething, multitudinous, worm-like movement of crawling shadows. They seemed to boil up in the darkness; and then, over the broad threshold of the vault, there poured the verminous vanguard of a countless army: things that were kindred to the monstrous, diabolic leech I had torn from Octave's eaten head. Some were thin and flat, like writhing, doubling disks of cloth or leather, and others were more or less poddy, and crawled with glutted slowness. What they had found to feed on in the sealed, eternal midnight I do not know; and I pray that I never shall know.

I sprang back and away from them, electrified with terror, sick with loathing, and the black army inched itself unendingly with nightmare swiftness from the unsealed abyss, like the nauseous vomit of horror-sated hells. As it poured toward us, burying Octave's body from sight in a writhing wave, I saw a stir of life from the seemingly dead thing I had cast aside, and saw the loathly struggle which it made to right itself and join the others.

But neither I nor my companions could endure to look longer. We turned and ran between the mighty rows of urns, with the slithering mass of demon leeches close upon us, and scattered in blind panic when we came to the first division of the vaults. Heedless of each other or of anything but the urgency of flight, we plunged into the ramifying passages at random. Behind me, I heard some one stumble and go down, with a curse that mounted to an insane shrieking; but I knew that if I halted and went back, it would be only to invite the same baleful doom that had overtaken the hindmost of our party.

Still clutching the electric torch and my open clasp-knife, I ran along a minor passage which, I seemed to remember, would conduct with more or less directness upon the large outer vault with the painted floor. Here I found myself alone. The others had kept to the main catacombs; and I heard far off a muffled babel of mad cries, as if several of them had been seized by their pursuers.

It seemed that I must have been mistaken about the direction of the passage; for it turned and twisted in an unfamiliar manner, with many intersections, and I soon found that I was lost in the black labyrinth, where the dust had lain unstirred by living feet for inestimable generations. The cinerary warren had grown still once more; and I heard my own frenzied panting, loud and stertorous as that of a Titan in the dead silence.

Suddenly, as I went on, my torch disclosed a human figure coming toward me in the gloom. Before I could master my startlement, the figure had passed me with long, machine-like strides, as if returning to the inner vaults. I think it was Harper, since the height and build were about right for him; but I am not altogether sure, for the eyes and upper head were muffled by a dark, inflated cowl, and the pale lips were locked as if in a silence of tetanic torture—or death. Whoever he was, he had dropped his torch; and he was running blindfold, in utter darkness, beneath the impulsion of that unearthly vampirism, to seek the very fountain-head of the unloosed horror. I knew that he was beyond human help; and I did not even dream of trying to stop him.

Trembling violently, I resumed my flight, and was passed by two more of our party, stalking by with mechanical swiftness and sureness, and cowled with those Satanic leeches. The others must have returned by way of the main passages; for I did not meet them; and I was never to see them again.

The remainder of my flight is a blur of pandemonian terror. Once more, after thinking that I was near the outer cavern, I found myself astray, and fled through a ranged eternity of monstrous urns, in vaults that must have extended for an unknown distance beyond our explorations. It seemed that I had gone on for years; and my lungs were choking with the eon-dead air, and my legs were ready to crumble beneath me, when I saw far off a tiny point of blessed daylight. I ran toward it, with all the terrors of the alien darkness crowding behind me, and accursed shadows flittering before, and saw that the vault ended in a low, ruinous entrance, littered by rubble on which there fell an arc of thin sunshine.

It was another entrance than the one by which we had penetrated this lethal underworld. I was within a dozen feet of the opening when, without sound or other intimation, something dropped upon my head from the roof above, blinding me instantly and closing upon me like a tautened net. My brow and scalp, at the same time, were shot through with a million needle-like pangs—a manifold, ever-growing agony that seemed to pierce the very bone and converge from all sides upon my inmost brain.

The terror and suffering of that moment were worse than aught which the hells of earthly madness or delirium could ever contain. I felt the foul, vampiric clutch of an atrocious death—and of more than death.

I believe that I dropped the torch; but the fingers of my right hand had still retained the open knife. Instinctively—since I was hardly capable of conscious volition—I raised the knife and slashed blindly, again and again, many times, at the thing that had fastened its deadly folds upon me. The blade must have gone through and through the clinging monstrosity, to gash my own flesh in a score of places; but I did not feel the pain of those wounds in the million-throbbing torment that possessed me.

At last I saw light, and saw that a black strip, loosened from above my eyes and dripping with my own blood, was hanging down my cheek. It writhed a little, even as it hung, and I ripped it away, and ripped the other remnants of the thing, tatter by oozing, bloody tatter, from off my brow and head. Then I staggered toward the entrance; and the wan light turned to a far, receding, dancing flame before me as I lurched and fell outside the cavern—a flame that fled like the last star of creation above the yawning, sliding chaos and oblivion into which I descended...

I am told that my unconsciousness was of brief duration. I came to myself, with the cryptic faces of the two Martian guides bending over me. My head was full of lancinating pains, and half-remembered terrors closed upon my mind like the shadows of mustering harpies. I rolled over, and looked back toward the cavern-mouth, from which the Martians, after finding me, had seemingly dragged me for some little distance. The mouth was under the terraced angle of an outer building, and within sight of our camp.

I stared at the black opening with hideous fascination, and descried a shadowy stirring in the gloom—the writhing, verminous movement of things that pressed forward from the darkness but did not emerge into the light. Doubtless they could not endure the sun, those creatures of ultramundane night and cycle-sealed corruption.

It was then that the ultimate horror, the beginning madness, came upon me. Amid my crawling revulsion, my nausea-prompted desire to flee from that seething cavern-mouth, there rose an abhorrently conflicting impulse to return; to thread my backward way through all the catacombs, as the others had done; to go down where never men save they, the inconceivably doomed and accursed, had ever gone; to seek beneath that damnable compulsion a nether world that human thought can never picture. There was a black light, a soundless calling, in the vaults of my brain: the implanted summons of the Thing, like a permeating and sorcerous poison. It lured me to the subterranean door that was walled up by the dying people of Yoh-Vombis, to immure those hellish and immortal leeches, those dark parasites that engraft their own abominable life on the half-eaten brains of the dead. It called me to the depths beyond, where dwell the noisome, necromantic Ones, of whom the leeches, with all their powers of vampirism and diabolism, are but the merest minions...

It was only the two Aihais who prevented me from going back. I struggled, I fought them insanely as they strove to retard me with their spongy arms; but I must have been pretty thoroughly exhausted from all the superhuman adventures of the day; and I went down once more, after a little, into fathomless nothingness, from which I floated out at long intervals, to realize that I was being carried across the desert toward Ignarh.

Well, that is all my story. I have tried to tell it fully and coherently, at a cost that would be unimaginable to the sane... to tell it before the madness falls upon me again, as it will very soon—as it is doing now... Yes, I have told my story... and you have written it all out, haven't you? Now I must go back to Yoh-Vombis—back across the desert and down through all the catacombs to the vaster vaults beneath. Something is in my brain, that commands me and will direct me... I tell you, I must go...

POSTSCRIPT

As an intern in the territorial hospital at Ignarh, I had charge of the singular case of Rodney Severn, the one surviving member of the Octave Expedition to Yoh-Vombis, and took down the above story from his dictation. Severn had been brought to the hospital by the

Martian guides of the Expedition. He was suffering from a horribly lacerated and inflamed condition of the scalp and brow, and was wildly delirious part of the time and had to be held down in his bed during recurrent seizures of a mania whose violence was doubly inexplicable in view of his extreme debility.

The lacerations, as will have been learned from the story, were mainly self-inflicted. They were mingled with numerous small round wounds, easily distinguished from the knife-slashes, and arranged in regular circles, through which an unknown poison had been injected into Severn's scalp. The causation of these wounds was difficult to explain; unless one were to believe that Severn's story was true, and was no mere figment of his illness. Speaking for myself, in the light of what afterward occurred, I feel that I have no other resource than to believe it. There are strange things on the red planet; and I can only second the wish that was expressed by the doomed archaeologist in regard to future explorations.

The night after he had finished telling me his story, while another doctor than myself was supposedly on duty, Severn managed to escape from the hospital, doubtless in one of the strange seizures at which I have hinted: a most astonishing thing, for he had seemed weaker than ever after the long strain of his terrible narrative, and his demise had been hourly expected. More astonishing still, his bare footsteps were found in the desert, going toward Yoh-Vombis, till they vanished in the path of a light sandstorm; but no trace of Severn himself has yet been discovered.

1942

THE GREAT FOG

H. F. Heard

Henry Fitzgerald Heard, who also wrote as Gerald Heard, was born in South Hackney, London in 1889, and educated at Gonville & Caius College, Cambridge, where his Christian beliefs (he had originally planned to take holy orders) appear at some point to have been transmogrified or diverted into other channels including various forms of mysticism, esoteric philosophy, and psychical research. First making a reputation as a scientific journalist, in which capacity he was a pioneering broadcaster for a nascent BBC, Heard became a well-known figure in the intellectual milieu of interwar London, writing several popular works advocating for a "third morality" integrating the separate spheres of science and religion. Evelyn Waugh called him "the cleverest man in the world", and E. M. Forster's biographer P. N. Furbank paints a flamboyant portrait of Heard during those years: "He was reputed to read two thousand books a year and had an extraordinary flow of information about hygiene, sex, paranormal phenomena and the probable destiny of mankind. He... favour[ed] purple suede shoes and leather jackets with leopard-skin collars, and he had his eyelids painted with what looked like mascara (actually a specific against conjunctivitis). Strangers thought of him, nervously, as a sort of Wellesian supermind or 'man of the future.'" Like such close friends, admirers, and acolytes as Forster, Christopher Isherwood, and W. H. Auden, Heard was gay, and moved with his partner Christopher Wood, along with Aldous

Huxley, to California in 1937, where he remained until his death in 1971, authoring numerous works of fiction, religion, philosophy, and science (and pseudoscience).

Rather like the modern category of the Weird itself, Heard's fiction often blurred boundaries, particularly between supernatural horror, detection, and science fiction; he wrote a trilogy of Holmesian pastiches of which the most famous is the first, *A Taste for Honey*, as well as a weird novel, *The Black Fox*, which reads rather like a collaboration between M. R. James and Anthony Trollope. His shorter (though often longish) tales of the strange are collected in *The Great Fog and Other Weird Tales* (1944) and *The Lost Cavern and Other Tales of the Fantastic* (1947). "The Great Fog" is a remarkable story—something the H. G. Wells of the 1890s might have written had he been alive during World War II (Wells himself did, of course, live through the war, but the muse that had inspired the great scientific romances, and such short tales as "In the Abyss", had long since parted ways with him). The story's conception of anthropogenic climate change seems astonishingly prescient, while its strikingly McLuhanesque speculations about the radically new media ecology of humanity "after the Fog" is as thought-provoking as it is unexpected.

"The Great Fog" first appeared in *Harper's Magazine* in 1943.

The first symptom was a mildew.

Very few people have ever looked carefully at such "moulds"; indeed, only a specialized branch of botanists knows about them. Nor is this knowledge—except rarely—of much use. Every now and then a low growth of this sort may attack a big cash crop. Then the mycologists, whose life-work is to study these spore growths, are called in by the growers. These botanists can sometimes find another mould which will eat its fellow. That closes the matter. The balance of life, which had been slightly upset, has been righted. It is not a matter of any general interest.

This particular mildew did not seem to have even that special importance. It did not, apparently, do any damage to the trees on which it grew. Indeed, most fruit growers never noticed it. The botanists found it themselves; no one called their attention to it. It was simply a form of spore growth different in its growth rate from any previously recorded. It did not seem to do any harm to any other form of life. But it did do amazingly well for itself. It was not a new plant, but a plant with quite a new power of growth.

It was this fact which puzzled the botanists, or rather that special branch of the botanists, the mycologists. That was why they finally called in the meteorologists. They asked for "another opinion," as baffled doctors say. What made the mycologists choose the meteorologists for consultation was this: Here was a mildew which spread faster than any other mould had ever been known to grow. It flourished in places where such mildews had been thought incapable of growing. But there seemed to be no botanical change either in the mould or in the plants it grew on. Therefore the cause must be climatic: only a weather change could account for the unprecedented growth.

The meteorologists saw the force of this argument. They became interested at once. The first thing to do, they said, was to study the mildew, not as a plant, but as a machine, an indicator. "You know," said Sersen the weatherman to Charles the botanist (they had been made colleagues for the duration of the study), "the astronomers have a thing called a thermo-couple that will tell the heat of a summer day on the equator of Mars. Well, here is a little gadget I've made. It's almost as sensitive to damp as the thermo-couple is to heat."

Sersen spent some time rigging it up and then "balancing" it, as he called it. "Find the normal humidity and then see how much the damp at a particular spot exceeds that." But he went on fiddling about far longer than Charles thought an expert who was handling his own gadget should. He was evidently puzzled. And after a while he confessed that he was.

"Queer, very queer," said Sersen. "Of course, I expected to get a good record of humidity around the mould itself. As you say, it can't grow without that: it wouldn't be here unless the extra damp was here too. But, look here," he said, pointing to a needle that quivered near a high number on a scale. "*That* is the humidity actually around the mould itself—what we might expect, if a trifle high. That's not the surprise. It's *this*." He had swung the whole instrument on its tripod until it pointed a foot or more from the mould; for the tree they were studying was a newly attacked one and, as far as Charles had been able to discover, had on it only this single specimen of the mildew.

Charles looked at the needle. It remained hovering about the high figure it had first chosen. "Well?" he queried.

"Don't you see?" urged Sersen. "This odd high humidity is present not only around the mould itself but for more than a foot beyond."

"I don't see much to that."

"I see two things," snapped Sersen; "one's odd; the other's damned odd. The odd one anyone not blind would see. The other one is perhaps too big to be seen until one can stand well back."

"Sorry to be stupid," said Charles, a gentle-spoken but close-minded little fellow; "we botanists are small-scale men."

"Sorry to be a snapper," apologized Sersen. "But, as I suppose you've guessed, I'm startled. I've got a queer feeling that we're on the track of something big, yes, and something maybe moving pretty fast. The first odd thing isn't a complete surprise: it's that you botanists have shown us what could turn out to be a meteorological instrument more delicate and more accurate than any we have been able to make. Perhaps we ought to have been on the outlook for some such find. After all, living things are always the most sensitive detectors—can always beat mechanical instruments when they want to. You know about the mitogenetic rays given out by breeding seeds. Those rays can be recorded only by yeast cells—which multiply rapidly when exposed to the rays, thus giving indication of their range and strength."

"Umph," said Charles. Sersen's illustration had been unfortunate, for Charles belonged to that majority of conservative botanists to whom the mitogenetic radiation was mere moonshine.

Sersen, again vexed, went on: "Well, whether you accept them or not, I still maintain that here we have a superdetector. This mildew can notice an increase in humidity long before any of our instruments. There's proof that something has changed in the climate. This mould is the first to know about it—and to profit by it. I prophesy it will soon be over the whole world."

"But your second discovery, or supposition?" Charles had no use for prophecy. These weathermen, he thought; well, after all, they aren't quite scientists, so one mustn't blame them, one supposes, for liking forecasts—forecasting is quite unscientific.

Charles was a courteous man, but Sersen was sensitive. "Well," he said defensively, "that's nothing but supposition." And yet, he thought to himself as he packed up his instrument, if it *is* true it may mean such a change that botany will be blasted and meteorology completely mystified. His small private joke relieved his temper. By the time they returned to headquarters he and Charles were friendly enough. They agreed to make a joint report which would stick severely to the facts.

Meanwhile, botanists everywhere were observing and recording the spreading of the mildew. Before long, they began to get its drift. It was spreading from a centre, spreading like a huge ripple from where a stone has been flung into a lake. The centre, there could be no doubt, was eastern Europe. Spain, Britain, and North Africa showed the same "high incidence." France showed an even higher one. The spread of the mould could be watched just as well in North or South America. Such and such a percentage of shrubs and trees was attacked on the Atlantic coasts; a proportionately lower percentage on the Pacific coasts; but everywhere the incidence was rising. On every sector of the vast and widening circle, America, Africa, India, the mildew was advancing rapidly.

Sersen continued his own research on the mould itself, on the "field of humidity" around each plant. He next made a number of calculations correlating the rapid rate of dispersal, the average increase of infestation of all vegetation by the mould, and the degree of humidity which must result. Then, having checked and counterchecked, at last he was ready to read his paper and give his conclusions at a joint meeting of the plant men and the weathermen.

Just before Sersen went up to the platform, he turned to Charles. "I'm ready now to face the music," he said, "because I believe we are up against something which makes scientific respectability nonsense. We've got to throw caution aside and tell the world." "That's serious," said Charles cautiously. "It's damned serious," said Sersen, and went up the steps to the rostrum.

When he came down, the audience was serious too; for a moment, as serious as he. He had begun by showing the world map with its spreading, dated lines showing where the mildew in its present profusion had reached; showing also where, in a couple of months, the two sides of the ripple would meet. Soon, almost every tree and shrub throughout the world would be infested, and, of course, the number of moulds per tree and bush would increase. That was interesting and queer, but of no popular concern. The moulds still remained harmless to their tree hosts and to animal life—indeed, some insects seemed rather happy about the botanical change. As far, then, as the change was only a change in mildew reproduction there was no cause for much concern, still less for alarm. The mould had gone ahead, because it was the first to benefit from some otherwise undetectable change in climate. The natural expectation would, then, be that insects, the host plants, or some other species of mould would in turn advance and so readjust the disturbed balance of nature.

But that was only the first part of Sersen's lecture. At that phrase, "balance of nature," he paused. He turned from the world map with its charting of the mould's growth. For a moment he glanced at another set of statistical charts; then he seemed to change his mind and touched the buzzer. The lights went out, and the beam from the stereopticon shot down through the darkened hall. The light screen showed a tree; on its branches and trunk a number of red crosses had been marked. Around each cross was a large circle, so large that some of the circles intersected.

"Gentlemen," said Sersen, "this is the discovery that really matters. Until now, perhaps unwisely, I have hesitated to communicate it. That the mould spreads, you know. That it is particularly sensitive to some otherwise undetected change in the weather, you know. Now, you must know a third fact about it—it is a weather *creator*. Literally, it can brew a climate of its own.

"I have proved that in each of these circles—and I am sure they are spreading circles—the mould is going far to create its own peculiar atmosphere—a curiously high and stable humidity. The statistically arranged readings which I have prepared, and which I have here, permit, I believe, of no other conclusion. I would also add that I believe we can see why this has happened. It is now clear what permitted this unprecedented change to get under way. We have pulled the trigger that has fired this mine. No doubt the mould first began to increase because a slight change in humidity helped it. But now it is—how shall I put it—co-operating. It is *making the humidity increase*.

"There has probably been present, these past few years, one of those small increases in atmospheric humidity which occur periodically. In itself, it would have made no difference to our lives and, indeed, would have passed unperceived. But it was at this meteorological moment that European scientists began to succeed in making a new kind of quick-growing mould which could create fats. It is, perhaps, the most remarkable of all the war efforts, perhaps the most powerful of all the new defensive weapons—against a human enemy. But in regard to the extra human world in which we live it may prove as dangerous as a naked flame in a mine chamber filled with fire damp. For, need I remind you, moulds are spore-reproducing growths. Fungus is by far the strongest form of life. It breeds incessantly and will grow under conditions no other form of life will endure. When you play with spore life you may at any moment let loose something the sheer power of which makes dynamite look like a damp squib. I believe what man has now done is precisely that—he has let the genie out of its bottle, and we may find ourselves utterly helpless before it."

Sersen paused. The lights came on. Dr. Charles rose and caught the chairman's eye. Dr. Charles begged to state on behalf of the botanical world that he hoped Dr. Sersen's dramatic remarks would not be taken gravely by the press or the public. Dr. Sersen had spoken of matters botanical. Dr. Charles wished to say that he and his colleagues had had the mildew under protracted observation. He could declare categorically that it was not dangerous.

Sersen had not left the platform. He strode back to the rostrum. "I am not speaking as a botanist," he exclaimed, "I am speaking as a meteorologist. I have told you of what I am sure—the balance of life has been upset. You take for granted that the only balance is life against life, animal against animal, vegetable against vegetable. You were right to call in a weatherman, but that's of no use unless you understand what he is telling you."

The audience shifted offendedly in its seats. It wasn't scientific to be as urgent as all that. Besides, hadn't Charles said there was no danger? But what was their queer guest now saying?

"I know, every meteorologist knows, that this nature-balance is far vaster and more delicately poised than you choose to suspect. All life is balanced against its environment. Cyclones are brought on, climate can change, a glacial age can begin as the result of atmospheric alterations far too small for the layman to notice. In our atmosphere, that wonderful veil and web under which we are sheltered and in which we grow, we have a condition of extraordinary delicacy. The right—or rather the precisely wrong—catalytic agent can send the whole thing suddenly into quite another arrangement, one which can well be desperately awkward for man. It has taken an amazing balance of forces to allow human beings to live. That's the balance you've upset. Look out."

He studied his audience. There they sat, complacent, assured, only a little upset that an over-excitable colleague should be behaving unscientifically—hysterically, almost. Suddenly, with a shock of despair, Sersen realized that it was no use hoping to stir these learned experts. These were the actual minds which had patiently, persistently, purblindly worked the very changes which must bring the house down on their heads. They'd never asked, never wished to ask, what might be the general and ultimate effects of their burrowing. We're just another sort of termite, thought Sersen, as he looked down on the rows of plump faces and dull-ivory-coloured pates. We tunnel away trying to turn everything into "consumable goods" until suddenly the whole structure of things collapses round us.

He left the rostrum, submitted to polite thanks, and went home. A week later his botanical hosts had ceased even to talk about his strange manners. Hardly anyone else heard of his speech.

The first report of trouble—or rumour rather (for such natural-history notes were far too trivial to get into the battle-crammed papers)—came from orchard growers in deep valleys. Then fruit growers began to gossip when the Imperial Valley, hot and dry as hell, began to report much the same thing. It was seen at night at the start and cleared off in the day; so it seemed no more than an odd, inconsequent little phenomenon. But if you went out at full moon you did see a queer sight. Every tree seemed to have a sort of iridescent envelope, a small white cloud or silver shroud all its own.

Of course, soon after that, the date growers had something to howl about. The dates wouldn't stand for damp—and each silver shroud was, for the tree about which it hung, a vapour bath. But the date growers, all the other growers decided, were done for anyway; they'd have made a howl in any case when the new Colorado water made the irrigation plans complete. The increase in humidity would inevitably spoil their crop when the valley became one great oasis.

The botanists didn't want to look into the matter again. Botanically, it was uninteresting. The inquiry had been officially closed. But the phenomenon continued to be noticed farther and farther afield.

The thing seemed then to reach a sort of saturation point. A new sort of precipitation took place. The cloud around each tree and bush, which now could be seen even during the day, would, at a certain moment, put out feeler-like wisps and join up with the other spreading and swelling ground clouds stretching out from the neighbouring trees. Sersen, who had thrown up his official job just to keep track of this thing, described that critical night when, with a grim prophetic pleasure, he saw his forecast fulfilled before his eyes. His last mouldering papers have remained just decipherable for his great-grandchildren.

"I stood," he said, "on a rock promontory south of Salton Sea. The full moon was rising behind me and lighted the entire Valley. I could see the orchards glistening, each tree surrounded by its own cloud. It was like a gargantuan dew; each dew-globule tree-size. And then, as I watched, just like a great tide, an obliterating flood of whiteness spread over everything. The globules ran into one another until I was looking down on a solid sea of curd-white, far denser than mist or fog. It looked as firm, beautiful, and dead as the high moon which looked down on it. 'A new Deluge,' I said to myself. 'May I not ask who has been right? Did I not foretell its coming and did not I say that man had brought it on his own head?'"

Certainly Sersen had been justified. For, the morning after his vigil, when the sun rose, the Fog did not. It lay undisturbed, level, dazzling white as a sheet of snow-covered ice, throwing back into space every ray of heat that fell on it. The air immediately above it was crystal clear. The valley was submerged under an element that looked solid enough to be walked on. The change was evidently so complete because it was a double one, a sudden reciprocal process. All the damp had been gathered below the Fog's surface, a surface as distinct as the surface of water. Conversely, all the cloud, mist, and aqueous vapour in the air above the Fog was evidently drained out of it by this new dense atmosphere. It was as though the old atmosphere had been milk. The mould acted as a kind of rennet, and so, instead of milk, there remained only this hard curd and the clear whey. The sky above the Fog was not so much the deepest of blues—it was almost a livid black, the sun in it was an intense, harsh white and most of the big stars were visible throughout the day. So, outside the Fog it was desperately cold. At night it was agonizingly so. Under that cold the Fog lay packed dense like a frozen drift of snow.

Beneath the surface of the Fog, conditions were even stranger. Passing into it was like going suddenly into night. All lights had to be kept on all day. But they were not much use. As in a bad old-fashioned fog, but now to a far worse degree, the lights would not penetrate the air. For instance, the rays of a car's headlights formed a three-foot cone, the base of which looked like a circular patch of light thrown on an opaque white screen. It was possible to move about in the Fog, but only at a slow walking pace—otherwise you kept running into things. It was a matter of groping about, with objects suddenly looming up at you—the kind of world in which a severe myopic case must live if he loses his spectacles.

Soon, of course, people began to notice with dismay the Fog's effect on crops and gardens, on houses and goods. Nothing was ever again dry. Objects did not become saturated, but they were, if at all absorbent, thoroughly damp. Paper moulded, wood rotted, iron rusted. But concrete, glass, pottery, all stone ware and ceramics remained unaffected. Cloth, too, served adequately, provided the wearer could stand its never being dry.

The first thought in the areas which had been first attacked was, naturally, to move out. But the Fog moved too. Every night some big valley area suddenly "went over." The tree fog around each tree would billow outward, join up with all its fellows, and so make a solid front and surface. Then came the turn for each fog-submerged valley, each fog-lake, to link with those adjacent to it. The general level of these lakes then rose. Instead of there being, as until now, large flooded areas of lowland, but still, in the main, areas of clear upland, this order was now reversed. The mountain ranges had become strings of islands which emerged from a shining ocean that covered the whole earth's surface, right up to the six-thousand-foot level.

Any further hope of air travel was extinguished. In the Fog, lack of visibility, of course, made it impossible. Above the Fog, you could see to the earth's edge: the horizons, cleared of every modulation of mist, seemed so close that you would have thought you could have touched them with your hand. As far as sight was concerned, above the Fog, near and far seemed one. But even if men could have lived in that thin air and "unscreened" light, no plane could be sustained by it.

Sea travel was hardly more open. True, the surface of the oceans lay under the Fog-blanket, as still as the water, a thousand fathoms down. But on that oily surface—that utterly featureless desert of motionless water—peering man, only a few yards from the shore, completely lost his way. Neither sun nor stars ever again appeared over the sea to give him his bearings. So man soon abandoned the sea beyond the closest inshore shallows. Even if he could have seen his way over the ocean, he could not have taken it. There was never a breath of wind to fill a sail, and the fumes from any steamship or motorboat would have hung around the vessel and would have almost suffocated the crew.

Retreat upward was cut off. For when the Fog stabilized at six thousand feet, it was no use thinking of attempting to live above it. Even if the limited areas could have given footing, let alone feeding, to the fugitive populations, no hope lay in that direction. For the cold was now so intense above the Fog that no plant would grow. And, worse, it was soon found, to the cost of those who ventured out there, that through this unscreened air—air which was so thin that it could scarcely be breathed—came also such intense ultraviolet radiations from the sun and outer space that a short exposure to them was fatal.

So the few ranges and plateaus which rose above the six-thousand-foot level stood gaunt as the ribs of a skeleton carcass under the untwinkling stars and the white glaring sun. After a very few exploratory expeditions out into that open, men realized that they must content themselves with a sub-surface life, a new kind of fish existence, nosing about on the floor of a pool which henceforth was to be their whole world. It might be a poor, confined way of living, but above that surface was death. A few explorers returned, but, though fish taken out of water may recover if put back soon enough, every above-the-Fog explorer succumbed from the effect. After a few days the lesions and sores of bad X-ray burning appeared. If, after that, the nervous system did not collapse, the wretched man literally began to fall to pieces.

Underneath the Fog-blanket men painfully, fumblingly worked out a new answer to living. Of course, it had to be done without preparation, so the cost was colossal. All who were liable to rheumatic damage and phthisis died off. Only a hardy few remained. Man had been clever enough to pull down the atmosphere-roof which had hung so loftily over his head, but he never learned again how to raise a cover as high, spacious, and pleasant as the sky's blue dome. The dividing out of the air was a final precipitation, a non-reversible change-down towards the final entropy. Man might stay on, but only at the price of being for the rest of his term on earth confined under a thick film of precipitated air. Maybe, even if he had been free and had had the power to move fast and see far, it would have been too great a task for him to have attempted to "raise the air." As he now found himself, pinned under the collapse he had caused, he had not a chance of even beginning to plan such a vast reconstruction.

His job, then, was just to work at making lurking liveable. And, within the limits imposed, it was not absolutely impossible. True, all his passion for speed and travel and seeing far and quick, all that had to go. He who had just begun to feel that it was natural to fly, now was confined not even to the pace of a brisk walk but to a crawl. It was a life on the lowest gear. Of course, great numbers died just in the first confusion, when the dark came on, before the permanent change in humidity and light swept off the other many millions who could not adapt themselves. But, after a while, not only men's health but their eyes became adapted to the perpetual dusk. They began to see that the gloom was not pitch-dark. Gradually, increasing numbers learned to be able to go about without lamps. Indeed, they found that they saw better if they cultivated this "nightsight," this ancient part of the eye so long neglected by man when he thought he was master of things. They were greatly helped also by a type of faint phosphorescence, a "cold-light," which (itself probably another mould-mutation) appeared on most surfaces if they were left untouched, and so outlined objects with faint, ghostly highlights.

So, as decentralized life worked itself out, men found that they had enough. War was gone, so that huge social haemorrhage stopped. Money went out of gear, and so that odd stranglehold on goods-exchange was loosed. Men just couldn't waste what they had, so they found they had much more than they thought. For one reason, it wasn't worth hoarding anything, holding back goods, real, edible, and wearable goods, for a rise in price. They rotted. The old medieval epitaph proved itself true in this new dark age: "What I spent I had: what I saved I lost." Altogether, life became more immediate and, what people had never suspected, more real because less diffused. It was no use having a number of things which had been thought to be necessities. Cars? You could not see to travel at more than four miles an hour, and not often at that. Radios? They just struck; either insulation against the damp was never adequate or the electric conditions, the radio-resonant layers of the upper atmosphere, had been completely altered. A wailing static was the only answer to any attempt to re-establish wireless communication.

It was a low-built, small-housed, pedestrian world. Even horses were too dashing; and they were blinder in the Fog than were men. As for your house, you could seldom see more than its front door. Metal was little used. Smelting it was troublesome (the fumes could hardly get away and nearly suffocated everyone within miles of a furnace), and when you got your iron and steel it began rusting at once. Glass knives were used instead. They were very sharp. Men learned again, after tens of thousands of years of neglect, how to flake flints, crystal, and all the silica rocks to make all manner of neat, sharp tools.

Man's one primary need, which had made for nearly all his hoarding, the animal craving to accumulate food stocks, that fear which, since the dawn of civilization, has made his granaries as vast as his fortresses, this need, this enemy, was wiped out by another freak botanical by-product of the Fog. The curious sub-fog climate made an edible fungus grow. It was a sort of manna. It rotted if you stored it. But it grew copiously everywhere, of itself. Indeed, it replaced grass: wherever grass had grown the fungus grew. Eaten raw, it was palatable and highly nutritious—more tasty and more wholesome than when cooked (which was a blessing in itself, since all fires burnt ill and any smoke was offensive in the dense air). Man, like the fishes, lived in a dim but fruitful element.

The mean temperature under the Fog stayed precisely at 67 degrees Fahrenheit, owing, evidently, to some basic balance, like that which keeps the sea below a certain depth always at 36 degrees, four degrees above freezing. Men, then, were never cold.

They stayed mainly at home, around their small settlements. What was the use of going about? All you needed and could use was at your door. There was nothing to see—your view was always limited to four feet. There was no use in trying to seize someone else's territory. You all had the same: you all had enough.

Art, too, changed. The art of objects was gone. So a purer, less collectible art took its place. Books would not last; and so memory increased enormously, and men carried their libraries in their heads— a cheaper way and much more convenient. As a result, academic accuracy, the continual quoting of authorities, disappeared. A new epic age resulted. Men in the dusk composed, extemporized, jointly developed great epics, sagas, and choruses, which grew like vast trees, generation after generation, flowering, bearing fruit, putting out new limbs. And, as pristine, bardic poetry returned, it united again with its nursery foster-brother, music. Wood winds and strings were ruined by the damp. But stone instruments, like those used by the dawn cultures, returned—giving beautiful pure notes. An orchestra of jade and marble flutes, lucid gongs, crystal-clear xylophones grew up. Just as the Arabs, nomads out on the ocean of sand, had had no plastic art, but, instead, a wonderful aural art of chant and singing verse, so the creative power of the men of the Umbral Epoch swung over from eye to ear. Indeed, the thick air which baffled the eye made fresh avenues and extensions for the ear. Men could hear for miles: their ears grew as keen as a dog's. And with this keenness went subtlety. They appreciated intervals of sound which to the old men of the open air would have been imperceptible. Men lived largely for music and felt they had made a good exchange when they peered at the last mouldering shreds of pictorial art.

"Yes," said Sersen's great-grandson, when the shock of the change was over and mankind had accustomed itself to its new conditions, "yes, I suspect we were not fit for the big views, the vast world into which the old men tumbled up. It was all right to give animal men the open. But, once they had got power without vision, then either they had to be shut up or they would have shot and bombed everything off the earth's surface. Why, they were already living in tunnels when the Fog came. And out in the open, men, powerful as never before, nevertheless died by millions, died the way insects used to die in a frost, but died by one another's hands. The plane drove men off the fields. That was the thing, I believe, that made Mind decide we were not fit any longer to be at large. We were going too fast and too high to see what we were actually doing. So, then, Mind let man fancy that all he had to do was to make food apart from the fields. That was the Edible Mould, and that led straight, as my great-grandfather saw, to the atmospheric upset, the meteorological revolution. It really was a catalyst, making the well-mixed air, which we had always taken for granted as the only possible atmosphere, divide out into two layers as distinct as water and air. We're safer as we are. Mind knew that, and already we are better for our Fog cure, though it had to be drastic.

"Perhaps, one day, when we have learned enough, the Fog will lift, the old high ceiling will be given back to us. Once more Mind may say: 'Try again. The Second Flood is over. Go forth and replenish the earth, and this time remember that you are all one.' Meanwhile I'm thankful that we are as we are."

1980

THE STAINS

Robert Aickman

"I don't know why people expect art to make sense", the late David Lynch is supposed to have said. "They accept the fact that life doesn't make sense." I don't know whether Lynch ever read any of Robert Fordyce Aickman's "strange stories" (as Aickman invariably called them, in preference to "ghost" or "horror" stories), but it would not be at all surprising given the affinities between their surreal, unsettling artistic visions. Born in London in 1914 (one day after the assassination of Archduke Franz Ferdinand plunged Europe into war), Aickman would write some half a hundred dreamlike, disturbing, confusing, frustrating, and yes, terrifying tales between 1951 and his death three decades later. Aickman's maternal grandfather was Richard Marsh, author of horror novels including *The Beetle* (a serious rival to Bram Stoker's *Dracula* in its day), though possibly this is a fact of interest only to Victorian scholars. In any case, Aickman's own tales owe far more to the ambiguous, nightmarish work of Walter de la Mare (1873–1956), and one of his very finest, albeit not one of his better-known, is "The Stains", a late story that first appeared in the 1980 collection *New Terrors*, edited by Ramsey Campbell.

After Elizabeth ultimately died, it was inevitable that many people should come forward with counsel, and doubtless equally inevitable that the counsel be so totally diverse. There were two broad and opposed schools.

The first considered that Stephen should "treasure the memory" (though it was not always put like that) for an indefinite period, which, it was implied, might conveniently last him out to the end of his own life. These people attached great importance to Stephen "not rushing anything." The second school urged that Stephen marry again as soon as he possibly could. They said that, above all, he must not just fall into apathy and let his life slide. They said he was a man made for marriage and all it meant.

Of course, both parties were absolutely right in every way. Stephen could see that perfectly well.

It made little difference. Planning, he considered, would be absurd in any case. Until further notice, the matter would have to be left to fate. The trouble was, of course, that fate's possible options were narrowing and dissolving almost weekly, as they had already been doing throughout Elizabeth's lengthy illness. For example (the obvious and most pressing example): how many women would want to marry Stephen now? A number, perhaps; but not a number that he would want to marry. Not after Elizabeth. That in particular.

They told him he should take a holiday, and he took one. They told him he should see his doctor, and he saw him. The man who had looked after Elizabeth had wanted to emigrate, had generously held back while Elizabeth had remained alive, and had then shot off at once. The new man was half-Sudanese, and Stephen found him difficult to communicate with, at least upon a first encounter, at least on immediate topics.

In the end, Stephen applied for and obtained a spell of compassionate leave, and went, as he usually did, to stay with his elder brother, Harewood, in the north. Harewood was in orders: the Reverend Harewood Hooper, B.D., M.A. Their father and grandfather had been in orders too, and had been incumbents of the same small church in that same small parish for thirty-nine years and forty-two years respectively. So far, Harewood had served for only twenty-three years. The patron of the living, a private individual, conscientious and very long lived, was relieved to be able to rely upon a succession of such dedicated men. Unfortunately, Harewood's own son, his one child, had dropped out, and was now believed to have disappeared into Nepal. Harewood himself cared more for rock growths than for controversies about South Africa or for other such fashionable Church preoccupations. He had published two important books on lichens. People often came to see him on the subject. He was modestly famous.

He fostered lichens on the flagstones leading up to the rectory front door; on the splendidly living stone walls, here grey stone, there yellow; even in the seldom used larders and pantries; assuredly on the roof, which, happily, was of stone slabs also.

As always when he visited his brother, Stephen found that he was spending much of his time out of doors; mainly, being the man he was, in long, solitary walks across the heathered uplands. This had nothing to do with Harewood's speciality. Harewood suffered badly from bronchitis and catarrh, and nowadays went out as little as possible. The domestic lichens, once introduced, required little attention—only observation.

Rather it was on account of Harewood's wife, Harriet, that Stephen roamed; a lady in whose company Stephen had never been at ease. She had always seemed to him a restless woman; jumpy and puzzling, the very reverse of all that had seemed best about Elizabeth. A doubtful asset, Stephen would have thought, in a diminishing rural parish; but Stephen himself, in a quiet and unobtruding way, had long been something of a sceptic. Be that as it might, he always found that Harriet seemed to be baiting and fussing him, not least when her husband was present; even, unforgivably, when Elizabeth, down in London, had been battling through her last dreadful years. On every visit, therefore, Stephen wandered about for long hours in the open, even when ice was in the air and snow on the tenuous tracks.

But Stephen did not see it as a particular hardship. Elizabeth, who might have done—though, for his sake, she could have been depended upon to conceal the fact—had seldom come on these visits at any time. She had never been a country girl, though fond of the sea. Stephen positively liked wandering unaccompanied on the moors, though he had little detailed knowledge of their flora and fauna, or even of their archaeology, largely industrial and fragmentary. By now he was familiar with most of the moorland routes from the rectory and the village, and, as commonly happens, there was one that he preferred to all the others, and nowadays found himself taking almost without having to make a decision. Sometimes even, asleep in his London flat that until just now had been *their* London flat, he found himself actually dreaming of that particular soaring trail, though he would have found it difficult to define what properties of beauty or poetry or convenience it had of which the other tracks had less. According to the map, it led to a spot named Burton's Clough.

There was a vague valley or extended hollow more or less in the place which the map indicated, but to Stephen it every time seemed too indefinite to be marked out for record. Every time he wondered whether this was indeed the place; whether there was not some more decisive declivity that he had never discovered. Or possibly the name derived from some event in local history. It was the upwards walk to the place that appealed to Stephen, and, to only slightly lesser extent, the first part of the slow descent homewards, supposing that the rectory could in any sense be called home: never the easily attainable but inconclusive supposed goal, the Clough. Of course there was always R. L. Stevenson's travelling hopefully to be inwardly quoted; and on most occasions hitherto Stephen had inwardly quoted it.

Never had there been any human being at, near, or visible from the terrain around Burton's Clough, let alone in the presumptive clough itself. There was no apparent reason why there should be. Stephen seldom met anyone at all on the moors. Only organizations go any distance afoot nowadays, and this was not an approved didactic district. All the work of agriculture is for a period being done by machines. Most of the cottages are peopled by transients. Everyone is supposed to have a car.

But that morning, Stephen's first in the field since his bereavement six weeks before, there *was* someone, and down at the bottom of the shallow clough itself. The person was dressed so as to be almost lost in the hues of autumn, plainly neither tripper nor trifler. The person was engaged in some task.

Stephen was in no state for company, but that very condition, and a certain particular reluctance that morning to return to the rectory before he had to, led him to advance further, not descending into the clough but skirting along the ridge to the west of it, where, indeed, his track continued.

If he had been in the Alps, his shadow might have fallen in the early-autumn sun across the figure below, but in the circumstances that idea would have been fanciful, because, at the moment, the sun was no more than a misty bag of gleams in a confused sky. None the less, as Stephen's figure passed, comparatively high above, the figure below glanced up at him. Stephen could see that it was the figure of a girl. She was wearing a fawn shirt and pale green trousers, but the nature of her activity remained uncertain.

Stephen glanced away, then glanced back.

She seemed still to be looking up at him, and suddenly he waved to her, though it was not altogether a kind of thing he normally did. She waved back at him. Stephen even fancied she smiled at him. It seemed quite likely. She resumed her task.

He waited for an instant, but she looked up no more. He continued on his way more slowly, and feeling more alive, even if only for moments. For these moments, it had been as if he still belonged to the human race, to the mass of mankind.

Only once or twice previously had he continued beyond the top of Burton's Clough, and never for any great distance. On the map (it had been his father's map), the track wavered on across a vast area of nothing very much, merely contour lines and occasional habitations with odd, possibly evocative, names: habitations which, as Stephen knew from experience, regularly proved, when approached, to be littered ruins or not to be detectable at all. He would not necessarily have been averse to the twelve or fourteen miles' solitary walk involved, at least while Elizabeth had been secure and alive, and at home in London; but conditions at the rectory had never permitted so long an absence. Harriet often made clear that she expected her guests to be present punctually at all meals and punctually at such other particular turning points of a particular day as the day itself might define.

On the present occasion, and at the slow pace into which he had subsided, Stephen knew that he should turn back within the next ten to fifteen minutes; but he half-understood that what he was really doing was calculating the best time for a second possible communication with the girl he had seen in the clough. If he reappeared too soon, he might be thought, at such a spot, to be pestering, even menacing: if too late, the girl might be gone. In any case, there was an obvious limit to the time he could give to such approach as might be possible.

As the whole matter crystallized within him, he turned on the instant. There was a stone beside the track at the point where he did it; perhaps aforetime a milepost, at the least a waymark. Its location seemed to justify his action. He noticed that it too was patched with lichen. When staying with Harewood, he always noticed; and more and more at other times too.

One might almost have thought that the girl had been waiting for him. She was standing at much the same spot, and looking upwards abstractedly. Stephen saw that beside her on the ground was a grey receptacle. He had not noticed it before, because its vague colour sank into the landscape, as did the girl herself, costumed as she was. The receptacle seemed to be half-filled with grey contents of some kind.

As soon as he came into her line of sight, and sometime before he stood immediately above her, the girl spoke.

"Are you lost? Are you looking for someone?"

She must have had a remarkably clear voice, because her words came floating up to Stephen like bubbles in water.

He continued along the ridge towards her while she watched him. Only when he was directly above her did he trust his own words to reach her.

"No. I'm really just filling in time. Thank you very much."

"If you go on to the top, there's a spring."

"I should think you have to have it pointed out to you. With all this heather."

She looked down for a moment, then up again. "Do you live here?"

"No. I'm staying with my brother. He's the rector. Perhaps you go to his church?"

She shook her head. "No. We don't go to any church."

That could not be followed up, Stephen felt, at his present distance and altitude. "What are you doing?" he asked.

"Collecting stones for my father."

"What does he do with them?"

"He wants the mosses and lichens."

"Then," cried Stephen, "you *must* know my brother. Or your father must know him. My brother is one of the great authorities on lichens." This unexpected link seemed to open a door; and, at least for a second, to open it surprisingly wide.

Stephen found himself bustling down the rough but not particularly steep slope towards her.

"My father's not an *authority*," said the girl, gazing seriously at the descending figure. "He's not an authority on anything."

"Oh, you misunderstand," said Stephen. "My brother is only an amateur too. I didn't mean he was a professor or anything like that. Still, I think your father must have heard of him."

"I don't think so," said the girl. "I'm almost sure not."

Stephen had nearly reached the bottom of the shallow vale. It was completely out of the wind down there, and surprisingly torrid.

"Let me see," he said, looking into the girl's basket, before he looked at the girl.

She lifted the basket off the ground. Her hand and forearm were brown.

"Some of the specimens are very small," he said, smiling. It was essential to keep the conversation going, and it was initially more difficult now that he was alone with her in the valley, and close to her.

"It's been a bad year," she said. "Some days I've found almost nothing. Nothing that could be taken home."

"All the same, the basket must be heavy. Please put it down." He saw that it was reinforced with stout metal strips, mostly rusty.

"Take a piece for yourself, if you like," said the girl. She spoke as if they were portions of iced cake, or homemade coconut fudge.

Stephen gazed full at the girl. She had a sensitive face with grey-green eyes and short reddish hair—no, auburn. The *démodé* word came to Stephen on the instant. Both her shirt and her trousers were worn and faded: familiar, Stephen felt. She was wearing serious shoes, but little cared for. She was part of nature.

"I'll take this piece," Stephen said. "It's conglomerate."

"Is it?" said the girl. Stephen was surprised that after so much ingathering, she did not know a fact so elementary.

"I might take this piece too, and show the stuff on it to my brother."

"Help yourself," said the girl. "But don't take them all."

Feeling had been building up in Stephen while he had been walking solitarily on the ridge above. For so long he had been isolated, insulated, incarcerated. Elizabeth had been everything to him, and no one could ever be like her, but "attractive" was not a word that he had used to himself about her, not for a long time; not attractive as this girl was attractive. Elizabeth had been a part of him, perhaps the greater part of him; but not mysterious, not fascinating.

"Well, I don't know," said Stephen. "How far do you have to carry that burden?"

"The basket isn't full yet. I must go on searching for a bit."

"I am sorry to say I can't offer to help. I have to go back."

All the same, Stephen had reached a decision.

The girl simply nodded. She had not yet picked up the basket again.

"Where do you live?"

"Quite near."

That seemed to Stephen to be almost impossible, but it was not the main point.

Stephen felt like a schoolboy; though not like himself as a schoolboy. "If I were to be here after lunch tomorrow, say at half past two, would you show me the spring? The spring you were talking about."

"Of course," she said. "If you like."

Stephen could not manage the response so obviously needed, gently confident; if possible, even gently witty. For a moment, in fact, he could say nothing. Then—"Look," he said. He brought an envelope out of his pocket and in pencil on the back of it he wrote. "Tomorrow. Here. 2:30 p.m. To visit the spring."

He said, "It's too big," and tore one end off the envelope, aware that the remaining section bore his name, and that the envelope had been addressed to him care of his brother. As a matter of fact, it had contained the final communication from the undertaking firm. He wished they had omitted his equivocal and rather ridiculous O.B.E.

He held the envelope out. She took it and inserted it, without a word, into a pocket of her shirt, buttoning down the flap. Stephen's heart beat at the gesture.

He was not exactly sure what to make of the situation or whether the appointment was to be depended upon. But at such moments in life, one is often sure of neither thing, nor of anything much else.

He looked at her. "What's your name?" he asked, as casually as he could.

"Nell," she answered.

He had not quite expected that, but then he had not particularly expected anything else either.

"I look forward to our walk, Nell," he said. He could not help adding, "I look forward to it very much."

She nodded and smiled.

He fancied that they had already looked at one another for a moment.

"I must go on searching," she said.

She picked up the heavy basket, seemingly without particular effort, and walked away from him, up the valley.

Insanely, he wondered about *her* lunch. Surely she must have some? She seemed so exceptionally healthy and strong.

His own meal was all scarlet runners, but he had lost his appetite in any case, something that had never previously happened since the funeral, as he had noticed with surprise on several occasions.

Luncheon was called lunch, but the evening meal was none the less called supper, perhaps from humility. At supper that evening, Harriet referred forcefully to Stephen's earlier abstemiousness.

"I trust you're not sickening, Stephen. It would be a bad moment. Dr. Gopalachari's on holiday. Perhaps I ought to warn you."

"Dr. Who?"

"No, not Dr. Who. Dr. Gopalachari. He's a West Bengali. We are lucky to have him."

Stephen's brother, Harewood, coughed forlornly.

*

For luncheon the next day, Stephen had even less appetite, even though it was mashed turnip, cooked, or at least served, with mixed peppers. Harriet loved all things oriental.

On an almost empty stomach, he hastened up the long but not steep ascent. He had not known he could still walk so fast uphill, but for some reason the knowledge did not make him particularly happy, as doubtless it should have done.

The girl, dressed as on the day before, was seated upon a low rock at the spot from which he had first spoken to her. It was not yet twenty past. He had discerned her seated shape from afar, but she had proved to be sitting with her back to the ascending track and to him. On the whole, he was glad that she had not been watching his exertions, inevitably comical, albeit triumphant.

She did not even look up until he actually stood before her. Of course this time she had no basket.

"Oh, hullo," she said.

He stood looking at her. "We're both punctual."

She nodded. He was panting quite strenuously, and glad to gain a little time.

He spoke. "Did you find many more suitable stones?"

She shook her head, then rose to her feet.

He found it difficult not to stretch out his arms and draw her to him.

"Why is this called Burton's Clough, I wonder? It seems altogether too wide and shallow for a clough."

"I didn't know it was," said the girl.

"The map says it is. At least I think this is the place. Shall we go? Lead me to the magic spring."

She smiled at him. "Why do you call it *that*?"

"I'm sure it is magic. It must be."

"It's just clear water," said the girl, "and very, very deep."

Happily, the track was still wide enough for them to walk side by side, though Stephen realized that, further on, where he had not been, this might cease to be the case.

"How long are you staying here?" asked the girl.

"Perhaps for another fortnight. It depends."

"Are you married?"

"I *was* married, Nell, but my wife unfortunately died." It seemed unnecessary to put any date to it, and calculated only to cause stress.

"I'm sorry," said the girl.

"She was a wonderful woman and a very good wife."

To that the girl said nothing. What could she say.

"I am taking a period of leave from the civil service," Stephen volunteered. "Nothing very glamorous."

"What's the civil service?" asked the girl.

"You ought to know *that*," said Stephen in mock reproof: more or less mock. After all, she was not a child, or not exactly. All the same, he produced a childlike explanation. "The civil service is what looks after the country. The country would hardly carry on without us. Not nowadays. Nothing would run properly."

"Really not?"

"No. Not run *properly*." With her it was practicable to be lightly profane.

"Father says that all politicians are evil. I don't know anything about it."

"Civil servants are not politicians, Nell. But perhaps this is not the best moment to go into it all." He said that partly because he suspected she had no wish to learn.

There was a pause.

"Do you like walking?" she asked.

"Very much. I could easily walk all day. Would you come with me?"

"I *do* walk all day, or most of it. Of course I have to sleep at night. I lie in front of the fire."

"But it's too warm for a fire at this time of year." He said it to keep the conversation going, but, in fact, he was far from certain. He himself was not particularly warm at that very moment. He had no doubt cooled off after speeding up the ascent, but the two of them were, none the less, walking reasonably fast, and still he felt chilly, perhaps perilously so.

"Father always likes a fire," said the girl. "He's a cold mortal."

They had reached the decayed milestone or waymark at which Stephen had turned on the previous day. The girl had stopped and was fingering the lichens with which it was spattered. She knelt against the stone with her left arm round the back of it.

"Can you put a name to them?" asked Stephen.

"Yes, to some of them."

"I am sure your father has one of my brother's books on his shelf."

"I don't think so," said the girl. "We have no shelves. Father can't read."

She straightened up and glanced at Stephen.

"Oh, but surely—"

For example, and among other things, the girl herself was perfectly well spoken. As a matter of fact, hers was a noticeably beautiful voice. Stephen had noticed it, and even thrilled to it, when first he had heard it, floating up from the bottom of the so-called clough. He had thrilled to it ever since, despite the curious things the girl sometimes said.

They resumed their way.

"Father has no eyes," said the girl.

"That is terrible," said Stephen. "I hadn't realized."

The girl said nothing.

Stephen felt his first real qualm, as distinct from mere habitual self-doubt. "Am I taking you away from him? Should you go back to him?"

"I'm never with him by day," said the girl. "He finds his way about."

"I know that does happen," said Stephen guardedly. "All the same—"

"Father doesn't need a civil service to run him," said the girl. The way she spoke convinced Stephen that she had known all along what the civil service was and did. He had from the first supposed that to be so. Everyone knew.

"You said your dead wife was a wonderful woman," said the girl.

"Yes, she was."

"My father is a wonderful man."

"Yes," said Stephen. "I am only sorry about his affliction."

"It's not an affliction," said the girl.

Stephen did not know what to say to that. The last thing to be desired was an argument of any kind whatever, other perhaps than a fun argument.

"Father doesn't need to get things out of books," said the girl.

"There are certainly other ways of learning," said Stephen. "I expect that was one of the things you yourself learned at school."

He suspected she would say she had never been to school. His had been a half-fishing remark.

But all she replied was, "Yes."

Stephen looked around him for a moment. Already, he had gone considerably further along the track than ever before. "It really is beautiful up here." It seemed a complete wilderness. The track had wound among the wide folds of the hill, so that nothing but wilderness was visible in any direction.

"I should like to live here," said Stephen. "I should like it *now*." He knew that he partly meant "now that Elizabeth was dead".

"There are empty houses everywhere," said the girl. "You can just move into one. It's what Father and I did, and now it's our home."

Stephen supposed that that at least explained something. It possibly elucidated one of the earliest of her odd remarks.

"I'll help you find one, if you like," said the girl. "Father says that none of them have been lived in for hundreds of years. I know where all the best ones are."

"I'll have to think about that," said Stephen. "I have my job, you must remember." He wanted her to be rude about his job.

But she only said, "We'll look now, if you like."

"Tomorrow, perhaps. We're looking for the spring now."

"Are you tired?" asked the girl, with apparently genuine concern, and presumably forgetting altogether what he had told her about his longing to walk all day.

"Not at all tired," said Stephen, smiling at her.

"Then why were you looking at your watch?"

"A bad habit picked up in the civil service. We all do it."

He had observed long before that she had no watch on her lovely brown forearm, no bracelet; only the marks of thorn scratches and the incisions of sharp stones. The light golden bloom on her arms filled him with delight and with desire.

In fact, he had omitted to time their progression, though he timed most things, so that the habit had wrecked his natural faculty. Perhaps another twenty or thirty minutes passed, while they continued to walk side by side, the track having as yet shown no particular sign of narrowing, so that one might think it still led somewhere, and that people still went there. As they advanced, they said little more of consequence for the moment; or so it seemed to Stephen. He surmised that there was now what is termed an understanding between them, even though in a sense he himself understood very little. It was more a phase for pleasant nothings, he deemed, always supposing that he could evolve a sufficient supply of them, than for meaningful questions and reasonable responses.

Suddenly, the track seemed not to narrow, but to stop, even to vanish. Hereunto it had been surprisingly well trodden. Now he could see nothing but knee-high heather.

"The spring's over there," said the girl in a matter of fact way, and pointing. Such simple and natural gestures are often the most beautiful.

"How right I was in saying that I could never find it alone!" remarked Stephen.

He could not see why the main track should not lead to the spring—if there really was a spring. Why else should the track be beaten to this spot? The mystery was akin to the Burton's Clough mystery. The uplands had been settled under other conditions than ours. Stephen, on his perambulations, had always felt that, everywhere.

But the girl was standing among the heather a few yards away, and Stephen saw that there was a curious serpentine rabbit-run that he had failed to notice—except that rabbits do not run like serpents. There were several fair-sized birds flying overhead in silence. Stephen fancied they were kites.

He wriggled his way down the rabbit path, with little dignity.

There was the most beautiful small pool imaginable: clear, deep, lustrous, gently heaving at its centre, or near its centre. It stood in a small clearing.

All the rivers in Britain might be taken as rising here, and thus flowing until the first moment of their pollution.

Stephen became aware that now the sun really *was* shining. He had not noticed before. The girl stood on the far side of the pool in her faded shirt and trousers, smiling seraphically. The pool pleased her, so that suddenly everything pleased her.

"Have you kept the note I gave you?" asked Stephen.

She put her hand lightly on her breast pocket, and therefore on her breast.

"I'm glad," said Stephen.

If the pool had not been between them, he would have seized her, whatever the consequences.

"Just clear water," said the girl.

The sun brought out new colours in her hair. The shape of her head was absolutely perfect.

"The track," said Stephen, "seems to be quite well used. Is this where the people come?"

"No," said the girl. "They come to and from the places where they live."

"I thought you said all the houses were empty."

"What I said was there are many empty houses."

"That *is* what you said. I'm sorry. But the track seems to come to an end. What do the people do then?"

"They find their way," said the girl. "Stop worrying about them."

The water was still between them. Stephen was no longer in doubt that there was indeed something else between them. Really there was. The pool was intermittently throwing up tiny golden waves in the pure breeze, then losing them again.

"We haven't seen anybody," said Stephen. "I never do see anyone."

The girl looked puzzled.

Stephen realized that the way he had put it, the statement that he never saw anyone might have been tactless. "When I go for my long walks alone," he added.

"Not only then," said the girl.

Stephen's heart turned over slightly.

"Possibly," he said. "I daresay you are very right."

The kites were still flapping like torn pieces of charred pasteboard in the high air, though in the lower part of it.

"You haven't even looked to the bottom of the pool yet," said the girl.

"I suppose not." Stephen fell on his knees, as the girl had done at the milestone or waymark, and gazed downwards through the pellucid near-nothingness beneath the shifting golden rods. There were a few polished stones round the sides, but little else that he could see, and nothing that seemed of significance. How should there be, of course? Unless the girl had put it there, as Stephen realized might have been possible.

Stephen looked up. "It's a splendid pool," he said.

But now his eye caught something else; something other than the girl and the pool. On the edge of the rising ground behind the girl stood a small stone house. It was something else that Stephen had not previously noticed. Indeed, he had been reasonably sure that there had been nothing and no one, not so much as a hint of mankind, not for a quite long way, a quite long time.

"Is that where one of the people lives?" he asked, and in his turn pointed. "Or perhaps more than one?"

"It's empty," said the girl.

"Should we go and look?"

"If you like," said the girl. Stephen quite saw that his expressed response to the glorious little spring had been inadequate. He had lost the trick of feeling, years and years ago.

"It's a splendid pool," he said again, a little self-consciously.

Despite what the girl had said, Stephen had thought that to reach the house above them, they would have to scramble through the high heather. But he realized at once that there was a path, which was one further thing he had not previously noticed.

The girl went before, weaving backwards and forwards up the hillside. Following her, with his thoughts more free to wander, as the exertion made talking difficult, Stephen suddenly apprehended that the need to return for Harriet's teatime had for a season passed completely from his mind.

Apprehending it now, he did not even look at his watch. Apart from anything else, the struggle upwards was too intense for even the smallest distraction or secondary effort. The best thing might be for his watch simply to stop.

They were at the summit, with a wider horizon, but still Stephen could see no other structure than the one before him, though this time he gazed around with a certain care. From here, the pool below them seemed to catch the full sun all over its surface. It gleamed among the heathered rocks like a vast luminous sea anemone among weeds.

Stephen could see at once that the house appeared basically habitable. He had expected jagged holes in the walls, broken panes in the windows, less than half a roof, ubiquitous litter.

The door simply stood open, but it was a door, not a mere gap; a door in faded green, like the girl's trousers. Inside, the floorboards were present and there was even a certain amount of simple furniture, though, as an estate agent would at once have pointed out with apologies, no curtains and no carpets.

"Nell. Somebody lives here already," Stephen said sharply, before they had even gone upstairs.

"Already?" queried the girl.

Stephen made the necessary correction. "Someone lives here."

"No," said the girl. "No one. Not for centuries."

Of course that was particularly absurd and childish. Much of this furniture, Stephen thought, was of the kind offered by the furnishing department of a good Co-op. Stephen had sometimes come upon such articles on visits paid in the course of his work. He had to admit, however, that he had little idea when such houses as this actually were built at these odd spots on the moors. Possibly as long ago as in the seventeenth century? Possibly only sixty or eighty years ago? Possibly—?

They went upstairs. There were two very low rooms, hardly as much as half lighted from one small and dirty window in each. One room was totally unfurnished. The sole content of the other was a double bed which absorbed much of the cubic capacity available. It was a quite handsome country object, with a carved head and foot. It even offered a seemingly intact mattress, badly in need of a wash.

"Someone *must* be living here," said Stephen. "At least sometimes. Perhaps the owners come here for the weekend. Or perhaps they're just moving in."

As soon as he spoke, it occurred to him that the evidence was equally consistent with their moving out, but he did not continue.

"Lots of the houses are like this," said the girl. "No one lives in them."

Stephen wondered vaguely whether the clear air or some factor of that kind might preserve things as if they were still in use. It was a familiar enough notion, though, in this case, somewhat unspecific. It would be simpler to disbelieve the girl, who was young and without experience, though perfectly eager. They returned downstairs.

"Shall we see some more houses?" asked the girl.

"I don't think I have the time."

"You said you had a fortnight. I know what a fortnight is."

"Yes." He simply could not tell her that he had to report for Harriet's astringent teatime; nor, even now, was that in the forefront of his mind. The truth was that whereas hitherto he had been trying to paddle in deep waters, he was now floundering in them.

The girl had a suggestion. "Why not live *here* for a fortnight?"

"I am committed to staying with my brother. He's not very fit. I should worry about him if I broke my word." He realized that he was speaking to her in a more adult way than before. It had really begun with her speaking similarly to him.

"Does your worrying about him do him any good?"

"Not much, I'm afraid."

"Does your worrying about everything do *you* any good?"

"None whatever, Nell. None at all."

He turned aside and looked out of the window; the parlour window might not be too grand a term, for all its need of cleaning.

He addressed her firmly. "Would you give me a hand with all the things that need to be done? Even for a tenancy of a fortnight?"

"If you like."

"We should have to do a lot of shopping."

The girl, standing behind him, remained silent. It was an unusual nonresponse.

"I should have to cook on a primus stove," said Stephen. "I wonder if we can buy one? I used to be quite good with them." Rapture was beginning.

The girl said nothing.

"We might need new locks on the doors."

The girl spoke. There is only one door."

"So there is," said Stephen. "In towns, houses have two, a front door and a back door. When trouble comes in at one, you can do a bolt through the other."

"People don't need a lock," said the girl. "Why should they?"

He turned away from the filthy window and gazed straight at her. "Suppose I was to fall in love with you?" he said.

"Then you would not have to go back after a fortnight."

It could hardly have been a straighter reply.

He put one arm round her shoulders, one hand on her breast, so that the note he had written her lay between them. He remembered that the first letter written to a woman is always a love letter. "Would you promise to visit me every day?"

"I might be unable to do that."

"I don't want to seem unkind, but you did say that your father could manage?"

"If he discovers, he will keep me at home and send my sister out instead. He has powers. He's very frightening."

Stephen relaxed his hold a little. He had been all along well aware how sadly impracticable was the entire idea.

For example: he could hardly even drive up to this place with supplies; even had his car not been in the course of an opportune overhaul in London, a very complete overhaul after all this anxious time. And that was only one thing; one among very many.

"Well, what's the answer?" Stephen said, smiling at her in the wrong way, longing for her in a very different way.

"I can't come and go the whole time," said the girl.

"I see," said Stephen.

He who had missed so many opportunities, always for excellent reasons, and for one excellent reason in particular, clearly saw that this might be his last opportunity, and almost certainly was.

"How should we live?" he asked. "I mean how should we eat and manage?"

"As the birds do," said the girl.

Stephen did not enquire of her how she came to know Shakespeare, as people put it. He might ask her that later. In the meantime, he could see that the flat, floating birds he had taken to be kites, were indeed drifting past the dirty window, and round and round the house, as it seemed. Of course his questions had been mere routine in any case.

He could well have killed himself if she had made a merely routine response.

"Let's see," he said. He gently took her hand. He kissed her softly on the lips. He returned with her upstairs.

It would perhaps have been more suitable if he had been leading the party, but that might be a trifle. Even the damp discoloration of the mattress might be a trifle. Harriet's teatime could not, in truth, be forced from the mind, but it was provisionally overruled. One learned the trick in the course of one's work, or one would break altogether.

There were of course only the bed and the mattress; no sheets or blankets; no Spanish or Kashmiri rugs; no entangling silkiness, no singing save that of the moor. Elizabeth had never wished to make love like that. She had liked to turn on the record player, almost always Brahms or Schumann (the Rhenish Symphony was her particular favourite), and to ascend slowly into a deep fully made bed. But the matter had not seriously arisen for years. Stephen had often wondered why not.

Nell was lying on her front. Seemingly expectant and resistant at the same time, she clung like a clam. Her body was as brown as pale chestnut, but it was a strong and well-made body. Her short hair was wavy rather than curly. Stephen was ravished by the line of it on her strong neck. He was ravished by her relaxed shoulder blade. He was ravished by her perfect waist and thighs. He was ravished by her youth and youthful smell.

"Please turn over," he said, after tugging at her intermittently, and not very effectively.

Fortunately, he was not too displeased by his own appearance. The hair on his body was bleaching and fading, but otherwise he could, quite sincerely, see little difference from when he had been twenty-four, and had married Elizabeth. He knew, however, that at these times sincerity is not enough; nor objectivity either. When are they?

"Please," he said softly in Nell's ear. Her ears were a slightly unusual shape, and the most beautiful he had ever beheld, or beheld so intently.

He put his hand lightly on her neck. "Please," he said.

She wriggled over in a single swift movement, like a light stab from an invisible knife. He saw that her eyes were neither closed nor open, neither looking at him, nor looking at anything but him.

On the skin between her right shoulder and her right breast was a curious, brownish, greyish, bluish irregular mark or patch, which had been hidden by her shirt, though Stephen could not quite see how. It was more demanding of attention than it might have been, partly because of its position, and partly, where Stephen was concerned, because of something vaguely else. In any case, it would mean that the poor girl could not reposefully wear a low-cut dress, should the need arise. Though it was by no means a birthmark in the usual sense, Nell had probably been lying on her front through chagrin about it. Upon Stephen, however, the effect was to make him love her more deeply; perhaps love her for the first time. He did not want her or her body to be quite perfect. In a real person, it would be almost vulgar. At this point, Harriet and Harriet's teatime came more prominently into view for a few seconds.

Nell might say something about the mark sooner or later. He would never take an initiative.

At the moment, she said nothing at all. He simply could not make out whether she was watching him or not. Her mouth was long and generous in a marvellous degree. He could not even make out whether she was taut or relaxed. No small mystery was Nell after years and years of a perfect, but always slow-moving, relationship with Elizabeth!

He kissed her intimately. When she made no particular response, not even a grunt, he began to caress her, more or less as he had caressed his wife. He took care not to touch the peculiar blemish, or even to enter its area. There was no need to do so. It occurred to Stephen that the mark might be the consequence of an injury; and so might in due course disappear, or largely so. In the end that happened even to many of the strangest human markings. One day, as the nannies used to say.

Suddenly she made a wild plunge at him that took away his breath. The surprise was directly physical, but moral also. He had found it a little difficult to assess Nell's likely age, and enquiry was out of the question; but he had supposed it probable that she was a virgin, and had quite deliberately resolved to accept the implication. Or so he had believed of himself.

Now she was behaving as a maenad.

As an oread, rather; Stephen thought at a later hour. For surely those moors were mountains, often above the thousand-foot contour; boundless uplands peopled solely by unwedded nymphs and their monstrous progenitors? Stephen had received a proper education at a proper place: in Stephen's first days, one had not made the grade, Stephen's grade, otherwise. Stephen's parents had undertaken sacrifices so immense that no one had fully recovered from them.

The last vestige of initiative had passed from Stephen like a limb. And yet, he fancied, it was not because Nell was what Elizabeth would have called unfeminine, but merely because she was young, and perhaps because she lived with contamination, merging into the aspect and mutability of remote places. So, at least, he could only suppose.

Soon he ceased to suppose anything. He knew bliss unequalled, unprecedented, assuredly unimagined. Moreover, the wonder lasted for longer than he would have conceived of as possible. That particularly struck him.

Nell's flawed body was celestial. Nell herself was more wonderful than the dream of death. Nell could not possibly exist.

He was fondling her and feeling a trifle cold; much as Elizabeth would have felt. Not that it mattered in the very least. Nell was no maenad or oread. She was a half-frightened child, sweetly soft, responsive to his every thought, sometimes before he had fully given birth to it. She was a waif, a foundling. And it was he who had found her. And only yesterday.

"Tell me about your sister," said Stephen. He realized that it was growing dark as well as chilly.

"She's not like *me*. You wouldn't like her."

Stephen knew that ordinary, normal girls always responded much like that.

He smiled at Nell. "But what *is* she like?"

"She's made quite differently. You wouldn't care for her."

"Has she a name?"

"Of a sort."

"What do you and your father call her?"

"We call her different things at different times. You're cold."

She was a human, after all, Stephen thought.

She herself had very little to put on. Two fairly light garments, a pair of stout socks, her solid shoes.

They went downstairs.

"Would you care to borrow my sweater?" asked Stephen. "Until tomorrow?"

She made no reply, but simply stared at him through the dusk in the downstairs room, the living place, the parlour, the *salon*.

"Take it," said Stephen. It was a heavy garment. Elizabeth had spent nearly four months knitting it continuously, while slowly recovering from her very first disintegration. It was in thick complex stitches and meant to last for ever. When staying with Harewood, Stephen wore it constantly.

Nell took the sweater but did not put it on. She was still staring at him. At such a moment her grey-green eyes were almost luminous.

"We'll meet again tomorrow," said Stephen firmly. "We'll settle down here tomorrow. I must say something to my brother and sister-in-law, and I don't care what happens after that. Not now. At least I *do* care. I care very much. As you well know."

"It's risky," she said.

"Yes," he replied, because it was necessary to evade all discussion. "Yes, but it can't be helped. You come as early as you can, and I'll arrive with some provisions for us. We really need some blankets too, and some candles. I'll see if I can borrow a Land Rover from one of the farms." He trusted that his confidence and his firm, practical actions would override all doubts.

"I may be stopped," she said. "My father can't read books but he can read minds. He does it all the time."

"You must run away from him," said Stephen firmly. "We'll stay here for a little, and then you can come back to London with me."

She made no comment on that, but simply repeated, "My father can read *my* mind. I only have to be in the same room with him. He's frightening."

Her attitude to her father seemed to have changed considerably. It was the experience of love, Stephen supposed: first love.

"Obviously, you must try to be in a *different* room as much as possible. It's only for one more night. We've known each other now for two days."

"There's only one room."

Stephen had known that such would be her rejoinder.

He well knew also that his behaviour might seem unromantic and even cold-hearted. But the compulsion upon him could not be plainer: if he did not return to the rectory tonight, Harriet, weakly aided by Harewood, would have the police after him; dogs would be scurrying across the moors, as if after Hercules, and perhaps searchlights sweeping also. Nothing could more fatally upset any hope of a quiet and enduring compact with such a one as Nell. He was bound for a rough scene with Harriet and Harewood as it was. It being now long past teatime, he would be lucky if Harriet had not taken action before he could reappear. Speed was vital and, furthermore, little of the situation could be explained with any candour to Nell. First, she would simply not understand what he said (even though within her range she was shrewd enough, often shrewder than he). Second, in so far as she did understand, she would panic and vanish. And he had no means of tracking her down at all. She was as shy about her abode as about the mark on her body; though doubtless with as little reason, or so Stephen hoped. He recognized that parting from her at all might be as unwise as it would be painful, but it was the lesser peril. He could not take her to London tonight, or to anywhere, because there was no accessible transport. Not nowadays. He could not take her to the rectory, where Harriet might make Harewood lay an anathema upon her. They could not stay in the moorland house without food or warmth.

"I'll walk with you to the top of the clough," he said.

She shook her head. "It's not there I live."

"Where then?" he asked at once.

"Not that way at all."

"Will you get there?"

She nodded: in exactly what spirit it was hard to say.

He refrained from enquiring how she would explain the absence of specimens for her father. Two or three stones dragged from the walls of the house they were in might serve the purpose in any case, he thought: outside and inside were almost equally mossed, lichened, adorned, encumbered.

"Goodnight, Nell. We'll meet tomorrow morning. Here." He really had to go. Harriet was made anxious by the slightest irregularity, and when she became anxious, she became frenzied. His present irregularity was by no means slight already; assuredly not slight by Harriet's standards.

To his great relief, Nell nodded again. She had still not put on his sweater.

"In a few days' time, we'll go to London. We'll be together always." He could hardly believe his own ears listening to his own voice saying such things. After all this time! After Elizabeth! After so much inner peace and convinced adoration and asking for nothing more! After the fearful illness!

They parted with kisses but with little drama. Nell sped off into what the map depicted as virtual void.

"All the same," Stephen reflected, "I must look at the map again. I'll try to borrow Harewood's dividers."

He pushed back through the heather, rejoicing in his sense of direction, among so many other things to rejoice about, and began lumbering down the track homewards. The light was now so poor that he walked faster and faster; faster even than he had ascended. In the end, he was running uncontrollably.

Therefore, his heart was already pounding when he discovered that the rectory was in confusion; though, at the rectory, even confusion had a slightly wan quality.

During the afternoon, Harriet had had a seizure of some kind, and during the evening had been taken off in a public ambulance.

"What time did it happen?" asked Stephen. He knew from all too much experience that it was the kind of thing that people did ask.

"I don't really know, Stephen," replied Harewood. "I was in my specimens room reading the *Journal*, and I fear that a considerable time may have passed before I came upon her. I was too distressed to look at my watch even then. Besides, between ourselves, my watch loses rather badly."

Though Stephen tried to help in some way, the improvised evening meal was upsetting. Harriet had planned rissoles sautéed in ghee, but neither of the men really knew how to cook with ghee. The homemade Congress Pudding was nothing less than nauseous. Very probably, some decisive final touches had been omitted.

"You see how it is, young Stephen," said Harewood, after they had munched miserably but briefly. "The prognosis cannot be described as hopeful. I may have to give up the living."

"You can't possibly do that, Harewood, whatever happens. There is Father's memory to think about. I'm sure I should think about him more often myself." Stephen's thoughts were, in fact, upon quite specially different topics.

"I don't wish to go, I assure you, Stephen. I've been very happy here."

The statement surprised Stephen, but was of course thoroughly welcome and appropriate.

"There is always prayer, Harewood."

"Yes, Stephen, indeed. I may well have been remiss. That might explain much."

They had been unable to discover where Harriet hid the coffee, so sat for moments in reverent and reflective silence, one on either side of the bleak table: a gift from the nearest branch of the Free India League.

Stephen embarked upon a tentative *démarche*. "I need hardly say that I don't want to leave you in the lurch."

"It speaks for itself that there can be no question of that."

Stephen drew in a quantity of air. "To put it absolutely plainly, I feel that for a spell you would be better off at this time without me around to clutter up the place and make endless demands."

For a second time within hours, Stephen recognized quite clearly that his line of procedure could well be seen as cold-blooded; but, for a second time, he was acting under extreme compulsion—compulsion more extreme than he had expected ever again to encounter, at least on the hither side of the Styx.

"I should never deem you to be doing that, young Stephen. Blood is at all times, even the most embarrassing times, thicker than water. It was Cardinal Newman, by the way, who first said that; a prelate of a different soteriology."

Stephen simply did not believe it, but he said nothing. Harewood often came forward with such assertions, but they were almost invariably erroneous. Stephen sometimes doubted whether Harewood could be completely relied upon even in the context of his private speciality, the lichens.

"I think I had better leave tomorrow morning and so reduce the load for a span. I am sure Doreen will appreciate it." Doreen was the intermittent help; a little brash, where in former days no doubt she would have been a little simple. Stephen had always supposed that brashness might make it more possible to serve Harriet. Doreen had been deserted, childless, by her young husband; but there had been a proper divorce. Harewood was supposed to be taking a keen interest in Doreen, who was no longer in her absolutely first youth.

"You will be rather more dependent upon Doreen for a time," added Stephen.

"I suppose that may well be," said Harewood. Stephen fancied that his brother almost smiled. He quite saw that he might have thought so because of the ideas in his own mind, at which he himself was smiling continuously.

"You must do whatever you think best for all concerned, Stephen," said Harewood. "Including, of course, your sister-in-law, dear Harriet."

"I think I should go now and perhaps come back a little later."

"As you will, Stephen. I have always recognized that you have a mind trained both academically and by your work. I am a much less coordinated spirit. Oh yes, I know it well. I should rely very much upon your judgement in almost any serious matter."

Circumstanced as at the moment he was, Stephen almost blushed.

But Harewood made things all right by adding, "Except perhaps in certain matters of the spirit which, in the nature of things, lie quite particularly between my Maker and myself alone."

"Oh, naturally," said Stephen.

"Otherwise," continued Harewood, "and now that Harriet is unavailable—for very short time only, we must hope—it is upon you, Stephen, that I propose to rely foremost, in many pressing concerns of this world."

Beyond doubt, Harewood now was not all but smiling. He was smiling nearly at full strength. He explained this immediately.

"My catarrh seems very much better," he said. "I might consider setting forth in splendour one of these days. Seeking specimens, I mean."

Stephen plunged upon impulse.

"It may seem a bit odd in the circumstances, but I should be glad to have the use of a Land Rover. There's a building up on the moors I should like to look at again before I go, and it's too far to walk in the time. There's a perfectly good track to quite near it. Is there anyone you know of in the parish who would lend me such a thing? Just for an hour or two, of course."

Harewood responded at once. "You might try Tom Jarrold. I regret to say that he's usually too drunk to drive. Indeed, one could never guarantee that his vehicle will even leave the ground."

Possibly it was not exactly the right reference, but what an excellent and informed parish priest Harewood was suddenly proving to be!

Harewood had reopened the latest number of the *Journal*, which he had been sitting on in the chair all the time. His perusal had of course been interrupted by the afternoon's events.

"Don't feel called upon to stop talking," said Harewood. "I can read and listen at the same time perfectly well."

Stephen reflected that the attempt had not often been made when Harriet had been in the room.

"I don't think there's anything more to say at the moment. We seem to have settled everything that *can* be settled."

"I shall be depending upon you in many different matters, remember," said Harewood, but without looking up from the speckled diagrams.

As soon as Stephen turned on the hanging light in his bedroom, he noticed the new patch on the wall-paper; if only because it was immediately above his bed. The wall-paper had always been lowering anyway. He was the more certain that the particular path was new because, naturally, he made his own bed each morning, which involved daily confrontation with that particular surface. Of course there had always been the other such patches among the marks on the walls.

Still, the new arrival was undoubtedly among the reasons why Stephen slept very little that night, even though, in his own estimation, he needed sleep so badly. There again, however, few do sleep in the first phase of what is felt to be a reciprocated relationship; equally fulfilling and perilous, always deceptive, and always somewhere known to be. The mixed ingredients of the last two days churned within Stephen, as in Harriet's battered cookpot; one rising as another fell. He was treating Harewood as he himself would not wish to be treated; and who could tell what had really led to Harriet's collapse?

In the end, bliss drove out bewilderment, and seemed the one thing sure, as perhaps it was.

Later still, when daylight was all too visible through the frail curtains, Stephen half-dreamed that he was lying inert on some surface he could not define and that Nell was administering water to him from a chalice. But the chalice, doubtless a consecrated object to begin with, and certainly of fairest silver from the Spanish mines, was blotched and blemished. Stephen wanted to turn away, to close his eyes properly, to expostulate, but could do none of these things. As Nell gently kissed his brow, he awoke fully with a compelling thirst. He had heard of people waking thirsty in the night, but to himself he could not remember it ever before happening. He had never lived like that.

There was no water in the room, because the house was just sufficiently advanced to make visitors go to the bathroom. Stephen walked quietly down the passage, then hesitated. He recollected that nowadays the bathroom door opened with an appalling wrench and scream.

It would be very wrong indeed to take the risk of waking poor Harewood, in his new isolation. Stephen crept on down the stairs towards the scullery, and there *was* Harewood, sleeping like the dead, not in the least sprawling, but, on the contrary, touchingly compressed and compact in the worn chair. For a moment, he looked like a schoolboy, though of course in that curtained light.

Harewood was murmuring contentedly. "Turn over. No, right over. You can trust me"; then, almost ecstatically, almost like a juvenile, "It's beautiful. Oh, it's beautiful."

Stephen stole away to the back quarters, where both the luncheon and the supper washing-up, even the washing-up after tea, all awaited the touch of a vanished hand.

The cold tap jerked and jarred as it always did, but when Stephen went back, Harewood was slumbering still. His self-converse was now so ideal that it had fallen into incoherence. The cheap figure on the mantel of Shiva or somebody, which Stephen had always detested, sneered animatedly.

But there Nell really was; really was.

In his soul, Stephen was astonished. Things do not go like that in real life, least of all in the dreaded demesne of the heart.

However, they unloaded the Land Rover, as if everything were perfectly real; toiling up the heather paths with heavy loads. Nell always ahead, always as strong as he: which was really rather necessary.

"I must take the Rover back. Come with me."

He had not for a moment supposed that she would, but she did, and with no demur.

"It's rough going," he said. But she merely put her brown hand on his thigh, as she sat and bumped beside him.

They were a pair now.

"It won't take a moment while I settle with the man."

He was determined that it should not. It must be undesirable that the two of them be seen together in the village. Probably it was undesirable that he himself, even alone, be seen there before a long time had passed. He might perhaps steal back one distant day like Enoch Arden, and take Harewood completely by surprise, both of them now bearded, shaggily or skimpily. What by then would have become of Nell?

They walked upwards hand in hand. Every now and then he said something amorous or amusing to her, but not very often because, as he had foreseen, the words did not come to him readily. He was bound to become more fluent as his heart reopened. She was now speaking more often than he was: not merely more shrewd, but more explicit.

"I'm as close to you as that," she said, pointing with her free hand to a patch of rocky ground with something growing on it—growing quite profusely, almost exuberantly. She had spoken in reply to one of his questions.

He returned the squeeze of the hand he was holding.

"We'll be like the holly and the ivy," she volunteered later, "and then we'll be like the pebble and the shard."

He thought that both comparisons were, like Harewood's comparisons, somewhat inexact, but, in her case, all the more adorable by reason of it. He kissed her.

At first he could not see their house, though, as they neared it, his eyes seemed to wander round the entire horizon: limited in range, however, by the fact that they were mounting quite steeply. But Nell led the way through the rabbit and snake paths, first to the spring, then upwards once more; and there, needless to say, the house was. Earlier that afternoon they had already toiled up and down several times with the baggage. The earlier occupants had been sturdy folk; men and women alike; aboriginals.

It was somewhere near the spring that Nell, this time, made her possibly crucial declaration.

"I've run away," she said, as if previously she had been afraid to speak the words. "Take care of me."

They entered.

When they had been lugging in the food and the blankets and the cressets and the pans, he had of policy refrained from even glancing at the walls of the house; but what could it matter now? For the glorious and overwhelming moment at least? And, judging by recent experience, the moment might even prove a noticeably long moment. Time might again stand still. Time sometimes did if one had not expected it.

Therefore, from as soon as they entered, he stared round at intervals quite brazenly, though not when Nell was looking at him, as for so much of the time she was now doing.

The upshot was anti-climax: here was not the stark, familiar bedroom in the rectory, and Stephen realized that he had not yet acquired points, or areas, of reference and comparison. He was at liberty to deem that they might never be needed.

Nell was ordering things, arranging things, even beginning to prepare things: all as if she had been a *diplomée* of a domestic college; as if she had been blessed with a dedicated mamma or aunt. After all, thought Stephen, as he watched her and intercepted her, her appearance is largely that of an ordinary modern girl.

He loved her.

He turned his back upon her earlier curious intimations. She had run away from it all; and had even stated as much, unasked and unprompted. Henceforth, an ordinary modern girl was what for him she should firmly be; though loyaller, tenderer, stronger than any other.

When, in the end, languishingly they went upstairs, this time they wrapt themselves in lovely new blankets, but Stephen was in no doubt at all that still there was only the one mark on her. Conceivably, even, it was a slightly smaller mark.

He would no longer detect, no longer speculate, no longer be anxious, no longer imagine. No more mortal marks and corruptions. For example, he would quite possibly never sleep in that room at the rectory again.

Thus, for a week, he counted the good things only, as does a sundial. They were many and the silken sequence of them seemed to extend over a lifetime. He recollected the Christian Science teaching that evil is a mere illusion. He clung to the thesis that time is no absolute.

Nell had the knack of supplementing the food he had purchased with fauna and flora that she brought back from the moor. While, at a vague hour of the morning, he lay long among the blankets, simultaneously awake and asleep, she went forth, and never did she return empty-handed, seldom, indeed, other than laden. He was at last learning not from talk but from experience, even though from someone else's experience, how long it really was possible to live without shops, without bureaucratically and commercially modified products, without even watered cash. All that was needed was to be alone in the right place with the right person.

He even saw it as possible that the two of them might remain in the house indefinitely: were it not that his "disappearance" would inevitably be "reported" by someone, doubtless first by Arthur Thread in the office, so that his early exposure was inevitable. That, after all, was a main purpose of science: to make things of all kinds happen sooner than they otherwise would.

Each morning, after Nell had returned from her sorties and had set things in the house to rights, she descended naked to the spring and sank beneath its waters. She liked Stephen to linger at the rim watching her, and to him it seemed that she disappeared in the pool altogether, vanished from sight, and clear though the water was, the clearest, Stephen surmised, that he had ever lighted upon. Beyond doubt, therefore, the little pool really was peculiarly deep, as Nell had always said: it would be difficult to distinguish between the natural movements of its ever-gleaming surface, and movements that might emanate from a submerged naiad. It gave Stephen special pleasure that they drank exclusively from the pool in which Nell splashed about, but, partly for that reason, he confined his own lustrations to dabblings from the edge, like a tripper. Stephen learned by experience, a new experience, the difference between drinking natural water and drinking safeguarded water, as from a sanitized public convenience. When she emerged from the pool, Nell each day shook her short hair like one glad to be alive, and each day her hair seemed to be dry in no time.

One morning, she washed her shirt and trousers in the pool, having no replacements as far as Stephen could see. The garments took longer to dry than she did, and Nell remained unclothed for most of the day, even though there were clouds in the sky. Clouds made little difference anyway, nor quite steady rain, nor drifting mountain mist. The last named merely fortified the peace and happiness.

"Where did you get those clothes?" asked Stephen, even though as a rule he no longer asked anything.

"I found them. They're nice."

He said nothing for a moment.

"*Aren't* they nice?" she enquired anxiously.

"Everything to do with you and in and about and around you is nice in every possible way. You are perfect. Everything concerned with you is perfect."

She smiled gratefully and went back, still unclothed, to the house, where she was stewing up everything together in one of the new pots.

The pot had already leaked, and it had been she who had mended the leak, with a preparation she had hammered and kneaded while Stephen had merely looked on in delighted receptivity, wanting her as she worked.

He had a number of books in his bag, reasonably well chosen, because he had supposed that on most evenings at the rectory he would be retiring early; but now he had no wish to read anything. He conjectured that he would care little if the capacity to read somehow faded from him. He even went so far as to think that, given only a quite short time, it might possibly do so.

At moments, they wandered together about the moor; he, as like as not, with his hand on her breast, on that breast pocket of hers which contained his original and only letter to her, and which she had carefully taken out and given to him when washing the garment, and later carefully replaced. Than these perambulations few excursions could be more uplifting, but Stephen was wary all the same, knowing that if they were to meet anyone, however blameless, the spell might break, and paradise end.

Deep happiness can but be slighted by third parties, whosoever, without exception, they be. No one is so pure as to constitute an exception.

And every night the moon shone through the small windows and fell across their bed and their bodies in wide streaks, oddly angled.

"You are like a long, sweet parsnip," Stephen said. "Succulent but really rather tough."

"I know nothing at all," she replied. "I only know you."

The mark below her shoulder stood out darkly, but, God be praised, in isolation. What did the rapidly deteriorating state of the walls and appurtenances matter by comparison with that?

*

But in due course, the moon, upon which the seeding and growth of plants and of the affections largely depend, had entered its dangerous third quarter.

Stephen had decided that the thing he had to do was take Nell back quickly and quietly to London, and return as soon as possible with his reinvigorated car, approaching as near as he could, in order to collect their possessions in the house. The machine would go there, after all, if he drove it with proper vigour; though it might be as well to do it at a carefully chosen hour, in order to evade Harewood, Doreen, and the general life of the village.

He saw no reason simply to abandon all his purchases and, besides, he felt obscurely certain that it was unlucky to do so, though he had been unable to recall the precise belief. Finally, it would seem likely that some of the varied accessories in the house might be useful in Stephen's new life with Nell. One still had to be practical at times, just as one had to be firm at times.

Nell listened to what he had to say, and then said she would do whatever he wanted. The weather was entirely fair for the moment.

When the purchased food had finally run out, and they were supposedly dependent altogether upon what Nell could bring in off the moor, they departed from the house, though not, truthfully, for that reason. They left everything behind them and walked down at dusk past Burton's Clough to the village. Stephen knew the time of the last bus which connected with a train to London. It was something he knew wherever he was. In a general way, he had of course always liked the train journey and disliked the bus journey.

It was hard to imagine what Nell would make of such experiences, and of those inevitably to come. Though she always said she knew nothing, she seemed surprised by nothing either. Always she brought back to Stephen the theories that there were two kinds of knowledge; sometimes of the same things.

All the others in the bus were old-age pensioners. They had been visiting younger people and were now returning. They sat alone, each as far from each as space allowed. In the end, Stephen counted them. There seemed to be eight, though it was hard to be sure in the bad light, and with several pensioners already slumped forward.

There were at least two kinds of bad light also; the beautiful dim light of the house on the moor, and the depressing light in a nationalized bus. Stephen recalled Ellen Terry's detestation of all electric light. And of course there were ominous marks on the dirty ceiling of the bus and on such of the side panels as Stephen could see, including that on the far side of Nell, who sat beside him, with her head on his shoulder, more like an ordinary modern girl than ever. Where could she have learned that when one was travelling on a slow, ill-lighted bus with the man one loved, one put one's head on his shoulder?

But it was far more that she had somewhere, somehow learned. The slightest physical contact with her induced in Stephen a third dichotomy: the reasonable, rather cautious person his whole life and career surely proved him to be, was displaced by an all but criminal visionary. Everything turned upon such capacity as he might have left to change the nature of time.

The conductor crept down the dingy passage and sibilated in Stephen's ear. "We've got to stop here. Driver must go home. Got a sick kid. There'll be a reserve bus in twenty minutes. All right?"

The conductor didn't bother to explain to the pensioners. They would hardly have understood. For them, the experience itself would be ample. A few minutes later, everyone was outside in the dark, though no one risked a roll call. The lights in the bus had been finally snuffed out, and the crew were making off, aclank with the accoutrements of their tenure, spanners, and irregular metal boxes, and enamelled mugs.

Even now, Nell seemed unsurprised and unindignant. She, at least, appeared to acknowledge that all things have an end, and to be acting on that intimation. As usual, Stephen persuaded her to don his heavy sweater.

It was very late indeed, before they were home; though Stephen could hardly use the word now that not only was Elizabeth gone, but also there was somewhere else, luminously better—or, at least, so decisively different—and, of course, a new person too.

Fortunately, the train had been very late, owing to signal trouble, so that they had caught it and been spared a whole dark night of it at the station, as in a story. Stephen and Nell had sat together in the buffet, until they had been ejected, and the striplighting quelled. Nell had never faltered. She had not commented even when the train, deprived of what railwaymen call its "path", had fumbled its way to London, shunting backward nearly as often as running forward. In the long, almost empty, excursion-type coach had been what Stephen could by now almost complacently regard as the usual smears and blotches.

"Darling, aren't you cold?" He had other, earlier sweaters to lend.

She shook her head quite vigorously.

After that, it had been easy for Stephen to close his eyes almost all the way. The other passenger had appeared to be a fireman in uniform, though of course without helmet. It was hard to believe that he would suddenly rise and rob them, especially as he was so silently slumbering. Perhaps he was all the time a hospital porter or a special messenger or an archangel.

On the Benares table which filled the hall of the flat (a wedding present from Harewood and poor Harriet, who, having been engaged in their teens, had married long ahead of Stephen and Elizabeth), was a parcel, weighty but neat.

"Forgive me," said Stephen. "I never can live with unopened parcels or letters."

He snapped the plastic string in a second and tore through the Glyptal wrapping. It was a burly tome entitled *Lichen, Moss, and Wrack. Usage and Abusage in Peace and War. A Military and Medical Abstract.* Scientific works so often have more title than imaginative works.

Stephen flung the book back on the table. It fell with a heavy clang.

"Meant for my brother. It's always happening. People don't seem to know there's a difference between us."

He gazed at her. He wanted to see nothing else.

She looked unbelievably strange in her faded trousers and the sweater Elizabeth had made. Elizabeth would have seen a ghost and fainted. Elizabeth did tend to faint in the sudden presence of the occult.

"We are not going to take it to him. It'll have to be posted. I'll get the Department to do it tomorrow."

He paused. She smiled at him, late though it was.

Late or early? What difference did it make? It was not what mattered.

"I told you that I should have to go to the Department tomorrow. There's a lot to explain."

She nodded. "And then we'll go back?" She had been anxious about that ever since they had started. He had not known what to expect.

"Yes. After a few days."

Whatever he intended in the first place, he had never made it clear to her where they would be living in the longer run. This was partly because he did not know himself. The flat, without Elizabeth, really was rather horrible. Stephen had not forgotten Elizabeth for a moment. How could he have done? Nor could Stephen wonder that Nell did not wish to live in the flat. The flat was disfigured and puny.

Nell still smiled with her usual seeming understanding. He had feared that by now she would demur at his reference to a few days, and had therefore proclaimed it purposefully.

He smiled back at her. "I'll buy you a dress."

She seemed a trifle alarmed.

"It's time you owned one."

"I don't own anything."

"Yes, you do. You own me. Let's go to bed, shall we?"

But she spoke. "What's this?"

As so often happens, Nell had picked up and taken an interest in the thing he would least have wished.

It was a large, lumpy shopping bag from a craft room in Burnham-on-Sea, where Elizabeth and he had spent an unwise week in their early days. What the Orient was to Harriet, the seaside had been to Elizabeth. Sisters-in-law often show affinities. The shopping bag had continued in regular use ever since, and not only for shopping, until Elizabeth had been no longer mobile.

"It's a bag made of natural fibres," said Stephen. "It belonged to my late wife."

"It smells. It reminds me."

"Many things here remind *me*," said Stephen. "But a new page had been turned." He kept forgetting that Nell was unaccustomed to book metaphors.

She appeared to be holding the bag out to him. Though not altogether knowing why, he took it from her. He then regretted doing so.

It was not so much the smell of the bag. He was entirely accustomed to that. It was that, in his absence, the bag had become sodden with dark growths, outside and inside. It had changed character completely.

Certainly the bag had been perfectly strong and serviceable when last he had been in contact with it; though for the moment he could not recollect when that had been. He had made little use of the bag when not under Elizabeth's direction.

He let the fetid mass fall on top of the book on the brass table.

"Let's forget everything," he said. "We still have a few hours."

"Where do I go?" she asked, smiling prettily.

"Not in there," he cried, as she put her hand on one of the doors. He very well knew that he must seem far too excitable. He took a pull on himself. "Try *this* room."

When Elizabeth had become ill, the double bed had been moved into the spare room. It had been years since Stephen had slept in that bed, though, once again, he could not in the least recall how many years. The first step towards mastering time is always to make time meaningless.

It was naturally wonderful to be at long last in a fully equipped deep double bed with Nell. She had shown no expectation of being invited to borrow one of Elizabeth's expensive nightdresses. Nell was a primitive still, and it was life or death to keep her so. He had never cared much for flowing, gracious bedwear in any case; nor had the wonder that was Elizabeth seemed to him to need such embellishments.

But he could not pretend, as he lay in Nell's strong arms and she in his, that the condition of the spare room was in the least reassuring. Before he had quickly turned off the small bedside light, the new marks on the walls had seemed like huge inhuman faces; and the effect was all the more alarming in that these walls had been painted, inevitably long ago, by Elizabeth in person, and had even been her particular domestic display piece. The stained overall she had worn for the task still hung in the cupboard next door, lest the need arise again.

It was always the trouble. So long as one was far from the place once called home, one could successfully cast secondary matters from the mind, or at least from the hurting part of it; but from the moment of return, in fact from some little while before that, one simply had to recognize that, for most of one's life, secondary matters were just about all there were. Stephen had learned ages ago that secondary matters were always the menace.

Desperation, therefore, possibly made its contribution to the mutual passion that changed the few hours available to them.

Within a week, the walls might be darkened all over; and what could the development after *that* conceivably be?

Stephen strongly suspected that the mossiness, the malady, would become more conspicuously three dimensional at any moment. Only as a first move, of course.

He managed to close his mind against all secondary considerations and to give love its fullest licence yet.

Thread was in the office before Stephen, even though Stephen had risen most mortifyingly early, and almost sleepless. It was a commonplace that the higher one ascended in the service, the earlier one had to rise, in order to ascend higher still. The lamas never slept at all.

"Feeling better?" Thread could ask such questions with unique irony.

"Much better, thank you."

"You still look a bit peaky." Thread was keeping his finger at the place he had reached in the particular file.

"I had a tiresome journey back. I've slept very little."

"It's always the trouble. Morag and I make sure of a few days to settle in before we return to full schedule."

"Elizabeth and I used to do that also. It's a bit different now."

Thread looked Stephen straight in the eyes, or very nearly.

"Let me advise, for what my advice is worth. I recommend you to lose yourself in your work for the next two or three years at the least. Lose yourself completely. Forget everything else. In my opinion, it's always the best thing at these times. Probably the only thing."

"Work doesn't mean to me what it did."

"Take yourself in hand, and it soon will again. After all, very real responsibilities do rest in this room. We both understand that quite well. We've reached that sort of level, Stephen. What we do nowadays *matters*. If you keep that in mind at all times, and I do mean at *all* times, the thought will see you through. I know what I'm talking about."

Thread's eyes were now looking steadily at his finger, lest it had made some move on its own.

"Yes," said Stephen, "but you're talking about yourself, you know."

Stephen was very well aware that the sudden death some years before of Arthur Thread's mother had not deflected Thread for a day from the tasks appointed. Even the funeral had taken place during the weekend; for which Thread had departed on the Friday evening with several major files in his briefcase, as usual. As for Thread's wife, Morag, she was a senior civil servant too, though of course in a very different department. The pair took very little leave in any case, and hardly any of it together. Their two girls were at an expensive boarding school on the far side of France, almost in Switzerland.

"I speak from my own experience," corrected Thread.

"It appears to me," said Stephen, "that I have reached the male climacteric. It must be what's happening to me."

"I advise you to think again," said Thread. "There's no such thing. Anyway you're too young for when it's supposed to be. It's not till you're sixty-three; within two years of retirement."

Thread could keep his finger in position no longer, lest his arm fall off. "If you'll forgive me, I'm rather in the middle of something. Put yourself absolutely at ease. I'll be very pleased to have another talk later."

"What's that mark?" asked Stephen, pointing to the wall above Thread's rather narrow headpiece. So often the trouble seemed to begin above the head. "Was it there before?"

"I'm sure I don't know. Never forget the whole place is going to be completely done over next year. Now do let me concentrate for a bit."

As the time for luncheon drew near, another man, Mark Tremble, peeped in.

"Glad to see you back, Stephen. I really am."

"Thank you, Mark. I wish I could more sincerely say I was glad to *be* back."

"Who could be? Come and swim?"

Stephen had regularly done it with Mark Tremble and a shifting group of others; usually at lunchtime on several days a week. It had been one of twenty devices for lightening momentarily the weight of Elizabeth's desperation. The bath was in the basement of the building. Soon the bath was to be extended and standardized, and made available at times to additional grades.

"Very well."

Stephen had at one time proposed to tear back; to be with Nell for a few moments; perhaps to buy that dress; but during the long morning he had decided against all of it.

His real task was to put down his foot with the establishment; to secure such modified pension as he was entitled to; to concentrate, as Thread always concentrated; to depart.

He had not so far said a word about it to anyone in the place.

The two seniors changed in the sketchy cubicles, and emerged almost at the same moment in swimming trunks. There seemed to be no one else in or around the pool that day, though the ebbing and flowing of table tennis were audible through the partition.

"I say, Stephen. What's that thing on your back?"

Stephen stopped dead on the wet tiled floor. "What thing?"

"It's a bit peculiar. I'm sure it wasn't there before. Before you went away. I'm extremely sorry to mention it."

"What's it look like?" asked Stephen. "Can you describe it?"

"The best I can do is that it looks rather like the sort of thing you occasionally see on trees. I think it may simply be something stuck on to you. Would you like me to give it a tug?"

"I think not," said Stephen. "I am sorry it upsets you. I'll go back and dress. I think it would be better."

"Yes," said Mark Tremble. "It does upset me. It's best to admit it. Either it's something that will just come off with a good rub, or you'd better see a doctor, Stephen."

"I'll see what I can do," said Stephen.

"I don't feel so much like a swim, after all," said Mark Tremble. "I'll dress too and then we'll both have a drink. I feel we could both do with one."

"I'm very sorry about it," said Stephen. "I apologize."

"What have *you* been doing all day?" asked Stephen, as soon as he was back and had changed out of the garments currently normal in the civil service, casual and characterless. "I hope you've been happy."

"I found this on the roof." Nell was holding it in both her hands; which were still very brown. It was a huge lump: mineral, vegetable, who could tell? Or conceivably a proportion of each.

"Your father would be interested."

Nell recoiled. "Don't talk like that. It's unlucky." Indeed, she had nearly dropped the dense mass.

It had been an idiotic response on Stephen's part; mainly the consequence of his not knowing what else to say. He was aware that it was perfectly possible to attain the roof of the building by way of the iron fire ladder, to which, by law, access had to be open to tenants at all hours.

"I could do with a drink," said Stephen, though he had been drinking virtually the whole afternoon, without Thread even noticing, or without sparing time to acknowledge that he had noticed. Moira, the coloured girl from the typing area, had simply winked her big left eye at Stephen. "I've had a difficult day."

"Oh!" Nell's cry was so sincere and eloquent that it was as if he had been mangled in a traffic accident.

"*How* difficult?" she asked.

"It's just that it's been difficult for me to make the arrangements to get away, to leave the place."

"But we *are* going?" He knew it was what she was thinking about.

"Yes, we are going. I promised."

He provided Nell with a token drink also. At first she had seemed to be completely new to liquor. Stephen had always found life black without it, but his need for it had become more habitual during Elizabeth's illness. He trusted that Nell and he would, with use, wont, and time, evolve a mutual equilibrium.

At the moment, he recognized that he was all but tight, though he fancied that at such times he made little external manifestation.

Certainly Nell would detect nothing; if only because presumably she lacked data. Until now, he had never really been in the sitting room of the flat since his return. Here, the new tendrils on the walls and ceiling struck him as resembling a Portuguese man-o'-war's equipment; the coloured, insensate creature that can sting a swimmer to death at thirty feet distance, and had done so more than once when Elizabeth and he, being extravagant, had stayed at Cannes for a couple of weeks. It had been there that Elizabeth told him finally she could never have a child. Really that was what they were doing there, though he had not realized it. The man-o'-war business, the two victims, had seemed to have an absurd part in their little drama. No one in the hotel had talked of anything else.

"Let's go to bed *now*," said Stephen to Nell. "We can get up again later to eat."

She put her right hand in his left hand.

Her acquiescence, quiet and beautiful, made him feel compunctious.

"Or are you hungry?" he asked. "Shall we have something to eat first? I wasn't thinking."

She shook her head. "I've been foraging."

She seemed to know so many quite literary words. He gave no time to wondering where exactly the forage could have taken place. It would be unprofitable. Whatever Nell had brought in would be wholesomer, inestimably better in every way, than food from any shop.

As soon as she was naked, he tried, in the electric light, to scrutinize her. There still seemed to be only the one mark on her body, truly a quite small mark by the standards of the moment, though he could not fully convince himself that it really was contracting.

However, the examination was difficult; he could not let Nell realize what exactly he was doing; the light was not very powerful, because latterly Elizabeth had disliked a strong light anywhere, and he had felt unable to argue; most of all, he had to prevent Nell seeing whatever Mark Tremble had seen on his own person, had himself all the time to lie facing Nell or flat on his back. In any case, he wondered always how much Nell saw that he saw; how much, whatever her utterances and evidences, she analysed of the things that he analysed.

The heavy curtains, chosen and hung by Elizabeth, had it seemed, remained drawn all day; and by now the simplest thing was for Stephen to switch off what light there was.

Nell, he had thought during the last ten days or ten aeons, was at her very best when the darkness was total.

He knew that heavy drinking was said to increase desire and to diminish performance; and he also knew that it was high time in his life for him to begin worrying about such things. He had even so hinted to Arthur Thread; albeit mainly to startle Thread, and to foretoken his, Stephen's, new life course; even though any such intimation to Thread would be virtually useless. There can be very few to whom most of one's uttered remarks can count for very much.

None the less, Nell and Stephen omitted that evening to arise later; even though Stephen had fully and sincerely intended it.

The next morning, very early the next morning, Nell vouchsafed to Stephen an unusual but wonderful breakfast—if one could apply so blurred a noun to so far-fetched a repast.

Stephen piled into his civil service raiment, systematically noncommittal. He was taking particular trouble not to see his own bare back in any looking-glass. Fortunately, there was no such thing in the dim bathroom.

"Goodbye, my Nell. Before the weekend we shall be free."

He supposed that she knew what a weekend was. By now, it could hardly be clearer that she knew almost everything that mattered in the least.

But, during that one night, the whole flat seemed to have become dark green, dark grey, plain black: patched everywhere, instead of only locally, as when they had arrived. Stephen felt that the walls, floors, and ceilings were beginning to advance towards one another. The knick-knacks were dematerializing most speedily. When life once begins to move, it can scarcely be prevented from setting its own pace. The very idea of intervention becomes ridiculous.

What was Nell making of these swift and strange occurrences? All Stephen was sure of was that it would be unwise to take too much for granted. He must hew his way out; if necessary, with a bloody axe, as the man in the play put it.

Stephen kissed Nell ecstatically. She was smiling as he shut the door. She might smile, off and on, all day, he thought; smile as she foraged.

By that evening, he had drawn a curtain, thick enough even for Elizabeth to have selected, between his homebound self and the events of the daylight.

There was no technical obstacle to his retirement, and never had been. It was mainly the size of his pension that was affected; and in his new life he seemed able to thrive on very little. A hundred costly substitutes for direct experience could be rejected. An intense reality, as new as it was old, was burning down on him like clear sunlight or heavenly fire or poetry.

It was only to be expected that his colleagues should shrink back a little. None the less, Stephen had been disconcerted by how far some of them had gone. They would have been very much less concerned, he fancied, had he been an acknowledged defector, about to stand trial. Such cases were now all in the day's work: there were routines to be complied with, though not too strictly. Stephen realized that his appearance was probably against him. He was not sure what he looked like from hour to hour, and he was taking no steps to find out.

Still, the only remark that was passed, came from Toby Strand, who regularly passed remarks.

"Good God, Stephen, you're looking like death warmed up. I should go home to the wife. You don't want to pass out in this place."

Stephen looked at him.

"Oh God, I forgot. Accept my apology."

"That's perfectly all right, Toby," said Stephen. "And as for the other business, you'll be interested to learn that I've decided to retire."

"Roll on the day for one and all," said Toby Strand, ever the *vox populi*.

Mercifully, Stephen's car had been restored to a measure of health, so that the discreet bodywork gleamed slightly in the evening lustre as he drove into the rented parking space.

"Nell, we can leave at cockcrow!"

"I forgot about buying you that dress."

He was standing in his bath gown, looking at her in the wide bed. The whole flat was narrowing and blackening, and at that early hour the electric light was even weaker than usual.

"I shan't need a dress."

"You must want a change sometime."

"No. I want nothing to change."

He gazed at her. As so often, he had no commensurate words.

"We'll stop somewhere on the way," he said.

They packed the rehabilitated car with essentials for the simple life; with things to eat and drink on the journey and after arrival. Stephen, though proposing to buy Nell a dress, because one never knew what need might arise, was resolved against dragging her into a roadside foodplace. He took all he could, including, surreptitiously, some sad souvenirs of Elizabeth, but he recognized plainly enough that there was almost everything remaining to be done with the flat, and that he would have to return one day to do it, whether or not Nell came with him. In the meantime, it was difficult to surmount what was happening to the flat, or to him. Only Nell was sweet, calm, and changeless in her simple clothes. If only the nature of time were entirely different!

"You'll be terribly cold."

She seemed never to say it first, never to think of it.

He covered her with sweaters and rugs. He thought of offering her a pair of his own warm trousers, but they would be so hopelessly too wide and long.

Islington was a misty marsh, as they flitted through; Holloway pink as a desert flamingo. The scholarly prison building was wrapped in fire. Finsbury Park was crystal as a steppe; Manor House deserted as old age.

When, swift as thoughts of love, they reached Grantham, they turned aside to buy Nell's dress. She chose a rough-textured white one, with the square neck outlined in black, and would accept nothing else, nothing else at all. She even refused to try on the dress and she refused to wear it out of the shop. Stephen concurred, not without a certain relief, and carried the dress to the car in a plastic bag. The car was so congested that a problem arose.

"I'll sit on it," said Nell.

Thus the day went by as in a dream: though there are few such dreams in one lifetime. Stephen, for sure, had never known a journey so rapt, even though he could seldom desist from staring and squinting for uncovenanted blemishes upon and around the bright coachwork. Stephen recognized that, like everyone else, he had spent his life without living; even though he had had Elizabeth for much of the time to help him through, as she alone was able.

Northwards, they ran into a horse fair. The horses were everywhere, and, among them, burlesques of men bawling raucously, and a few excited girls.

"Oh!" cried Nell.

"Shall we stop?"

"No," said Nell. "Not stop."

She was plainly upset.

"Few fairs like that one are left," said Stephen, as he sat intimately, eternally beside her. "The motors have been their knell."

"Knell," said Nell.

Always it was impossible to judge how much she knew.

"Nell," said Stephen affectionately. But it was at about that moment he first saw a dark, juicy crack in the polished metalwork of the bonnet.

"Nell," said Stephen again; and clasped her hand, always brown, always warm, always living and loving. The huge geometrical trucks were everywhere, and it was an uncircumspect move for Stephen to make. But it was once more too misty for the authorities to see very much, to take evidence that could be sworn to.

The mist was more like fog as they wound through Harewood's depopulated community. Harewood really should marry Doreen as soon as it becomes possible, thought Stephen, and make a completely new start in life, perhaps have a much better type of youngster, possibly and properly for the cloth.

Stephen was struck with horror to recollect that he had forgotten all about the costly book which had been almost certainly intended for

Harewood, and which Harewood would be among the very few fully to appreciate and rejoice in. The book had not really been noticeable at first light in the eroding flat, but his lapse perturbed Stephen greatly.

"A fungus and an alga living in a mutually beneficial relationship," he said under his breath.

"What's that?" asked Nell.

"It's the fundamental description of a lichen. You should know that."

"Don't talk about it."

He saw that she shuddered; she who never even quaked from the cold.

"It's unlucky," she said.

"I'm sorry, Nell. I was thinking of the book we left behind, and the words slipped out."

"We're better without the book."

"It wasn't really our book."

"We did right in leaving it."

He realized that it had been the second time when, without thinking, he had seemed ungracious about the big step she had taken for him: the second time at least.

Therefore, he simply answered. "I expect so."

He remained uneasy. He had taken due care not to drive past the crumbling rectory, but nothing could prevent the non-delivery of Harewood's expensive book being an odious default, a matter of only a few hundred yards. To confirm the guilt, a middle-aged solitary woman at the end of the settlement suddenly pressed both hands to her eyes, as if to prevent herself from seeing the passing car, even in the poor light.

The ascending track was rougher and rockier than on any of Stephen's previous transits. It was only to be expected, Stephen realized. Moreover, to mist was now added dusk. At the putative Burton's Clough, he had to take care not to drive over the edge of the declivity; and thereafter he concentrated upon not colliding with the overgrown stony waymark. Shapeless creatures were beginning to emerge which may no longer appear by daylight even in so relatively remote a region. Caution was compelled upon every count.

Thus it was full night when somehow they reached the spot where the track seemed simply to end—with no good reason supplied, as Stephen had always thought. Elizabeth would have been seriously upset if somehow she had seen at such a spot the familiar car in which she had taken so many unforgettable outings, even when a virtual invalid. She might have concluded that at long last she had reached the final bourne.

The moon, still in its third quarter, managed to glimmer, like a fragrance, through the mist; but there could be no visible stars. Stephen switched on his flash, an item of official supply.

"We don't need it," said Nell. "Please not."

Nell was uncaring of cold, of storm, of fog, of fatigue. Her inner strength was superb, and Stephen loved it. But her indifference to such darkness as this reminded Stephen of her father, that wonderful entity, whom it was so unlucky ever to mention, probably even to think of. None the less, Stephen turned back the switch. He had noticed before that he was doing everything she said.

As best he could, he helped her to unload the car, and followed her along the narrow paths through the damp heather. Naturally, he could not see a trace of the house, and he suddenly realized that, though they struggled in silence, he could not even hear the gently heaving spring. They were making a pile at the spot where the house must be; and Nell never put a foot wrong in finding the pile a second, third, and even fourth time. Much of the trip was steep, and Stephen was quite winded once more by his fourth climb in almost no moonlight at all, only the faint smell of moonlight; but when, that time, he followed Nell over the tangled brow, the mist fell away for a moment, as mist on mountains intermittently does, and at last Stephen could see the house quite clearly.

He looked at Nell standing there, pale and mysterious as the moonlight began to fade once more.

"Have you still got my letter?"

She put her hand on her breast pocket.

"Of course I have."

They re-entered the house, for which no key was ever deemed necessary. It might be just as well, for none was available.

Stephen realized at once that what they were doing was moving into the house pretty finally; not, as he had so recently proposed, preparing to move out of it in a short time. It was clear that once Nell truly and finally entered one's life, one had simply to accept the consequences. Stephen could perceive well enough that Nell was at every point moved by forces in comparison with which he was moved by inauthentic fads.

Acquiescence was the only possibility. The admixture in Nell of ignorance and wisdom, sometimes even surface sophistication, was continuously fascinating. In any case, she had left familiar surroundings and completely changed her way of life for him. He must do the same for her without end; and he wished it.

The moonlight was now insufficient to show the state of the walls or the curiously assorted furnishings or the few personal traps he had omitted to bear to London. Stephen had worn gloves to drive and had not removed them to lug. He wore them still.

None the less, when he said, "Shall we have a light now?" he spoke with some reluctance.

"Now," said Nell. "We're at home now."

He fired up some of the rough cressets he had managed to lay hands on when he had borrowed the sottish Jarrold's Land Rover.

Nell threw herself against him. She kissed him again and again.

As she did so, Stephen resolved to look at nothing more. To look was not necessarily to see. He even thought he apprehended a new vein of truth in what Nell had said on that second day, still only a very short time ago, about her father.

Nell went upstairs and changed into the dress he had bought her. She had done it without a hint, and he took for granted that she had done it entirely to give pleasure. In aspect, she was no longer a part of nature, merging into it, an oread. Not surprisingly, the dress did not fit very well, but on Nell it looked like a peplos. She was a sybil. Stephen was scarcely surprised. There was no need for him to see anything other than Nell's white and black robe, intuitively selected, prophetically insisted upon; quite divine, as ordinary normal girls used to say.

When he dashed off his gloves in order to caress her, he regarded only her eyes and her raiment; but later there was eating to be done, and it is difficult, in very primitive lighting, to eat without at moments noticing one's hands. These particular hands seemed at such moments to be decorated with horrid subfusc smears, quite new. Under the circumstances, they might well have come from inside Stephen's driving gloves; warm perhaps, but, like most modern products, of no precise or very wholesome origin. If ineradicable, the marks were appalling; not to be examined for a single second.

When Nell took off her new dress, Stephen saw at once (how else but at once?) that her own small single mark had vanished.

She was as totally honied as harvest home, and as luscious, and as rich.

Stephen resolved that in the morning, if there was one, he would throw away all the souvenirs of Elizabeth he had brought with him. They could be scattered on the moor as ashes in a memorial garden, but better far. The eyes that were watching from behind the marks on the walls and ceilings and utensils glinted back at him, one and all. The formless left hands were his to shake.

In the nature of things, love was *nonpareil* that night; and there was music too. Nell's inner being, when one knew her, when one really knew her, was as matchless as her unsullied body. Goodness is the most powerful aphrodisiac there is, though few have the opportunity of learning. Stephen had learned long before from the example of Elizabeth, and now he was learning again.

Time finally lost all power.

The music became endlessly more intimate.

"God!" cried Stephen suddenly. "That's Schumann!" He had all but leapt in the air. Ridiculously.

"Where?" asked Nell. Stephen realized that he was virtually sitting on her. He dragged himself up and was standing on the floor.

"That music. It's Schumann."

"I hear no music."

"I don't suppose you do."

Stephen spoke drily and unkindly, as he too often did, but he knew that everything was dissolving.

For example, he could see on the dark wall the large portrait of Elizabeth by a pupil of Philip de Laszlo which had hung in their conjugal bedroom. The simulacrum was faint and ghostly, like the music, but he could see it clearly enough for present purposes, dimly self-illuminated.

He had taken that picture down with his own hands, years and years ago; and the reason had been, as he now instantly recalled, that the light paintwork had speedily become blotched and suffused. They had naturally supposed it to be something wrong with the pigments, and had spoken between themselves of vegetable dyes and the superiorities of Giotto and Mantegna. Stephen had hidden the festering canvas in the communal basement storeroom, and had forgotten about it immediately. Now he could see it perfectly well, not over the bed, but in front of it, as always.

"Come back," said Nell. "Come back to me."

The music, which once, beyond doubt, had been the music of love, was dying away. In its place, was a persistent snuffling sound, as if the house from outside, or the room from inside, were being cased by a wolf.

"What's that noise? That noise of an animal?"

"Come back to me," said Nell. "Come back, Stephen." Perhaps she was quite consciously dramatizing a trifle.

He had gone to the window, but of course could see nothing save the misleading huge shapes of the flapping birds.

He went back to the bed and stretched out both his hands to Nell. He was very cold.

Though there was almost no light, Nell grasped his two hands and drew him down to her.

"You see and hear so many things, Stephen," she said.

As she spoke, he had, for moments, a vision of a different kind.

Very lucidly, he saw Nell and himself living together, but, as it might be, in idealized form, vaguely, intensely. He knew that it was an ideal of which she was wonderfully capable, perhaps because she was still so young. All that was required of him was some kind of trust.

Held by her strong hands and arms, he leant over her and faltered.

"But whatever animal is that?" he demanded.

She released his hands and curled up like a child in distress. She had begun to sob.

"Oh, Nell," he cried. He fell on her and tried to reach her. Her muscles were as iron, and he made no impression at all.

In any case, he could not stop attending to the snuffling, if that was the proper word for it. He thought it was louder now. The noise seemed quite to fill the small, low, dark, remote room; to leave no space for renewed love, however desperate the need, however urgent the case.

Suddenly, Stephen knew. A moment of insight had come to him, an instinctual happening.

He divined that outside or inside the little house was Nell's father.

It was one reason why Nell was twisted in misery and terror. Her father had his own ways of getting to the truth of things. She had said so.

Stephen sat down on the bed and put his hand on her shoulder. Though he was shivering dreadfully, he had become almost calm. The process of illumination was suggesting to him the simple truth that, for Nell too, the past must be ever present. And for her it was, in common terms, the terms after which he himself was so continuously half-aspiring, a past most absurdly recent. How could he tell what experiences were hers, parallel to, but never meeting, his own?

It would be no good even making the obvious suggestion that they should dwell far away. She could never willingly leave the moor, even if it should prove the death of her; no more than he had been able all those years to leave the flat, the job, the life, all of which he had hated, and been kept alive in only by Elizabeth.

"What's the best thing to do, Nell?" Stephen enquired of her. "Tell me and we'll do it exactly. Tell me. I think I'm going to dress while you do so. And then perhaps you'd better dress too."

After all, he began to think, there was little that Nell had ever said about her father or her sister which many girls might not have said when having in mind to break away. He would not have wanted a girl who had no independent judgement of her own family.

The processes of insight and illumination were serving him well, and the phantom portrait seemed to have dissipated completely. The snuffling and snorting continued. It was menacing and unfamiliar, but conceivably it was caused merely by a common or uncommon but essentially manageable creature of the moors. Stephen wished he had brought his revolver (another official issue), even though he had no experience in discharging it. He could not think how he had omitted it. Then he recollected the horrible furred-up flat, and shuddered anew, within his warm clothes.

For the first time it occurred to him that poor Elizabeth might be trying, from wherever she was, to warn him. Who could tell that Harriet had not made a miraculous recovery (she was, after all, in touch with many different faiths); and was not now ready once more to accept him for a spell into the life at the rectory?

Nell was being very silent.

Stephen went back to the bed.

"Nell."

He saw that she was not in the bed at all, but standing by the door.

"Nell."

"Hush," she said. "We must hide."

"Where do we do that?"

"I shall show you." He could see that she was back in her shirt and trousers; a part of the natural scene once more. Her white dress glinted on the boards of the floor.

To Stephen her proposal seemed anomalous. If it really was her father outside, he could penetrate everywhere, according to her own statement. If it was a lesser adversary, combat might be better than concealment.

Nell and Stephen went downstairs in the ever more noisy darkness, and Nell, seemingly without effort, lifted a stone slab in the kitchen floor. Stephen could not quite make out how she had done it. Even to find the right slab, under those conditions, was a feat.

"All the houses have a place like this," Nell explained.

"Why?" enquired Stephen. Surely Nell's father was an exceptional phenomenon? Certainly the supposed motion of him was akin to no other motion Stephen had ever heard.

"To keep their treasure," said Nell.

"You are my treasure," said Stephen.

"You are mine," responded Nell.

There were even a few hewn steps, or so they felt to him. Duly it was more a coffer than a room, Stephen apprehended; but in no time Nell had the stone roof down on them, almost with a flick of the elbow, weighty though the roof must have been.

Now the darkness was total; something distinctly different from the merely conventional darkness above. All the same, Stephen of all people could not be unaware that the stone sides and stone floor and stone ceiling of the apartment were lined with moss and lichen. No doubt he had developed sixth and seventh senses in that arena, but the odour could well have sufficed of itself.

"How do we breathe?"

"There is a sort of pipe. That's where the danger lies."

"You mean it might have become blocked up?"

"No."

He did not care next to suggest that it might now be blocked deliberately. He had already made too many tactless suggestions of that kind.

She saved him the trouble of suggesting anything. She spoke in the lowest possible voice.

"He might come through."

It was the first time she had admitted, even by implication, who it was: outside or inside—or both. Stephen fully realized that. It was difficult for him not to give way to the shakes once more, but he clung to the vague possibilities he had tried to sort out upstairs.

"I should hardly think so," he said. "But how long do you suggest we wait?"

"It will be better when it's day. He has to eat so often."

It would be utterly impossible for Stephen to enquire any further; not at the moment. He might succeed in finding his way to the bottom of it all later. He was already beginning to feel cramped, and the smell of the fungi and the algae were metaphorically choking him and the moss realistically tickling him; but he put his arm round Nell in the blackness, and could even feel his letter safe against her soft breast.

She snuggled back at him; as far as circumstances permitted. He had only a vague idea of how big or small their retreat really was.

Nell spoke again in that same lowest possible voice. She could communicate, even in the most pitchy of blackness, while hardly making a sound.

"He's directly above us. He's poised."

Stephen mustered up from his school days a grotesque recollection of some opera: the final scene. The Carl Rosa had done it: that one scene only; after the film in a cinema near Marble Arch. Elizabeth had thought the basic opera convention too far-fetched to be taken seriously; except perhaps for Mozart, who could always be taken seriously.

"I love you," said Stephen. No doubt the chap in the opera had said something to the like effect, but had taken more time over it.

Time: that was always the decisive factor. But time had been mastered at last.

"I love *you*," said Nell, snuggling even closer; manifesting her feeling in every way she could.

Curiously enough, it was at the verge of the small, lustrous pool that Stephen's body was ultimately found.

A poor old man, apparently resistant to full employment and even to the full security that goes with it, found the corpse, though, after all those days or weeks, the creatures and forces of the air and of the moor had done their worst to it, or their best. There was no ordinary skin anywhere. Many people in these busy times would not even have reported the find.

There were still, however, folk who believed, or at least had been told, that the pool was bottomless; and even at the inquest a theory was developed that Stephen had been wandering about on the moor and had died of sudden shock upon realizing at what brink he stood. The coroner, who was a doctor of medicine, soon disposed of that hypothesis.

None the less, the actual verdict had to be open; which satisfied nobody. In these times, people expect clear answers; whether right or wrong.

Harewood, almost his pristine self by then, enquired into the possibility of a memorial service in London, which he was perfectly prepared to come up and conduct. After all, Stephen was an O.B.E. already, and could reasonably hope for more.

The view taken was that Stephen had been missing for so long, so entirely out of the official eye, that the proper moment for the idea was regrettably, but irreversibly, past.

The funeral took place, therefore, in Harewood's own church, where the father and the grandfather of both the deceased and the officiant had shepherded so long with their own quiet distinction. People saw that no other solution had ever really been thinkable.

Doreen had by now duly become indispensable to the rector; in the mysterious absence of Stephen, to whom the rector had specifically allotted that function. At the funeral, she was the only person in full black. Not even the solitary young man from the Ministry emulated her there. It had not been thought appropriate to place Stephen's O.B.E. on the coffin, but during the service, the rector noticed a scrap of lichen thereon which was different entirely, he thought, from any of the species on the walls, rafters, and floors of the church. Performing his office, Harewood could not at once put a name to the specimen. The stuff that already lined the open grave was even more peculiar; and Harewood was more than a little relieved when the whole affair was finally over, the last tributes paid, and he free to stumble back to Doreen's marmite toast, and lilac peignoir. The newest number of the *Journal* had come in only just before, but Harewood did not so much as open it that evening.

As Stephen's will had been rendered ineffective by Elizabeth's decease, Harewood, as next of kin, had to play a part, whether he felt competent or not, in winding everything up. Fortunately, Doreen had been taking typing lessons, and had bought a secondhand machine with her own money.

The flat was found to be in the most shocking state, almost indescribable. It was as if there had been no visitors for years; which, as Harewood at once pointed out, had almost certainly been more or less the case, since the onset of Elizabeth's malady, an epoch ago.

A single, very unusual book about Harewood's own speciality was found. It had been published in a limited edition: a minute one, and at a price so high that Harewood himself had not been among the subscribers.

"Poor fellow!" said Harewood. "I never knew that he was really interested. One can make such mistakes."

The valuable book had of course to be disposed of for the benefit of the estate.

Stephen's car was so far gone that it could be sold only for scrap; but, in the event, it never was sold at all, because no one could be bothered to drag it away. If one knows where to look, one can see the bits of it still.

2008

CESARE THODOL: SOME LINES WRITTEN ON A WALL

Mark Samuels

Mark Samuels was born in London in 1968 and died, too soon, in 2023. His story collections include *The White Hands and Other Weird Tales* (2003), *Glyphotech and Other Macabre Processes* (2008), and *The Man Who Collected Machen and Other Stories* (2010); his novel *Witch-Cult Abbey* was published in 2021. Michael Dirda likens Samuels's work to the paranoid, gnostic vision of Philip K. Dick, with both writers posing deeply disconcerting questions about reality itself: "How can we distinguish between what is real and what isn't? Who is human or alive and who isn't? Might everything around us be a Potemkin Village, masking cosmic nothingness or some horrific truth?" Fungal entities play a sinister role in Samuels's apocalyptic "The Black Mould", as well as this story, more Gothic than cosmic in scope, first published in *Glyphotech*.

Of this one thing I am, at least, absolutely certain: no one is now more qualified than myself to write of the facts concerning Cesare Thodol.

It may be the case that they choose to ignore the findings I have recently made available for scrutiny. However, none of them are aware of the information known to me alone. Doubtless they will continue to dismiss what I have to say as a consequence of an over-active imagination, of a brain too deeply immersed in the outré minutiae of Thodoliana, to be objective. I can only retort by insisting that they consider the evidence. If they would take the time to examine this account and remember that I have previously expressed my doubts as to the claims of parapsychology, then they might realize that I came to my conclusions from an initial basis as sceptical then as is their own now.

Let me begin by restating the biographical information concerning Cesare Thodol that is accepted by everyone. He was born in Düsseldorf in 1870, one of two twins, brother and sister. His parents were Gerhard Thodol and Eva Thodol (née Hess), the former a lawyer and the latter the daughter of the wealthy industrialist Johann Hess. Eva Thodol died giving birth to the twins, Cesare and Elsa. They were sickly children, confined for much of their adolescence to the gloomy chambers of the family home. Cesare's fevered imagination found succour in the fairy tales of the Brothers Grimm and in the *Struwwelpeter* of Dr. Heinrich Hoffman.

Educated privately by tutors, he had reached twenty-three years of age before he showed any signs of wishing to leave the family home. His intense attachment to his twin sister made the suspicion of an incestuous relationship having developed between them all the more credible given that later correspondence showed Cesare's fanatical hatred for his detail-obsessed and drunken father. The old widower had died after a mysterious fall in the family home in 1885, and neither Cesare nor his sister showed the least sign of remorse at his passing. Indeed, the two's virtually total seclusion between the years 1885 and 1893 and the horrible intimacy that existed between brother and sister were remarked upon by all those private tutors who had attended to Cesare's schooling.

Only after his sister's death via consumption did the young Thodol venture forth into the world. An inheritance passed to Cesare, and he took the opportunity to emigrate from Germany to England, settling in London during 1894 and leaving the scandal that had by then attached itself to the Thodol name in his wake.

By this time already the author of several weird metaphysical essays in German, Thodol's love of the strange and horrible led him to the works of Edgar Allan Poe, Charles Baudelaire, Joris-Karl Huysmans, and Ambrose Bierce. Poe's "The Fall of the House of Usher" exerted an influence on his mind that Thodol himself described as "forming the single most important impetus to my writing, nay, my life, that I have ever experienced."

During the year before the trial of Oscar Wilde brought down the curtain on all things decadent in the Victorian era, Thodol, as if sensing its end was close, threw himself into the lifestyle with a fervour to rival even that of Count Stenbock. Thodol's descent into drug-fuelled excess and sexual debauchery continued for a period of nearly ten years, taking a terrible physical and psychological toll on him. The fact that Thodol locked himself away with his perversions, keeping them out of the public gaze, doubtless spared him any outside interference.

But it was his eventual refusal to admit anyone at all into his London home that drew comments from the society papers of the day and led to his downfall. There were rumours that his only companion in his chambers was a waxwork dummy that he had commissioned from Madame Tussaud's. The thing had been formed according to Thodol's own specifications. It was said that the simulacrum was an exact representation of his dead sister and that he spoke to it as if it were alive.

When finally the alienists were called to see for themselves the degree to which Thodol had succumbed to madness, they were at once set upon by the German refugee, who believed that they, and not the waxwork dummy he entertained, were imitations of humanity.

Apparently this wax mannequin was in a shocking state, though Thodol pleaded with his captors that he might be allowed to take it with him. Its mottled face was infested by a fine webwork of tiny fungi. The German had been unable to arrest its deterioration himself and refused to call upon outside help. He could not bear the thought of anyone else seeing, let alone touching, what he thought to be his dead twin sister.

When his financial status was examined it was found that Thodol was effectively a pauper. He had exhausted his inheritance on drugs and on incredibly naïve investments that brought no return, and spent what remained on dresses, flowers, and gaudy trinkets for the fantastically elaborate waxwork of his sister. At this time, in London, the principal terminus for the destitute insane was Colney Hatch Asylum, and it was there, in 1905, that Thodol was taken in a horse-drawn carriage with barred windows. And there he remained until his death in 1938.

The above are the bare facts commonly known to history. What happened to Cesare Thodol during the thirty-three years of his incarceration in Colney Hatch has remained untold. For most Thodolian scholars the story of his life is over by 1905, and they have contented themselves with just a paragraph or two of speculation relating to his existence amongst the deranged in that huge citadel on the outskirts of the city. One or two have mentioned that Thodol believed that all the inmates and staff of the asylum were wax dummies come to life, and that he screamed at the sight of any person, but of the bizarre writings he produced whilst incarcerated there is no account. However, during that time he wrote—not on paper, but on the walls of his cell, until he had covered much of them with his tiny, crabbed handwriting.

One of the psychiatric doctors at Colney Hatch, Sidney Rhodes, took photographs of the writing on the walls after Thodol's death, transcribing them for possible use in a monograph that he was preparing on the creative impulses of the mentally disturbed. It is by thorough analysis of the phantasmal imaginings Thodol sought to preserve in this most desperate of fashions that we can separate truth from fiction. Since I alone now have access to the Rhodes papers, I alone am able to speak with authority on the subject.

The diagnosis of Thodol's mental illness in 1905 was "acute hallucinatory disorder," but this is vague, unsatisfactory, and more suited to the time when the insane were treated by those terming themselves "alienists" rather than by psychiatrists. However, I believe that even the psychiatry of today would produce a diagnosis just as useless. One can, with some legitimacy, point to the organic degeneration in Thodol's body caused by his habitual abuse of intoxicants, but this is little more than a side issue: the reality is terrifying.

The psychiatrist's fascination with the cell in which Thodol had been kept seems to have developed over quite a length of time. During Thodol's incarceration Rhodes, although intrigued by the patient, had very little direct contact with him. Thodol was only calm when left alone, since, as I have already remarked, he was driven into hysterics by the approach of any human being. Treatment of the patient was actually counterproductive, since it was personal interaction and face-to-face contact itself that resulted in phobic reactions. When sedatives were used (these were hidden in the food left for him outside the small hatch at the foot of his cell door) they proved of little benefit. Although physically docile, Thodol's eyes still had in them a crazed fear, and he would reveal nothing to the doctors except that he earnestly desired total solitude.

Finally it was decided that an extreme shock was the last recourse left by way of treatment. Since Thodol had been absented from the waxwork dummy of his sister there had been no improvement whatsoever in his case. Perhaps, it was argued, contact with what appeared to be the cause of his dementia might jolt his mind back into a state where communication was possible. Certainly the doctors had nothing to lose.

Tracing the whereabouts of the simulacrum was not easy, since most of Thodol's former belongings were sold at auction in order to pay creditors. It transpired that the owner of a small waxworks exhibition that toured the country had purchased this particular lot number. He had made a tidy sum displaying the thing and telling the story of Thodol's disgrace and morbid fascination with it. However, since the scandal had been a number of years ago, interest in the matter had inevitably waned and the owner was prepared to turn it over for a pittance in the interests of good publicity. For several months he had, in any case, kept the dummy locked away in a trunk.

It was by now in an even worse state than when it had last been in Thodol's possession. Indeed, the more ghastly it was, the more horrible a fascination it exerted over the paying public, so the waxwork exhibitor had reported.

It is very easy, in hindsight, to state that reuniting Thodol with the object was bound to result in tragedy. And yet, it was genuinely felt that nothing but the most desperate measures remained. What occurred when two orderlies carried the dummy down the corridor accompanied by the psychiatrist in charge of the case, unlocked Thodol's cell, and entered is clearly recorded.

The German stared at the thing, got to his feet, and, ignoring all those around him for once, flattened himself against the wall at his back. The orderlies and the doctor withdrew, leaving him alone with it, though watching the proceedings through the observation hole in the door. Thodol spasmodically tottered forward, as if with great effort. His features twisted into a loathsome smirk of welcome. His eyes were riveted on the fungi-ridden and corroded parody of the female form. He took it in his arms, brushed away the mass of straggly hair covering one side of its mottled face, and began to whisper into its ear.

The men outside withdrew altogether for several minutes, satisfied that no damage had been done. Complete privacy seemed the next logical step. But when they returned to the cell there was no trace of the dummy. Thodol himself was not in any state to give an account of what had transpired. Yet the thing that repelled all three was that he had undergone some horrible physical alteration. His hair actually appeared to be much longer, and his gait stiff-backed and awkward. Moreover, his skin was riddled with a widespread dermatitis that had erupted only during the three men's short absence.

No one could explain what had happened to the waxwork of his sister Elsa. However, psychosomatic trauma was finally listed as the cause of his physical symptoms. Evidently allowing Thodol to be reunited with the dummy had not produced the beneficial mental jolt, but something even worse.

Rhodes has pointed out that the fungus did not appear elsewhere in the Colney Hatch asylum; that, for some reason, it was confined, like Thodol, to one cell. The German had no means of nurturing it, and the reappearance of the growth on the cell walls, mere hours after apparent eradication by carbolic acid, was unaccountable. Moreover, it was evident that the fungus multiplied only whilst Thodol was present. When he was not in close proximity it remained dormant, neither expanding nor contracting over the area it had come to occupy.

The fungus had a peculiar hue. No one could identify its actual colour, saying that it seemed to be both monochrome and ultraviolet. Staring at it for longer than a half a minute induced severe nausea, although Thodol himself appeared unaffected by the sight of the morbid growth. Its propensity to spread over the written characters that he scrawled on the walls, as if tracing their design, led Rhodes to speculate that it sprang from some rogue toxin in the India ink Thodol used. Later he came to a quite different conclusion.

There was also the matter of the stench. Again, this seemed not to bother Thodol himself, and all attempts by nurses to approach his cell and rid the place of the infestation were met with frenzy. It was an unfortunate set of circumstances, and one that lent itself to Thodol's being abandoned for longer and longer periods of time.

His genuine, unshakable belief was that he himself was not mad; rather, it was the world around him that had gone insane. Although this is not an uncommon delusion amongst mental patients, and they can often be very thorough in creating elaborate conspiracy theories that they use to self-validate their delusions, in Thodol's case we cannot rely upon the common interpretation.

The end was of course predictable. Whether by design or not, Thodol was left alone and unattended for a period of well over two weeks. The short corridor in which his cell was located contained no other inmates, since even the noise of footsteps drove Thodol crazy with fear at the thought that the waxworks were closing in on him. Rhodes was one of the few honest enough to admit that Thodol's German nationality created a great deal of resentment towards him, and he overheard at least one other doctor say that it would be no great shame if "that Kraut was ignored and left to rot." This remark caused the doctor who uttered it a great deal of satisfaction once the Nazi policy of exterminating the mentally ill was fully documented after World War II. I doubt that he saw the irony of it.

When the cell was finally opened the stench that emanated from within was unbearable. The fungus had completely overrun the interior, covering the walls, the ceiling, and the sparse furniture. Thodol himself had been dead for more than a week. He had been forced to resort to eating the growth, scraping it away from a corner of the room with his fingers and consuming it as a substitute for food. But it was not hunger that had killed him. His corpse lay curled up in a contorted foetal position. The shocking grimace upon his face indicated the effects of poisoning and a slow, agonizing death. His features were covered by a webwork of the fungi.

Thodol was buried in a plot in the asylum's graveyard marked only with a metal plate bearing his case number. Like the other inmates who had died whilst in confinement in the institution, his name was not even recorded on the meagre memorial. There was no scandal.

The cell was thoroughly cleaned, and all trace of the writings that he had scrawled on the walls disappeared along with the fungus that covered it. Rhodes, however, without official permission, managed to take numerous photographs of the growth before the fungicidal chemicals did their work and then while the demented text they had obscured was briefly revealed. Where the markings were too faint to be photographed he reproduced them (as best he could) in a notebook. He even managed to salvage a small piece of the fungus, storing it in a jar of formaldehyde for subsequent examination. Alas, none of these are extant.

It is not necessary for me to go into any great detail as to the circumstances that led to my seeking out what information I could about Sidney Rhodes. If I say that I noted a curious parallel between his derided 1942 speculative-medical treatise *On Brain Fungus* and Cesare Thodol's 1899 tale entitled "Inside the Fungi Mind," doubtless readers familiar with the latter will understand my determination to interview Dr. Rhodes. I could not help but speculate that the one owed much to the other. At the time I had no idea that Rhodes had come into direct contact with Thodol at the Colney Hatch asylum.

I attempted to trace further details concerning Rhodes through the usual channels—the BMA register, telephone directories, and via the offices of the specialist publishing house that had issued *On Brain Fungus*. However, these were in vain. Rhodes seemed to have disappeared after 1943. It was a chance remark over the telephone by one of his long-lived relatives that put me on the right track. A cousin whom I had traced, Frank Sutton, although not willing to be interviewed, had told me before he hung up that lunacy is contagious and I was wasting my time.

On a hunch I went back to the Colney Hatch records in order to try and determine who had occupied Thodol's cell after his death. The answer was shrouded in evasive, patchy hospital records, and yet I half knew what it would be. Dr. Rhodes had never left Colney Hatch. By 1943 he had instead become a patient there.

The transition from doctor to inmate must have occurred gradually, and I cannot help but imagine that the German's neglect had preyed upon Rhodes's mind. Although his contact with Thodol was of the slightest, somehow he had allowed himself to become too emotionally involved with the fate of the patient, a pitfall against which those working in the psychiatric profession are warned. The reason why he was treated at Colney Hatch (it was after all an institution designed specifically for the treatment of the poorest in society) is easy to explain. It would have led to a scandal had one of their doctors succumbed to insanity. That was hardly the type of publicity the asylum sought. Incredibly, the committee there agreed to shut Rhodes away and deal with the matter internally, though on a semi-official basis.

It appears that Rhodes even acquiesced in the outcome, for he is listed as a voluntary admission. Moreover, it seems that the suggestion that he be domiciled in Thodol's old cell came directly from Rhodes himself (though whether in a lucid or deranged moment I cannot say). Perhaps it was felt that such occupancy might allow the psychiatrist to come to terms with what formed the source of his neurosis.

The most incredible aspect of Rhodes's case is that his delusions exactly duplicated those of Cesare Thodol. He too believed himself to be surrounded by waxworks masquerading as the living. Moreover, he was convinced that the German had been right all along and that the whole process of psychiatric treatment had nothing to do with curing the patient but with forcing a false model of reality upon his perception of the world. The best that could be achieved was that the individual was sufficiently indoctrinated so that he might function in outside society; Rhodes therefore implied that his mental state was a consequence of a verifiable ontological nightmare. He laid particular emphasis on the hitherto unsuspected sentience of fungi growing within the skulls of human simulacra.

Rhodes believed that Thodol had attempted to communicate the truth by writing it on the walls of his cell. But the fungus had obscured his account, tracing a pattern over his words, covering them with its noxious presence. At some point the growth had emerged from its hosts' skulls, after usurping the brains within and shaping new waxen forms from the old tissue and flesh of their bodies. But no one had realized that the change had taken place. It was all a bizarre, incomprehensible joke that the fungi played upon each other—a game of charades whereby they pretended to act as human beings for their own amusement.

The revulsion that the animate waxworks had displayed at the fungus was just one aspect of their horrible antics, another jest they used to further torment those unfortunates under their supervision. The Electro-Convulsive Therapy that Thodol had undergone over a period of years was not designed to shock his brain into functioning normally; in fact, it was an attempt to accelerate the production of spores inside the skull by the layer of fungus that already coated the cerebral hemispheres.

Now here it must be admitted that it is difficult to accept the idea of Rhodes submitting voluntarily to the custodianship of the Colney Hatch Asylum if he really believed in Thodol's morbidly fantastic interpretation of events. However, I suggest that there was still enough doubt in his mind, even at that stage, for him to fall back on his training as a psychiatrist and hope that the terrifying ideas racing uncontrollably through his mind might have their origin in some nervous or organic disorder. To be incarcerated in the very institution where he had treated others was awful, but remember that he may have thought he could more easily escape outside publicity and that he was used to being there.

Rhodes did not ultimately benefit from what treatment he received in the asylum. How could he have done so? For a good number of years he was very much the focus of attention amongst the other psychiatrists who, one might imagine, would be fascinated and appalled at the psychological deterioration of one of their own. This was in spite, or perhaps because, of the fact that Rhodes experienced the selfsame horror Cesare Thodol had felt when becoming aware of other persons in his vicinity. But as time passed no improvement in his condition was evident. His case was increasingly like that of Thodol, even to the extent that, despite having no previous knowledge of the language, he was often overheard muttering to himself in German, as if the dead madman's personality had transferred itself to Rhodes's body.

But if even this aspect might be explained in terms of a guilt-complex connected with Thodol's death, then what remained inexplicable (except if one maintains the view that Rhodes was the victim of a malign conspiracy) was the reappearance of the fungus in the cell. And although it was certain that Rhodes had no writing apparatus available, when the fungus was destroyed script was discovered beneath and not in the former psychiatrist's handwriting at all. True, it seemed to be that of Thodol. And indeed, when compared it was found to be in the exact style of the script that had appeared previously when the German author had occupied the cell. But one of the more inquisitive of the doctors had discovered another twist to the puzzle.

No one had thought to check at the time of the first infestation whether Thodol's own handwriting tallied with the scribbling on the walls. It did not. Even if Rhodes had copied it, thinking it was in Thodol's style, who was the true begetter? Why was the pathologist's autopsy file on Rhodes destroyed within days of his death in October

1959? And why was it an unwritten rule in the institution that the cell must not be occupied in the future?

Colney Hatch Asylum was finally shut down in 1994. Even renaming the institution "Friern Barnet Hospital" could not dispel its notoriety. By then the vogue was for "Care in the Community" rather than confinement. It cost the Tory government less money. The grounds, which had formerly been extensive, and boasting gardens, courtyards, and outbuildings, were redeveloped shortly afterwards. A warren of cul-de-sacs with ugly modern houses was built there. Only the main building now stands intact. Its lofty domed tower and cupola can be seen for miles around and dominates the view in the area, rising above the dreary North Circular Road and the American-style Retail Park. The main building bears no indication of its former purpose and has become an exclusive housing community for the wealthy. Where the reception area and hall used to be, there is a gym and health club for residents and fitness fanatics from outside.

Ironically though, the place is still surrounded by walls and fences. They yet serve their original purpose: to separate residents from society. However, their function has now been reversed. They keep the public out rather than keep the inmates inside. Moreover, in a cabin-office at the main gates is a uniformed security guard, the grounds are patrolled, and every section is under twenty-four-hour CCTV surveillance. Approaching from these main gates one might not notice any significant change. That familiar façade is as impressive as ever, with its terraced portico sheltering five archways, the twin pillared towers flanking the domed central tower set further back, and its bow windows reflecting the mood of the sky. The ornate fountain in the driveway is still there; so too the pagoda, Victorian lampposts, and the willow trees on the front lawn. It is only behind the imposing length of the main building, at the back where the clock tower stands, that one encounters the ugly housing estate that has replaced the remains of the institution.

I came to see what remained of the structure and found myself unaccountably drawn to it. A few of the flats in the main building were unoccupied, and I resolved to explore the possibility of my moving into one. I think it no coincidence—in fact, I now know it was no coincidence—that still currently on the market was an apartment in precisely the location where once had been Thodol's and then Rhodes's own fungi-ridden cell.

In order to dwell in what remained of the asylum it was necessary for me to draw heavily on my savings. The rent I paid was ridiculously expensive, and yet I was in the grip of an obsession that made all other considerations insignificant. I felt certain that my desire to understand what had happened to the two men was intimately connected with the very walls at which they had stared day after day.

Consulting blueprints of the original building in the archives of the local council, I determined that the cell had formerly been where my bedroom was now situated. Its dimensions had not altered, although a connecting door had been added through which access was gained to the other rooms in the flat. I furnished the place with the cheapest items I could find, and a small library of dog-eared paperbacks formed my only source of diversion.

I think that, from the first hour of my tenancy, I was waiting for its reappearance. My gaze roved the walls, the ceiling, and the corners of the bedroom seeking evidence of the slightest discoloured stain or tiny blemish on the recently painted white surfaces.

While I made my minute observations of my surroundings, my thoughts keep returning to the idea that both Thodol and Rhodes had harboured about animate waxworks whose skulls housed not brains but a mass of sentient fungi. I could not account for it, but found that despite my resolution not to succumb to the same irrational phobia I too shunned contact with society. It seemed to me that what faces I saw beyond the windows *were* somewhat like waxen masks, rigid and dehumanized. And in their eyes did I not now detect the hint of an eerie glow, as if a phosphorescent fungus lurked within?

The first growth sprouted in the top left corner of the room, a single toadstool of violet-grey. It looked diseased, but within a matter of a few hours a cluster of them had grown and formed a line along the edge of the corner, following the angle of the wall inwards. From the fungi there wafted a musty, nauseous odour.

When I scraped some of it away, I found the following words beneath:

"Of this one thing I am, at least, absolutely certain: no one is now more qualified than myself to write of the facts concerning my dear brother Cesare Thodol."

And so I sit and watch the inexorable spread of the fungi across the walls and the ceiling. Soon I will have to eat something. My food ran out yesterday and I am quite tormented by hunger.

2025

THE MYKOPHAGOI

Aaron Worth

If, I repeat if, the reader should have the stomach for more, one final fungal tale is offered here. N. B.—as any experienced forager will tell you, "If you aren't sure, *leave it alone*."

"The Mykophagoi" appears here for the first time.

"Oh, Yorkshire pudding's well enough," agreed the man in the stern of the whaleboat. Slowly he pulled up the oars, laid them deliberately across the gunwales, and leaned forward to rest upon them. Gazing intently across the expanse of sky-blue ocean that stretched without end in all directions, he wiped his parched mouth with the back of a sunburnt hand. "It's fine. I've no objection whatever to Yorkshire pudding. But you said, *one* dish—anything in the whole wide world—'wiv a pistol clapped to me 'ed'—those, Jim, were your very words. One's own idea of the pinnacle of culinary perfection. And under those conditions, I believe I should have to choose—let me see—" He leaned back and closed his eyes, like one in a reverie. "Yes, it would have to be a big, brimming bowl of *tete de veau*—prepared *en tortue*, by choice."

"Tortoo?" repeated the lean, leathery man in the bow, opening his eyes comically wide. "Tetty Voo? Christ, what a name! Who's 'e when 'e's at 'ome?" And the Cockney roared with laughter.

"Easy, Jim, easy, you'll upset the dam' boat," growled the rower good-naturedly; then, taking up the oars again:

"It's a Belgian dish. When I was a boy, our cook—a little, barrel-shaped martinet from Maastricht—would make it once a month, regular as a Flemish clock. It's a head of veal, simmered with leeks and mushrooms in a tomato sauce." He ran the tip of a dry tongue over dry lips. "Oh, how grateful was the odour that used to fill the house!"

But the other was shaking his head with vigorous decision. "No, none of your cow's brains for me, Master Nick. Me uncle kept a stall in Billingsgate, and I 'ad me fill of brains of every sort.

"Mushrooms, now, I don't mind mushrooms. On toast, plen-ty of butter. Me mum useter take me along to gather 'em, up in 'ampstead 'eath. Great big whacking ones, Master Nick, like that!" And he held up a bony, sun-browned fist.

He said "Master Nick" half from habit, and half in friendly jest; for whatever differences in station might have existed between the two men had they ever met back home in England had been largely washed away, as sins are said to be washed away by the blood of the Lamb, over the course of the long journey from Portsmouth to Botany Bay, then effaced all but entirely by two years' hard labour in one of New South Wales's more infamous penal colonies. It hardly seemed to matter, under the circumstances, how great a social gulf had once yawned between James Sugg, housebreaker and receiver of stolen goods, and Nicholas Yates, Oxford graduate and painter of promise, whose watercolour sketches of the Welsh coastline had been exhibited at the Academy, and compared by the anonymous *Times* reviewer, not unfavourably, to Turner's early work.

All that had been in another life, as it were, before Nicholas had attempted to pay a debt to a fellow member of the Zeuxis Club with a forged cheque. Now both men belonged to what Nicholas called "the sodality of the transported"; and among the members of that unfortunate brotherhood, as he liked to say, "there was neither Greek nor Jew, neither delver nor gentleman."

At the colony, the two men had shared a cell, within whose damp and reeking concrete walls they had, in the fullness of time, conceived and evolved a complicated plan of escape, one in which an artfully bent piece of wire, a rope made from patiently accumulated scraps of sailcloth, and a purloined whaleboat were each called upon in turn to play a crucial role. Against all odds—against, indeed, even their own expectations—this plan had succeeded, with the result that now, four days later, the two men found themselves at liberty.

At liberty—and adrift, somewhere in the vast expanse of the Pacific Ocean.

(There had been a third man in with them, a plump, jolly Fenian named O'Connor, but he had a horror of the sea, and so had parted from them on the beach, with a general shaking of hands and a genial exchanging of dooms. Likely he had been recaptured by now. How they envied him!)

Their plan, so admirably detailed with respect to the departure from the colony itself, was rather hazier when it came to the subsequent journey by water. Neither man was a sailor by any conceivable definition of the word, and knowing literally nothing about navigation, their vague intention had been to strike north while keeping in sight of land. Eventually, after landing "somewhere up the coast," they had hoped to make their way to Port Stephens, where they thought they could melt into the growing population of "respectable" colonists being encouraged by the Government to settle there.

Of course, this scheme, such as it was, depended on fair weather and good visibility, and on the night of their escape they had neither. A strong wind from the west lashed them with curtains of rain, driving their boat farther and farther away from a shore that had, in any event, been swallowed up in darkness almost as soon as they put to sea.

The rain had stopped by morning, but dawn found them drifting in a mass of fog so thick that the boat made up their entire world. This, in turn, passed off by afternoon, but they were already long out of sight of land, with a sky so overcast that they could scarcely be sure of the sun by day, while that night they dared not do anything but sit and drift beneath a starless, moonless sky.

On the third morning the sun had finally appeared, blinding white in a dazzling blue sky, but the damage had been done. All their energies were now directed towards rowing westwards, praying that they might find the coast again before hunger and, more urgently, thirst, finished them off. They had long eaten the few crusts of bread they had brought with them, and all that was left of the rainwater that had gathered in the curved bottom of the boat was a salty, green slime.

Some perverse impulse had led them to discourse upon matters culinary, and this discussion might have gone on for the rest of the day, which was already well advanced, had not Jim suddenly gasped and pointed a quivering finger over the rower's shoulder.

"Look! Look, Master Nick! It's land—land, by the Lord Jesus!"

Quickly Nicholas twisted round and squinted at a dark speck on the horizon. "An island, anyway," he agreed.

"'Ere, Master Nick." Jim scrambled towards Nicholas as though he meant to attack him. "Let me 'ave them oars—I'm fresh!"

Good as his word, Jim pulled for all he was worth, and it took something less than an hour for them to reach the island, but to Nicholas, at least, it seemed far longer. He watched it grow by painfully slow degrees from a tiny blot to a green, three-humped mass of land, perhaps two or three miles across.

"Three silent pinnacles rose, sunset-flushed," murmured Nicholas.

"What's that?"

"Oh, nothing. Something from Tennyson, I think, and doubtless I've bungled it. Look here, Jim, make for that bit of beach there."

They were close to the island now, close enough to see the surf foaming to cream along the narrow band of white sand that marked the shore. Close behind the beach loomed a high wall of green, the edge of a thick forest of pine and palm trees. With a rush of renewed energy Jim pulled hard for half a dozen final strokes, and then they were out of the boat, running in shallow warm water, collapsing gratefully on the hot sand. Then they stood on shaky legs, dragged the boat up onto the beach and, after a single, wild look at each other, plunged together into the dense, semitropical forest, which enfolded them immediately in a sweltering, humid embrace.

Wordlessly, they staggered on through the dense wood for some time, searching for something—anything—to eat, to drink. Once they came into a little clearing where the aerial roots of an enormous banyan tree reared up into shafts of sunlight like the pipes of a mighty organ in a cathedral; often, one or both of them tripped in the dense tangled underbrush and fell; always, their hands and faces were lashed with branches and pricking vines.

Then all at once the thick sea of vegetation parted as if by magic, and they half-stumbled, half-fell into a roughly circular enclosure or grotto.

It was a queer place. All round the perimeter rose the great palms and pines, their heads meeting together in the centre, high above, as if in eldritch conclave, nearly blotting out the sun. It was cooler here, and there was an unpleasant odour, quite different from the rank vegetable smell of the forest. It was a difficult odour to put a name to—dank, sweetish, yet with an acrid undertone.

Just within the ring of trees ran a narrow carpet of thick moss, on which they stood; beyond this there was no vegetation at all, only a mottled brown, undulating surface that Nicholas at first took for dark, lichen-spotted rock, almost flat but rising to a slight mound in the centre, and pitted all over with little hollows or craters.

There was something decidedly unearthly about the place; it reminded Nicholas of one of the plates illustrating the copy of Godwin's *Man in the Moone* which he had loved as a child.

Those pictured lunar landscapes, however, had been devoid of water, while here he saw dozens of little black pools, where rainwater had gathered in the hollows.

"Thank 'eaven," croaked Jim, staggering to one of these. He fell to his knees like a penitent, then lowered his head to the ground and drank noisily.

After only a moment's hesitation Nicholas followed him onto the mottled brown surface, and was immediately surprised to find that it gave springily under his feet. Not rock, then. Some sort of fungus, he thought, quite unlike any he had ever seen, or heard of, before.

But that was hardly important now. Stumbling over the rubbery, uneven substance, he knelt before one of the craters. Looking down, he saw that the surface of the water was darkly opalescent, with an oily swirl on it, mingled with something like pollen. He filled his cupped hands with the liquid and sipped tentatively at it, then coughed violently.

"Lord, it's bitter," he gasped.

"It's water," returned Jim shortly.

There was nothing to be said to this, so Nicholas filled his hands again, and both men lapped, slurped, and gulped down the bitter fluid until, their thirst satiated, they rolled onto their backs and lay panting in utter exhaustion.

"Blimey, Master Nick," gasped Jim. "I'm about all in."

Nicholas grunted agreement. His own eyelids already felt heavy as lead, and before many more minutes had passed, both men lay fast asleep in the dim grotto.

When Nicholas awoke, some hours had evidently passed; it was perceptibly darker in the grotto, and the few irregular patches of sky showing through the vegetable firmament above had changed colour, from a brilliant blue to a deep indigo. But there was light enough to see by, and he could see Jim sitting up, cross-legged, near the pool from which he had drunk, some dozen or so yards away. In his hands he held a large fragment of the mottled brown fungus which, rather to Nicholas's surprise, he was eating. He ate with obvious relish, and as the smacking sounds reached Nicholas's ears, he became aware of a ravenous hunger within himself—no longer a dull gnawing ache but a sharp, agonizing pain stabbing deeply into his guts.

He groaned slightly, and Jim looked up from his repast.

"Awake, are we?" He sucked at a finger and grinned. "Look 'ere, Master Nick, you've just got to try this stuff." He took another bite and said, with his mouth full: "It beats any mushroom *I've* ever 'ad, right 'ollow it does!"

Nicholas frowned. "Careful, Jim. We know nothing about it; it may well be poisonous."

Jim swallowed, belched, and winked. "Put it to you this way, Master Nick. It's bloody delicious, and I ain't dead yet!" And he bent to his meal once more.

Hunger twisted its blade in Nicholas's belly again, and he decided that Jim's reasoning was sound.

Peering down at the rubbery surface on which he sat, he now saw smallish protuberances of varying shape and size which he had not noticed before. He turned his attention to the nearest of these, a tiny orb like a brown, speckled gooseberry sprouting up near his right hand. Tentatively he poked at it with his thumb, and a ripple of mild revulsion passed through him at its thick, gelatinous texture. But hunger once again won out, and gripping it between fingers and thumb, he tugged at it until it came free, put it in his mouth, and chewed.

Jim was right—it *was* delicious. Nicholas gave a little grunt of enjoyment, and even before the morsel was fairly down his throat

THE MYKOPHAGOI

he was scanning the surface again for more. After a minute he found another of the berry-like growths, which soon followed the first.

By now he was beginning to feel the most delicious warmth spreading throughout his body. It radiated outward from his belly, making his extremities tingle. It beat every meal he'd ever had, every spirit he'd ever drunk. "Beat 'em 'ollow," as Jim had said.

"Good, ain't it?" grunted Jim.

"Good? It's grand—pos'tively heavenly. Ambrosia's nothing to it. And as for manna—manna's a rotten, er, onion." With which fatuous pronouncement, and vaguely conscious of a rather idiotic grin that was spreading across his own face, he searched avidly about for more of the gooseberry-like things.

Of these could find no more, but there, to his left, sprouted a cluster of longer growths, rather like smallish sausages. With no hesitation at all this time, he tore these up and sank his teeth into them. Punctuating the sounds of mastication that followed were faint moans of pleasure which, he realized absently, issued from his own mouth.

At length, having gobbled down the last of the sausages, he lay back, stretched himself out on the rubbery carpet, and exhaled slowly. Jim, he could see, had done the same, and for a long time they lay like this, in a state of perfect contentment, while the last of the light in the grotto slowly died, and the cool of night crept in upon them. Neither man was inclined for further conversation. For Jim's part, he could not remember having ever felt so sated before, so repleted—so utterly at peace with the world.

Time passed. The grotto was black as pitch when one of them spoke again.

It was Jim: "Look 'ere, Master Nick," he said, dreamily. "If we ever get back to Lunnon, we oughter open a restaurant in Soho, an' serve nuffink but this stuff. Eight bloomin' courses, ev'ry one of 'em fungus. 'What'll you 'ave, sir? Fungus, side of fungus? Very good, sir.' Be bloody millionaires within a week, mark me words."

Nicholas agreed, though possibly only in his mind, and before long he fell into another, even deeper slumber. He dreamed that he was back in his cell at the colony, but finding that the walls were not made of concrete after all but liver-coloured fungus, he began to eat his way out, only to find that the wall seemed to go on forever, and so he ate and ate, tunnelling for miles in sheer ecstasy, and it was in a state of strange excitement that he awoke, to see thin shafts of sunlight weakly penetrating into the grotto.

Turning his head, he saw Jim on all fours like a dog, head down, biting into a mound of the fungus which jutted up like a large, speckled molehill.

Without changing his canine attitude, Jim looked up and grinned.

"Mornin', Master Nick. 'ave a spot of breakfast?"

Doing his best to ignore the spasms of sudden hunger that had begun to twist his belly anew, Nicholas said: "Yes, yes—in a bit. But Jim, don't you think we should make some sort of a plan first—review our options? After all, we can't stay here forever, lying about and eating fungus!"

"N-o," said Jim, rather dubiously. Slowly he raised himself back to a sitting position, wiped his mouth. "No, 'course not. But it 'ardly makes sense to go making plans on an empty stomach, does it, mate?"

"No, I suppose not," replied Nicholas, his eyes already creeping hungrily over the mottled surface of the fungus. Then he added, rather sententiously: "The mind, after all, needs food as well as the body." And a minute later he had torn free a roughly oblong chunk of fungus, about a foot in length, and was biting greedily into it.

The eating of it, and of several more very like it, seemed to go on for hours; and indeed, when at last he had finished, he looked up sluggishly, and was astonished to see that it was dark again. How was that possible?

"Jim," he heard himself croaking weakly into the darkness, "Jim, we've lost another day, somehow."

Silence.

"D'you hear me, Jim? We've got to get out of this place... there's something... something *wrong* here. Very, very wrong."

For a long time the darkness did not answer. Then Jim's voice came back: "There's plenty of time to think about that later, Master Nick."

Another long silence, and then: "As a matter of fact, Master Nick... I don't think I want to leave here at all. Do you?"

Nicholas tried to frame a reply but found that he could not. That sensation of pure satiety was washing over his body again, lulling him back into drowsiness.

Of course he wanted to leave. Of course they *would* leave. In time.

But when? murmured a little voice in his head. Then a second voice chimed in: *And why?*

And he tried to think of answers to these questions, but he could not, and anyway, the work of thinking was vexing in the extreme, and very soon sleep washed over him once more.

Again he dreamed. This time he dreamed that he was a boy, visiting his Uncle Jeffrey at his place in Surrey. He was lying on his stomach on the great hearth-rug in the library, and his uncle was sitting in the big arm-chair beside the fire, reading from an enormous book that lay open on his lap. At least—he had *thought* that it was his uncle; but really the figure in the chair looked more like Lord Tennyson, except the face was not flesh but fungus, corpse-white and blood-freckled, and the fingers that held the book were leprous and rubbery. And when the figure opened its mouth, brittle bits broke off from the lips and fell, silent as snow, into the great white beard.

"We will return no more," intoned the thing in the chair, very slowly and solemnly. "Our island home is far beyond the wave; we will no longer roam."

In the hearth a mottled, half-devoured log dropped silent cinders upon rubbery stones.

Then suddenly the speaker turned a pair of black, empty eye-sockets to Nicholas and roared in a terrible inhuman voice, *We will return no more*, and Nicholas woke in terror.

Heart pounding, he lay for a minute in paralysed silence.

It was, he dimly realized, twilight again in the grotto—though whether the twilight of morning or of evening he could not tell.

He was about to call out to Jim when the sound of a voice stopped him. It was the voice of a man, talking low, apparently to himself. Perhaps it was this voice that had awakened him. At first he thought it must be Jim. To be sure, it sounded nothing like him—but who else could it be? When he looked around the grotto, he could see no one else *but* Jim, who lay, apparently sleeping, in his usual place, his back turned to Nicholas.

Besides, the voice issued from another direction altogether. It was accompanied by a sound like a pencil scratching on paper. It said:

"...it has been eight years, gentlemen, since my previous letter. (Only eight? Egad, it seems longer—much longer!) In it, I wrote, you may recall, of an entirely novel species of the *Cryptogamia* family which I had discovered upon an island, situated some eighty or ninety miles to the south-east of Lord Howe's Isle.

"The island was then, and remains now, uninhabited except for myself. As I told you before, I came here to establish a mission, a project which I was compelled to abandon soon after my arrival, owing to an incident related to the above-mentioned discovery. I shall not dwell upon that incident here, except to repeat that it occasioned the loss not only of the three men whom I brought with me, but also of my own religious faith, without which no man (as I am sure you will agree) is justified in attempting to christianize other men.

"As I say, that was eight years ago. I write now, gentlemen, because the thing has happened again..."

Here Nicholas, who had been listening in growing confusion, called out sharply:

"Who's there?"

There came an answering cry of surprise—a cry of shock and, he thought, of horror.

Again, Nicholas looked all around him, but could see no one. The cry had sounded very near indeed—it seemed to come from the very patch of moss on which he and Jim had stood only a few days ago; or had it been weeks? Time seemed to have no meaning at all any longer...

But there was no one there; unless perhaps the owner of the voice was lurking unseen in the trees, just beyond?

He tried again.

"Please," he said. "Is there someone there? We want help—want it very badly."

There was another, longer pause, and then the voice could be heard again, this time in a whisper, and now there was no mistaking the horror and loathing in it.

"Alive," it said. "One of them is still alive. Alive and conscious. Oh, merciful God!"

Still Nicholas could see no one. "Please," he groaned, "won't you come out?" Then he yelled, in a sudden rage born of panic: "Damn you, why don't you show yourself?"

"What shall I tell him?" murmured the voice. "The poor devil. He cannot see me, of course—yet he thinks he ought to be able to.

I am right here," it went on, louder, addressing Nicholas now. "I am here, and no ghost, believe me. I am standing not ten yards from you.

"I was just writing to the Royal Society, you see," the voice added hastily, as though this explained something. "I wrote them before, you know, about—the thing. But none of that august fraternity, I am afraid, stooped to make reply. No, stay, there was one—a Mr. Derwin. Or was it Darwin?

"He was cordial enough, but sceptical to a degree. I rather suspect, indeed, that he believed me to be mad. I have sometimes wondered that myself, in the years since. I wish I *were* mad, my poor friend, oh yes indeed. For your sake, if nothing else."

"Please," said Nicholas, who understood none of this, and was beginning to agree with the judgment of Mr. Derwin (or Darwin). "Whoever you are, you must help us get out of this place. We can't—can't manage it ourselves. We're ill, or something—I mean to say, there's something wrong with the place."

A sigh. "Even if I could, my dear fellow, I'm afraid that it would do you no good, no good at all. (Why, he sounds quite young! The poor, poor devil!)

"Besides," continued the voice, "I daren't come any closer than this, you know. Mind you, I *think* it's safe enough if one doesn't touch the water, but—well, I simply daren't. You understand, don't you?"

A pause, and then: "You *did* drink the water, didn't you? Of course you did. Probably mad with thirst. That's how it gets you. Yes, it's the water that starts all the mischief. The seeds *in* the water, rather. The—what d'ye call 'em—the spores, that's the word."

"What the devil are you babbling on about? Just get us out of this, man, if you have a heart in your breast!"

A low murmur that might have been a prayer, and then:

"If it is at all a comfort to you, my son—and believe me, I mean to be comforting—you cannot have very much time left. Soon you will join your friend in—in the presence of our maker. (And yet—and yet—dear God in Heaven, what kind of a maker must it be, to countenance such a thing!)"

"Jim? Why, he's only sleeping..." Nicholas cast an anxious glance at his companion. Surely Jim was not really... no, Nicholas could see his back, slowly rising and falling. "Sleeping," he repeated, turning back to the voice in triumph. "Why, man, don't you see him right over there?"

"*I* see him," said the voice, and the emphasis which was placed on the personal pronoun was somehow unsettling. "I am afraid, however, that you do not. Not as—as he truly is."

"As he truly—nonsense!" Nicholas returned irritably. "What damned nonsense you are talking. All right, then, you—you sneak—perhaps you will be good enough to tell me what it is that *you* see?"

Instead of answering, the voice mused to itself, like one who pieces together a puzzle: "Of course, the poor fellow sees (so to speak) only what *it* wants him to see. He is imprisoned in a kind of waking dream. Terrible—oh God, how terrible—yet withal fascinating—yes, whatever else, undoubtedly that." Again came the sound of a pencil scratching on paper.

"It's the spores, you see," continued the voice, almost apologetically, addressing Nicholas once more. "As I said before. They have a phantasticating or, ah, hallucinatory effect. They must take root in the brain and—oh, the cunning of it! It's what the naturalists term, I believe, an adaptation. Oh, a most cunning and awful adaptation!"

"Adaptation?" repeated Nicholas blankly. "What the devil do you mean? What sort of adaptation? And for what conceivable purpose?"

"Why, as to that," returned the voice, "why does the porcupine have quills? Why does the rose-bush have thorns? It's a matter of self-defence, don't you see; simply put, it doesn't want to be eaten."

At this Nicholas could not help but laugh. "Doesn't want to be *eaten*?" he echoed, incredulously. "Why, man, we've been gorging ourselves on the stuff for days!"

He laughed again, a dreadful sound that echoed in the grotto before trailing off slowly, as the black shadow of an idea crept, uninvited, into his mind. Once there it began to lengthen and grow, and to take definite shape...

"*Haven't we?*"

ALSO AVAILABLE

Strangling vines and meat-hungry flora fill this unruly garden of strange stories, selected for their significance as the seeds of the villainous (or perhaps just misunderstood) 'killer plant' in fiction, film and video games.

Step within to marvel at Charlotte Perkins Gilman's giant wistaria and H. G. Wells' hungry orchid; hear the calls of the ethereal women of the wood, and the frightful drone of the moaning lily; and do tread carefully around E. Nesbit's wandering creepers...

Every strain of vegetable threat (and one deadly fungus) can be found within this new collection, representing the very best tales from the undergrowth of Gothic fiction.

ALSO AVAILABLE EDITED BY AARON WORTH

A mysterious news signal reports cosmic doom from an otherworldly location. X-ray evidence suggests the impossible truth that a sculptor is becoming one with his creation. A gramophone channels the venomous words of a churlish spirit and its cruel vengeance.

The ground-breaking new technologies of the nineteenth and twentieth centuries delivered their users into a world of unfathomable miracles and fresh nightmares—a world in which pioneers of weird fiction gave expression to anxieties generated by seemingly limitless communication and the capturing of images beyond the human eye.

Tracing this fiction of speculation and fear from the motion photography of the 1890s to 1950s television, this new collection presents seventeen tales of haunted and uncanny media from a range of writers inspired by its ghastly potential, including Marjorie Bowen, H. Russell Wakefield, H. P. Lovecraft and Rudyard Kipling.

For more Tales of the Weird titles
visit the British Library Shop (shop.bl.uk)

We welcome any suggestions, corrections or feedback you may have, and will aim to respond to all items addressed to the following:

The Editor (Tales of the Weird), British Library Publishing,
The British Library, 96 Euston Road, London NW1 2DB

We also welcome enquiries through our X (Twitter) account, @BL_Publishing.